Moving Targets

A Helen Black Mystery by

PAT WELCH

Bella
BOOKS

Ferndale, Michigan
2001

Bella Books, Inc.
P.O. Box 201007
Ferndale, MI 48220

Printed in the United States of America on acid-free paper
First Edition

Editor: Lila Empson
Cover designer: Bonnie Liss (Phoenix Graphics)

ISBN 0-9677753-6-1

*Dedicated with gratitude
and affection to Susan —
I couldn't have done it
without you.*

Prologue

Helen Black woke with a start. Her heart pounded against her ribs with painful clarity. Her hands, slick with sweat, slithered across the armrests of her uncomfortable economy-class seat. To her right, the storm slapped fat raindrops against the thick airplane window. The middle-aged business-man in the carefully tailored suit snored gently at her left, his plump fingers laced comfortably across his slight paunch.

She shook her head, trying to force herself into an alert state. She'd never been able to sleep well on airplanes — always too keyed up, unable to fully relax. Whenever she did drowse off in mid-flight, it was a fitful doze troubled by weird dreams. Dreams she could never recall clearly, but which left her shaken and uneasy on waking.

Helen made an unsuccessful attempt to shift to a more comfortable position in the seat. Damned if airplane seats hadn't shrunk in proportion over the last couple of years. She squirmed for a moment, then gave up. As she sank back against the cushions, she caught a glimpse of her pale blank face in the dark window — deep-set dark eyes ringed with purple-black that betrayed her exhaustion, hair flattened oddly from her sweating scalp pressed against the tiny pillow, mouth set in thin-lipped determination. Not a pretty sight. A flash of lightning obscured the reflection, and Helen slid the shade down, obliterating the image.

Lights flickered on in the cabin, and a disembodied voice intoned over the cabin speaker that the passengers needed to return to their seats and fasten their safety belts. The plane pitched suddenly, yawing with a jerk downward and to the right, as the pilot made some mysterious maneuver against the elements. Helen heard a soft, high-pitched squeal of dismay from behind her, a few muttered curses, and several sharp breath intakes. She glanced around the cabin, which was only about two-thirds full. Everyone seemed to be awake now.

Even her companion to the left had roused up with a snort. He fumbled at his seat belt and promptly went back to sleep. Helen gave him an envious glance, and then the plane careened wildly in a stomach-wrenching orbit.

"Jesus," she muttered. Her briefcase, which she'd held on her lap ever since they'd taken off from San Francisco, hurtled across her seatmate's ample tummy and landed with a slap on the thinly carpeted floor, spilling out an assortment of files and papers and notepads. He whiffed in mild surprise for a moment, then went back to sleep.

Helen sighed and closed her eyes. Terrific. *Why the hell I brought it with me, anyway, I'll never know.* She lectured herself for a few moments on her foolishness while the plane shuddered in the storm. Did she dare break the rules and climb out of her seat to retrieve the files? Maybe not — she'd probably be flailed around the cabin by another fit of air turbulence and end up with a broken neck or something. The papers weren't going anywhere, and neither was she, she reassured herself.

She paid little attention to the ill-concealed fear beneath the anger she heard in the other passengers' voices. Instead, her gaze fell idly on the bits and pieces that had fallen from her briefcase. Splinters of a life, she thought. A few files from the most recent cases she'd taken in Berkeley and San Francisco. There was the missing teenager from Modesto, wedged up against the legs of the seats in front of her. The insurance fraud lay wide open in the middle of the floor. And the one just beside her sleeping neighbor's feet — that was the man who suspected his wife of cheating on him. Just a few final notes on these three, she'd thought as she packed in a hurry for the trip to Mississippi, and the Helen Black Detective Agency will be all caught up.

Someone cried out as the lights dimmed, then came back up, then went off and stayed off. In the faint emergency lights glowing from the walls, Helen watched the pages of her daybook as it flapped open on the floor. Months of meetings with clients, business luncheons, and therapy sessions wheeled around each other in those small, cramped pages, the endlessly tearful crying jags on her shrink's sofa bumping up against plastic foam cups that marked off the hours spent tailing a subject. These in turn jostled the blank lines, day after day after day, for the long hours spent alone at night.

The plane veered off again, and Helen forced her mind to stay on those files, not on her queasy stomach and her own increasing fears. Yes, the agency was running smoothly, no pressing new cases, just these few for final notes and invoices, she thought in soothing litany. No problems, nothing to worry about — just a little turbulence, we'll get there shortly —

Then another fragment registered in her vision. This one was half in, half out of the briefcase — a small rectangle of patterned paper poking out of the red leather. The briefcase had landed sideways against the legs of the row of seats to Helen's left. Helen had an idea what it was but leaned over cautiously to get a better look. She winced with the effort. The scar tissue from her gunshot wound, stretching across her left side around her back, still twinged sometimes when she put pressure on it or moved in resistance to it. A glance at her neighbor assured her that he was still out of it, so Helen leaned further.

Her stomach clenched when she recognized the check from her ex-lover. Jesus, she thought, slumping back in her seat, hadn't she gotten rid of that yet? Helen had cleared out everything else the same day Alison left her life for good. Photographs, movie-ticket stubs, pressed flowers, even that silly plastic ring from the Cracker Jack box — nothing had remained. Now this frigging check. Helen pressed her hands down hard on the armrests as the plane whipped back and forth. A million times she'd taken the check in her hands to rip it up rather than accept Alison's half of the rent. A million times she'd reached for an envelope to mail it back to her — and a million times Helen had put it back in her briefcase. A small piece of unfinished business. No big deal. She'd get to it when she had time.

Suddenly the plane leveled off, its shimmy ended. They must have flown right through the storm, Helen thought. She slid the shade up. Just below, twinkling like tiny birthday candles on a black cake, the lights of Dallas and Fort Worth glowed. They'd be landing soon.

Helen scrambled awkwardly from her seat while the flight attendant's voice welcomed them to Dallas/Fort Worth International Airport. She fell over her neighbor and woke him up while the voice advised them that passengers going on to Memphis should stay aboard the plane since they'd be departing in forty minutes. She gathered up the files and stuffed Alison's check deep into the depths of her briefcase. As she stood up she noticed her seatmate, now wide awake, studying her ass and her legs.

4

Shit. Shouldn't have worn this suit, she thought as she edged her way back into her own seat. Should have taken enough time to change before driving to the airport. Oh well. With a smile that was more grimace than grin, Helen clutched the briefcase tightly and tried not to see how his gaze traveled up and down her torso.

"Here on business?"

"No." Her reticence wasn't going to stop this good old boy from trying, Helen realized. He smiled widely at her and twisted in his seat so he could peer into her face.

"Going on to Memphis?"

"I'm meeting relatives there."

"What a coincidence! So am I." She glanced down at his hand and saw the telltale pale width of skin around his left ring finger. Great. "More of a business trip, actually."

"Is that so?"

"So — this is a vacation for you, then?"

"No. I'm going to a funeral."

There, that shut him up. He sat back, his eyes widened in surprise, and cleared his throat. "Well, I'm really sorry to hear that. Close relative, was it?"

"Yes. My uncle."

"I see. Well, that's too bad." He looked genuinely sorry, and Helen felt a flicker of remorse. It wasn't entirely the truth. Uncle Loy wasn't dead yet, although he wasn't expected to last more than a couple of days.

Helen busied herself with rearranging the files in her briefcase while her neighbor took off for the john. Just as well — she needed a couple of moments to gather her thoughts, to be ready to meet Aunt Edna at the airport in Memphis and then drive down to Tupelo. Helen refused to think beyond that moment, refused to consider the final goal of this journey.

She gazed out at the rain-slick runway, barely noticing when her hefty seatmate returned. Beyond the asphalt, trees waved in the wind. They looked as if they would pick up roots and walk, shuffling across the soil and pavement, weaving their arms back and forth, maybe moaning. What was that thing she'd seen once, a painting from Tibet or Nepal — hungry ghosts. That's what those trees looked like. Hungry ghosts — eternally starving, crying out through pinhole mouths for sustenance they could never receive.

The plane lifted off gently, leaving Dallas/Fort Worth behind as it turned east toward Memphis, soaring up into the black sky. Helen felt an ache in her hands and looked down to find she'd been clenching the briefcase as if it were a lifeline. Her lifeline — her work. There wasn't anything else now. Soon there wouldn't even be Uncle Loy left to hold on to. She leaned her face against the cool surface of the windowpane and tried to see into the night. There were no stars, no light from below, no sign of life. Just the wind and the rain and the dark.

When they landed at Memphis, Helen waited until everyone else had left the cabin. She didn't have long to wait. People rushed off the plane, laughing in nervous relief at the scare they'd had, shoving each other in their eagerness to get the hell out of there. Then, as she finally stood, she fished Alison's check from her briefcase and tore it into tiny fragments. Bits of paper drifted from her fingers as she walked by the flight attendants with a smile glazed on her face. The cleaning crew would take care of it for her, she told herself. They were already waiting, in fact, three tired men of indeterminate age sporting dull gray coveralls huddled at the front of the cabin, laden with vacuum cleaners and dustcloths. There, Helen thought as she quickly made her through the empty plane. No problem. All done now.

Helen braced herself and walked off the plane.

Chapter One

Rain began to fall in thick warm drops onto the loose soil. Thunder surged beneath the minister's intonation. Lightning cracked thin streaks against a backdrop of iron-gray sky.

"I am the resurrection, and the life: he that believeth in me, though he were dead, yet shall he live." Wind ruffled the young preacher's wispy red hair as the storm moved closer. Helen tried to shut out the sound of rain pelting the glossy surface of her uncle's coffin. To her it sounded like someone getting their face slapped, over and over and over. The bucktoothed minister, who looked all of twelve with his light spray of acne and freckles on an unlined face, raised his voice to be heard over the rumble of the approaching storm.

The kid was skipping around, Helen realized, quoting from

a lot of different spots in the King James Version, a hodgepodge of vaguely familiar stock phrases she could recall from endless summers of vacation Bible school. "For now we see through a glass, darkly; but then face to face."

Face to face. She remembered Loy McCormick's face in his final hours. He'd insisted on coming home to die. Beneath the oxygen masks that gave meager relief, from the web of tubing and machinery that engulfed him in the hospital, her uncle had saved what was left of his breath to insist on being in his own bed for the end.

He'd looked at his wife, who sat beside the hospital bed in helpless tears, her voice worn out from weeping. "Loy, hon, these people can help you — they can make you better," she'd protested the first time he suggested going home. "Why, just the other day the doctor was talking about chemotherapy again." Helen could still see the way her aunt's trembling hands had clutched at the bedsheets, kneading them into a small rumpled knot. "And they come up with new things all the time, Loy. I wish you'd quit talking like that, honey."

As she'd spoken, Helen — having just arrived only four hours before — saw Loy turn his stare in her direction. With a sinking feeling, she'd been able to read his thoughts. Just like always. Ever since she'd been a kid, lonely and scared and unwanted by her own parents, Helen and her uncle had seemed able to communicate without words. It had happened more times than she could count. When they'd gone fishing — she'd not been more than seven or eight. When he'd found her the first time she'd run away from home, heading off on foot with only a lunch box, all of ten years old, down Highway 10 toward parts unknown. When he made sure she got to the doctor and the dentist because her parents forgot.

And, of course, the night she'd turned up on their doorstep with bruises all over her face and back. This was long before the trailer park in Tupelo, where the McCormicks had settled after Loy's retirement from Roberts and Farrell. They'd still been out in the small brick house down by Vicksburg then, and Uncle Loy had opened the door wearing his factory overalls and smelling of the oil and gasoline he worked with in maintaining the machinery there. It had been raining that night too — just like it was raining now, in periodic bursts of wind and water that spewed down with violence from a dark sky.

She'd stood on the steps, mute and trembling and exhausted from her four-hour trek through the mud. At first she'd been afraid her father would follow her, not content with beating her for kissing a girl but determined to kill her. After the first hour of aimless trudging, she'd known her father wouldn't chase her. And she knew the only place she could find refuge was with Uncle Loy and Aunt Edna.

Her uncle hadn't said a word — merely looked at her silently with a slight tightening of the jaw. He'd taken a deep drag on his cigarette as he stepped aside to let her in out of the rain. He'd never asked who had done it, or why. He'd just known.

In the hospital, looking down at him trapped in a swath of sheets and medical equipment and silence, once again Helen had known what her uncle was thinking. Aunt Edna continued to talk about her hopes for his recovery while Helen quietly left the room and went in search of the nurses station to ask some questions about how to get her uncle home to die.

The hospice people had been quick, quiet, and unobtrusive, Helen realized now. Without a lot of fuss and bother, they'd arranged for all the drugs that he'd needed to make him comfortable. And they'd been on hand in the background as Edna and Bobby and Helen had circled around the bed in the trailer's living room when Loy turned his face to them one last time.

Helen closed her eyes briefly. The young minister's words faded as the image of that gray, skeletal face burned in her memory. What the hell had he been trying to say to her? For his last look, with those tired, dark eyes, had been for his niece. His lips, cracked and dry, had moved, and some strange

9

murmur had come out. Helen recalled vividly that she had leaned forward, fighting back an involuntary urge to retch at the stench and the sound of his lungs straining for air. "What, Uncle Loy?" she'd whispered, putting her ear next to his lips.

Nothing. By the time she'd gotten that close it was over. His face, when she pulled away in shock, was calm and relaxed and amazingly young looking. The flat dull stare of his eyes had told her then that she wasn't ever going to know what he'd been trying to say.

She'd seen death often before, of course. Ugly deaths, serene ones, surprising ones, even the odd, blackly humorous ones. Life as a cop and then as a private investigator had given her plenty of exposure to the way people's lives ended. But something about her uncle lying on the narrow bed in the cheap double-wide trailer, at the edge of an asphalt lot in Mississippi, with her aunt sobbing behind her and her poor cousin yelling out in confusion at her side — something about this scene was wrong. This was her Uncle Loy, dammit. This was the man who had taken her in as a kid when her own father had beaten her and thrown her out of the house. This wasn't supposed to happen. She'd stared down at his body and felt herself trembling with rage. Thank god the hospice folks had been handy and had seen to her aunt and cousin. Helen hadn't felt up to much more than punching her fists through the flimsy walls of the trailer at that final moment.

A sudden break in the wind and rain brought the voice of the preacher back to her consciousness. "In my Father's house are many mansions," he droned on in a high-pitched voice calculated to reach the back of the crowd, huddled away from further soaking along one side of the canopy-covered grounds. "If it were not so, I would have told you."

Despite the rather fragmented nature of his oration, Helen decided it was better than a false eulogizing over a man this young preacher had never known. Uncle Loy used to say that Aunt Edna was religious for both of them. He'd dutifully taken his wife, however, to all the services at the Holy

Nazareth Pentecostal Assembly of Jesus Risen, according to the sympathetic brethren gathered at the interminable funeral an hour before.

Helen had stood between her aunt and cousin at the entrance to the church, shaking hands and nodding for what felt like eons. Mississippi in August was no time to be standing on the concrete steps of a church that shimmered in the heat. She'd been sweating steadily in her scratchy black wool suit and white silk blouse — the only appropriate wear she'd scrounged up from her closets at home in Berkeley as she'd stuffed a suitcase last week for the emergency trip. Helen had sighed, squirmed and fidgeted at the waist of her skirt, and smiled for the sake of her relatives as she greeted the good brothers and sisters one by one.

The only faces that stood out in her admittedly taxed memory were the ones that had been lit with curiosity and malice. She'd noted their hard little eyes shining with delighted hostility at her, their hands either clasping hers a moment too long or dropping away quickly as if touched with plague. Faces didn't stick in her mind, but their questions did.

"Yes, I'm Loy McCormick's niece. From California," she'd introduced herself repeatedly.

"Oh? I don't recall seeing you at church before," was one of the phrases she got in response, followed by curious stares. A small group had clustered around the entrance, lingering over the guest book and stealing surreptitious glances at her. The old ladies' contingent hovered around her aunt, and Helen had been on her own.

"No, I haven't been here until today."

"Well, we certainly hope to see you again on Sunday." That particular set had departed for the depths of the church only to be replaced by others. Helen leaned against the concrete wall that had soaked up all the heat of the day and felt her silk blouse sticking uncomfortably to her back. Of course, not everyone in the church had behaved like reporters for a tabloid — certainly a fair number had seemed genuinely concerned with Edna and Bobby, even behaved graciously toward Helen. As far as Helen had been able to tell, however, those had been few and far between. Even now, perched in an uncomfortable metal chair that slid on the wet grass of the cemetery, Helen imagined she could feel their stares and hear all their whispers. At least being pissed off gave her some relief from all the other emotions boiling inside her as she let her mind wander from the kid's Bible quotes.

She stole a glance at her Aunt Edna, sitting on the folding metal chair beside her. The older woman, clad in a too-tight black dress that caught and gathered in strained creases over her ample stomach, stared blankly at the wine-colored polished wood box that contained her husband's body. Edna's eyes streamed in an endless flow of tears, as if she were suffering from a bad case of the flu. The makeup she'd applied that morning with a trembling hand, under Helen's admittedly awkward guidance, had long since been wiped away. Only a couple of dark streaks lay embedded in the wrinkles around her eyes. Her hands lay slack in her lap, a wad of tissues lay loosely in her palm and her forgotten handbag lay tumbled at her feet on the springy grass.

Beside Aunt Edna, Helen's cousin Bobby sat rocking back and forth slightly in his chair, making tiny creaking sounds with each motion. Fortunately none of Helen's worst fears about Bobby had materialized during the funeral. There had been no tantrums, no outbursts of wailing, no confused, incessant, loud questions. Even though all the mourners present would have known that Bobby was "slow," a man of thirty frozen mentally at the age of six by spinal meningitis, the question of whether or not to allow his presence at the funeral had been debated up until that very morning.

"Helen, that's his daddy they're putting in the ground today." Aunt Edna's hands had gripped her coffee mug firmly as she and her niece traded stares across a kitchen table littered with half-empty cups and a plate of untouched,

12

congealing buttered biscuits no one had wanted. "He is going to be there to say good-bye to his daddy."

"Aunt Edna, I don't know if he understands."

"No, you don't understand." For the first time since Helen had arrived in Mississippi a week ago, Edna faced her with angry eyes and a firm set to her jaw. "That doesn't matter. He is going, and that's that. I'm still his mother."

Ashamed, Helen had nodded and gathered up cups and plates to set in the sink. She'd stared out over the backyard of the trailer, watching the clouds gather in the north. Who the hell was she, anyway, to come out here from California and take charge of anything? Just a relative who sailed in and out of the McCormick family's life at her pleasure, dipping into the generous emotional cache of acceptance when she felt like it and trotting off back to Berkeley when she'd had enough family life to last for a couple of years.

The same disgust at herself welled up like acid in her throat as the humid wind tore at the corners of the canopy set up over the graveside. It flapped wildly, cracking over the preacher's reedy voice with snapping sounds before tearing away in a sudden burst of wind and water that soaked the gaudy display of wreaths at the foot of the coffin. A couple of dark-suited ushers scurried to secure the canvas amid a general bustle of people rearranging themselves away from the danger zone. All the commotion, however, wasn't enough to hide the whispers that snaked through the gathering to Helen's ears.

"That's the niece, right? Helen Black?"

"Yes, the one from California. Berkeley, I think — where all those weirdos live."

"She looks older than I thought she'd be."

"So she really is one of those, um, you know . . ."

"Shh. Yes, that's what I heard. Don't you remember Peggy Beale saying about how Helen's own daddy kicked her out when he found her with another girl?"

13

"Oh, that one! Can't believe Edna and Loy would even have someone like that in their house."

"Well, they already have a crazy son — what does a perverted niece matter?"

"Shh!"

Helen managed to fight off the inclination to turn around and stare into the crowd behind them, to see who was whispering. She'd been here only a week, and already she'd heard enough whispers to last her a lifetime. Uncle Loy had died on Thursday, three days after her arrival, and now it was Monday again. Was this kind of talk going to continue for the duration of her visit? Then, as suddenly as it had flared up, her anger faded. What did it matter, anyway? She wasn't planning on staying very long as it was. And Aunt Edna and Cousin Bobby seemed oblivious to the gossip of the congregation. This was clearly a tight-knit little group, most of them having known one another for years. Why shouldn't the out-of-town relative cause a bit of gossip? Too bad the fact that until recently she'd been a private eye mattered a lot less to them than whom she fucked.

And she had a good idea how she appeared, anyway. Helen had been far too busy with Edna and Bobby and helping to make arrangements since she arrived to spend any time in front of mirrors — not that she'd ever had much use for them anyhow. Particularly in the past year. Yet another failed relationship, another big check from an uncomfortable situation, another string of insignificant shoe-leather jobs passed her way by local insurance agents, mourning parents of missing teenagers, or spouses sporting the wounds of infidelity — none of them earth-shattering events, but all adding up to a huge painful sore. It was like a blister situated at some sensitive spot on her heart. Dammit, Uncle Loy, she thought — why did you have to get that fucking tumor? *I'll kill you for this.*

As her anger receded, she realized that the kid was wrapping things up and gesturing at them. Confused at first,

Helen realized that Aunt Edna and Cousin Bobby were being invited to engage in a ritual of saying farewell. With a sigh, Helen helped her aunt to her feet and led her to the casket. Bobby shambled right behind her, a low moan welling up from his chest and buzzing through his lips in a ceaseless hum that set Helen's teeth on edge.

"Loy, honey, it's Edna." The old woman's voice cracked and she heaved a shaking sigh as she knelt awkwardly on the soil. Her swollen hands, the fingernails newly painted crimson for the occasion, stroked the coffin. Without turning her head, Helen could imagine the mourners craning their necks to watch with gruesome fascination. Bobby shuffled from foot to foot. Helen thought he was fortunate in not being able to understand what the hell was going on.

Aunt Edna murmured a few more words before groping for Helen's helping hands. She patted her niece on the shoulder and gently pushed her forward.

Helen bit her lip and stepped up to the coffin, well aware that all eyes were wondering what the wayward pervert from the land of fruits and nuts would do. In her hand she clutched the single white rose she'd purchased early that morning from the only florist open, the one at the big new mall outside Tupelo. Helen removed the tiny plastic, water-filled capsule fastened to the end of the stem. She felt the anger that had protected her from grief all day seep into a terrible longing to see her uncle again, to watch the slow smile steal over his lean face, to finally know what he'd been trying to say in his last moments. Why shouldn't they talk about her? And why should it matter? It wasn't really the whispering that upset her. That was just her way, she knew, of covering her rage and sorrow at this loss.

She leaned over the coffin, ignoring the vague rustle of the people crowded behind them, ignoring the watchful eye of the young preacher. *Fuck them. I don't care what they think of me. I'm saying good-bye to one of the few people in this world who ever really loved me.* Silently she dropped the white rose onto the casket. Moments after the blossom fluttered on the polished wood, a gust of wind chased by raindrops blew against the petals, scattering them across the damp dark earth heaped to the side of the grave.

Bobby distracted Helen for the rest of the burial. Her aunt, swallowed up in a sea of elderly ladies in black dresses, disappeared for the next half-hour while the minister and the rest of the congregation drifted over the soggy turf toward the parking lot outside the iron arches of the entrance. Helen steered her cousin to a safe distance from the crowd but made sure to keep Bobby's line of sight directed away from the group of caretakers taking down the canopy.

"My daddy won't be coming home anymore."

Helen linked her arm through Bobby's. They walked slowly through the silent landscape, carefully stepping around gray stone markers and monuments that dripped with rain. "No, honey, he won't."

"He was really sick and he got worse and he's dead. That means he won't be home anymore."

Helen peered into his face. He was calm and remote, as if he'd clarified something for himself. Whatever death meant for Bobby, at least he understood his father was gone. She'd been fearful of having to explain over and over that Loy would not be back. Although god knew what else he might come up with, what painful questions she and her aunt would have to attempt to answer in terms he could fathom.

Helen had made sure they trailed the last stragglers out of the cemetery so that when they reached her small rented car they were alone. Even Edna was nowhere to be seen, tucked away in one of the other cars that formed a caravan out to the highway and to the double-wide trailer outside Tupelo, where a repast had already been organized by some of the ladies of the church. Rain sheeted down now; lightning snaked through the murky clouds. The change in weather did nothing to lessen the heat. Helen got Bobby safely into the car, then eased out of the heavy jacket with relief. The water felt soothing on her body, at least for the moment. As she rounded the car and reached down to open the driver's side door, she got a good look at herself in the window.

"Like something the cat dragged in," she muttered to herself. With a shock she realized how much weight she'd lost in the past few months. For the first time it struck her that the suit wasn't just annoyingly hot and itchy — it hung loosely on a frame that usually had more bulk. Her cheekbones stood out sharply, accentuating dark, deep-set eyes. And her hair — well, she'd not gotten a haircut for several months. Dampened by rain, it hung lank and lifeless around her shoulders. Her mouth was a thin dark line with no hint of feeling given away.

"I look like shit. I look fucking angry."

"Helen?" Bobby's muffled voice sounded through the thick glass. He leaned across the gearshift and peered out at her. "How come you standing out there in the rain?"

Helen forced a smile as she slipped into the driver's seat. "Because your cousin Helen is silly sometimes, Bobby. That's why."

Bobby regarded her solemnly, then nodded. "Yeah. People are silly sometimes."

"Fasten your seat belt, hon. We're going to go home."

He fumbled with the buckle. Helen watched him as she got the car started, then reached over to help him. It struck her forcefully, as she got the buckle locked, that her cousin Bobby was now a middle-aged man. His blank, pale face, doughy with exhaustion and confusion, bore all the lines of maturity without any of the understanding etched into his features. Jesus, she thought as she pulled out onto the highway, what the fuck is Aunt Edna going to do with him?

She was distracted, however, by the presence of one other car in the parking lot. Helen drove past close enough to get a good look at the driver. Despite the pouring rain and the gathering darkness, she easily made out the features of Beth Wilks. Uh-oh. She hadn't seen Beth at the funeral. The woman must have slipped in late, maybe delayed by her work as a state trooper. Helen got only a glance as she went by the car, but it didn't look as though Beth was in uniform.

"Who's that, Helen?"

"Just a-an old friend, Bobby."

"Is she coming to my house too?"

Helen sighed. "I'm afraid so." Of course, describing her as an old friend wasn't entirely accurate, Helen realized. Especially since one of the last times Helen had seen Beth was when they were both naked in front of a fireplace screwing their brains out. "Yes, the whole gang is here now." Helen flipped the windshield wipers up to their highest speed and sped through the downpour to the wake.

Chapter Two

    Sunlight blazed down on the sere brown dead grass of the swath called a backyard behind the trailer. Aunt Edna's tomato plants had long since died in the August heat without anyone to tend them and give them the frequent soaking they required to survive the hell of summer in the deep South. Thin, wasted lengths of vine still curled around the wire frames where they'd been slowly dying. The recent storms hadn't done much more than turn them into mushy stems. A couple of fig trees straggled their limbs over the dying garden. The coiled snake of a garden hose lay between them, and Helen felt a pang of sadness. Maybe the fruit trees could be salvaged. She'd have to soak the roots a few times, see if they could be saved.

From the postage-stamp yard next door, the neighbors' twin Irish wolfhounds panted and drooled and stared at Helen, their flat, empty eyes gleaming with something — hunger? Disgust? Maybe just boredom — as they followed her progress across their line of sight. Their haunches settled on the gravel that covered the hard-baked clay soil of the property, grating the stones beneath their butts as they shifted to keep Helen in view. Not for the first time Helen noted the absence of cats or birds or squirrels in the vicinity of these beasts. No big surprise — they'd probably devoured anything that couldn't move fast enough to get away from those smelly jowls, and they certainly looked like they'd enjoy a taste of Helen.

Helen stood by the back door long enough to keep the flyspecked screen door from slamming behind her. Voices broke into the heat and silence of the afternoon, murmurs from all over the trailer as various church folk wandered around munching on sandwiches and odd-shaped little rolls and buns provided by some of the ladies who'd been hovering around Edna all day. Mere minutes ago Helen had marveled at the endless possibilities of Vienna sausage and Bisquick while making her selection. She wasn't in the least hungry but felt she had to make at least a pretense of picking at the food arrayed on the folding tables that took up most of the space in the trailer's front room.

Now Helen glanced back over her shoulder toward the tiny square window that marked Bobby's room. It was little more than a narrow galley, with just enough space for his bed and some shelves crammed with books and toys and a few odd treasures that made sense only to him. He'd dozed off in the car and mercifully went right to his room for a nap. And for the moment, at least, Aunt Edna was enthroned on the sofa and surrounded by a flutter of church friends. As she'd walked toward the back door, she'd gotten a look at her aunt's face, still frozen in shock. Better that way, Helen thought — just let her get through this afternoon. She'd grabbed a sandwich without really seeing what she was getting and looked around for something to drink.

It had been a disappointment to see that the punch was some kind of Kool-Aid and frozen juice concentrate mix, sparkling with ice cubes but definitely alcohol free. Of course, it was to be expected. A fundamentalist Protestant gathering wouldn't have anything stronger than carbonated soda to offer. The sandwich Helen now held in one hand contained some indescribable meat paste spread on limp white bread, cut artfully into a triangular shape with crusts sliced off. Helen attempted a second bite and managed to swallow it without gagging as she stepped outside.

"Here, guys. Knock your socks off," she muttered as she tossed the remains of her sandwich to the pair of dogs sitting sentinel next door. With a quickness belying their immobility of seconds before, they leaped after the bits of bread and meat. Muffled snarls rose up over the chain-link fence as they settled into a dance of dominance over the food.

Helen squinted up at the sun. Jesus, it was getting hot again. Her blouse, already uncomfortable from dried sweat, felt like it was melting into her skin. Too bad for the saints inside, she thought, unbuttoning the final button that hid her cleavage from the good folks of the church. She made for the corner of the yard where Uncle Loy's workshop stood, her pumps making crackling noises on the dead grass.

Workshop was perhaps a bit too kind a name for the lopsided wooden shed leaning against a sagging fence. Shaded by a huge magnolia tree that spread its shelter from the wooded lot next door, the corner offered the only bit of shade in the backyard besides the fig trees. Glossy leaves shone brightly in the sun, stray raindrops sparkling like crystal as the branches moved gently in the hot breeze that carried a scent of honeysuckle from somewhere. As she watched, Helen saw an enormous white magnolia blossom, big as a dinner plate, float to the red-brown dirt in front of the shed, its petals separating and drifting into the dust. Helen stepped around it and opened the door of the workshop, recoiling momentarily from the heat and dust that rolled out from its interior. With a final glance over her shoulder — no one else in sight, just the dogs that'd settled into silence again — she stepped inside.

Holding her breath she opened the two windows that faced away from the house, letting in a humid breeze through the torn screens. Sunlight illuminated dust motes that flowed in a steady stream, swirling around the square interior of the boxy shed. Helen sneezed, sneezed again, then took stock of her surroundings as she caught her breath.

The shed was another unspoken understanding she and her uncle had shared. Aunt Edna had, of course, long ago realized that her husband's on-and-off interest in wood-working or small-appliance repair or obsessive arrangement of his tackle box was the single escape he had from the demands of his life. Helen couldn't count the times she'd heard over the years her Aunt Edna pronounce, on being questioned as to the whereabouts of her husband, "He's out in his work shed right now." Or, "Loy is working out back. Don't bother him right now." And sometimes, "He's been out back for hours and hours. I declare, he loses all track of time when he's working." Even poor Bobby understood that the shed was Uncle Loy's kingdom, the one place where his privacy wouldn't be invaded nor the pressures of reality intrude. Helen guessed that he could leave all the hard truths of his life — his marriage to a sweet but simpleminded woman, the pain of the son he loved who would never be a man, the frustration of being trapped in a dead-end factory job that would allow only for survival just above poverty — at the crookedly hung wooden door of this shed for just a few hours.

And as she looked around the room Helen felt a flood of memories wash over her tired, sweating body with the force of tangible, tactile presence that reached beyond merely cerebral reflection. Was it the lingering scent of his unfiltered cigarettes? And the heavy odor of gasoline and thick oil beneath that. The bitter, clogging taste of sawdust on her

22

tongue from his many half-finished carpentry projects. She looked up to see the big bulb hanging from a hook over her head, but she didn't reach up to the strand of rusted metal that would switch it on with one pull. Helen could see just fine without it.

She took a step closer to the long bench that ran the length of the shed. She carefully avoided stacked cardboard boxes filled with old magazines, boxes of rusted tools, splintery wooden crates of empty Mason jars, and heaps of coiled and fraying rope that was rotted from heat and the passage of time. A variety of hand tools hung from hooks on the crumbling perfboard that teetered behind the workspace, and there was some kind of oddly cut piece of plywood still lodged in the big vise that gripped the edge of table.

Helen cautiously leaned against the table — yes, it still careened off to the left on the uneven floor — and looked at the calendar from the local bait shop that was pinned on the right side of the perfboard. It was four years old. Miss December, decently clad in waders and sporting an expensive rod and reel, smiled up from her motorboat with a toothy grin, her long curly blond hair flowing out from the bright red baseball cap advertising a line of sinkers guaranteed to land the user in the fishermen's hall of fame. Beside her lay a pile of gleaming fish, eyes wide and staring and mouths gaping as if caught in permanent surprise at their fate at the hands of such a lovely debutante.

Helen found herself smiling at this innocent version of cheesecake, perhaps the only nod to libido her uncle had ever indulged. Her attention was caught by a sudden plop as water dripped to the worktable, splattering the dust. Was it raining again? No, she realized, wiping her cheeks.

Helen sighed and turned away, suddenly enraged at the uncomfortable clothing she'd been compelled to wear all day long. A quick look out the shed windows assured her that the congregation was still inside the trailer, chewing their way through grief. She unbuttoned her blouse and flapped it a bit, creating a tiny bit of breeze against her sweating skin. Surely she could hear anyone coming, walking across the dead grass. She lifted her hair up off her neck — she really had to go get a haircut, although she didn't even want to attempt it while she was in Mississippi, hoping it would be tolerable until she got back to Berkeley. She scrabbled around for a rubber band from the dusty boxes of clips and staples stacked on the worktable. Once she found one that didn't crumble in her fingers, she pulled her hair back into it.

A cool breeze gusted through the open door. Maybe it was going to rain again, after all. God, if only it would cool off. Why did all her visits to Mississippi seem to take place in the summer? Helen sat down on the padded stool, safely in shadows away from the door, and let the air wash over her bare skin. She kicked off her shoes and stretched out her legs, looking down at her feet as they wiggled in the mottled sunlight coming from the windows. With a wry smile she realized she hadn't worn pantyhose in — well, she couldn't even remember the last time. In fact, it was the one thing she'd forgotten to throw in a suitcase during her hurried preparations for the flight a week ago. These had been purchased after she had arrived in Mississippi. "What the hell," Helen muttered as she tugged at the itchy, thin fabric. The hose were off in moments, and she sighed with relief as she stretched her legs again.

Pantyhose were not the only item she'd purchased. And this wasn't the first time she'd visited the work shed since her return last week. With an odd mingling of anxiety and relief, Helen reached under the worktable for the filing cabinet Uncle Loy used to hold up the end of the table. The lower drawer was deep enough to hold the stash of extension cords he'd stuffed away, just in case. And her two bottles of bourbon fit neatly behind the cords. The drawer squeaked as she slammed it shut.

Helen retrieved one of the bottles and twisted off the cap.

24

She tried to force her mind away from the vague unease she felt at keeping the bottles out here, but the thoughts pushed up, surfacing like dark fins through murky waters as she took a sip. It wasn't as if Aunt Edna would care, Helen was certain of that. It wouldn't be a big deal to anyone, as long as she herself didn't make a big deal about it. So what was she so worked up about? Why did she feel compelled to hide this little vice out here in the shed, where no one would see?

Helen took another deep swallow and savored the hot silky sensation of the liquor burning down her throat and hitting her stomach. The feeling spread with familiar comfort to her chest, and she could almost tell the moment her muscles began to relax. She leaned against the table and studied her bare toes, letting the images flow unhindered through her mind. Images of herself back at home, back in Berkeley, alone in her messy house and still messier office. Images of how her last relationship had ended, with Alison's tear-stained face pale in the darkness, slamming the door shut behind her. Worst of all, the image of herself taking a big fat check, loaded with lots of zeros behind a satisfyingly big number, to the bank for deposit just about six months ago. Watching the bank clerk cheerfully accept the deposit, her perky, smiling features beaming with corporate goodwill above the glass barrier as she handed Helen a receipt.

"Would you be interested in opening a time deposit, ma'am?"

Helen had just stared blankly at the young woman, wondering how she'd react if Helen told her the money was a reward for keeping her mouth shut about murder. A payoff for silence. A payoff that would enable her to quit her minimum-wage, security-guard job and get back into the business of snooping into other people's sordid mistakes and self-deceptions. An exchange of lies — you scratch my back and I'll buy your complicity.

"No, thanks. I'll be needing that money as soon as the

check clears," Helen had managed to mumble before hurrying out. And so she had — the lease to the new and improved office near the university, business cards and letterhead, a new computer and fax machine, even some new clothes. Alison had left for good just as Helen had hung up her shingle, taking the cat with her to her new apartment in Oakland.

Helen took another swig to drown out the memory of the cat yowling in the backseat of Alison's car. As she replaced the cap on the bottle she heard a familiar voice at the doorway.

"Mind some company?" Beth Wilks's tall frame filled the doorway, blocking the sunlight.

"What if I said yes?" Helen was suddenly aware of her unbuttoned blouse, her bare legs, the bottle of bourbon in her hands.

"I'd just come in anyhow."

Helen sighed, unable to stifle a wave of pleasure at seeing the other woman. Beth hadn't changed much in the past five years. Still tall, still well muscled, still blond and blue-eyed in a fresh-faced way that belied the hard set to her mouth. "You look different when you're not in your uniform. I don't think I've ever seen you in a skirt," she said, taking in the dark suit and low-heeled shoes.

Beth stepped inside and glanced down at herself. "I didn't want to show up at the church in work drag. That's why I was late getting there. Sorry about that." She moved further into the room, never taking her eyes off Helen.

Helen shrugged. "No problem. Nice of you to show up."

"I wouldn't stay away, Helen. Your uncle was always very good to me. To you, too, as I recall." Beth shrugged off her jacket, and Helen tried not to watch the muscles in her arms move beneath the tailored dark shirt. At least she was hot and sweaty too. Again, not a good thought to have floating through her mind, particularly when she was working hard at getting a decent buzz before returning to the trailer.

"So, how the hell are you these days, Beth? Still rounding

up the bad guys on the highway and busting stills on private property?"

She watched the slow, familiar grin steal across Beth's face. "Yep, still saving the world. As you would know if you ever read my letters."

"What do you mean? Of course I read them. All three of them."

Beth shrugged. "I might have sent more if you had ever answered those three. Seems like you still owe me a couple. Or a phone call. Or something."

Helen faced Beth squarely as she took another drink. "Well, I've been kind of busy."

"So Edna and Loy told me." Beth took a step closer, and Helen felt herself blushing under the other woman's scrutiny. "How long were you in the hospital, Helen?"

"Too long. Being gut-shot tends to put you out of commission for a while," Helen answered, hoping she'd managed a carefree tone. She had to look away as she spoke. Beth, a police officer herself, would know just how close Helen had come to death a couple of years ago. For some reason, Beth's understanding was harder to bear than all the shocked sympathy that she'd received from anyone else. Made it more difficult to keep up a cool facade, she realized. More difficult to keep from admitting to herself that in some sense her life had ended with those bullets, no matter how hard she'd tried to put it back together since that moment of pain and blood. "You should see the other guy," she went on. "The really tough part, though, was all the physical therapy. That was worse than being shot, I think." Please don't ask me about Alison, Helen prayed. Anything but that — anything but my ex-lover.

Fortunately Beth seemed willing to move on. "Well — sounds like you're back in business now."

"You betcha. You get to save the world this side of the river, and the western half is for me."

"Sounds good. Hope I'm managing my end okay." Beth kept her eyes on the bottle as it made its journey back and forth.

"Oh yes, it's a real showplace out here, Beth. Just take a look at what's stalking around the trailer."

"Hey — these people care about your aunt. They're mostly decent folks, Helen."

"Huh." Helen took another drink to swallow down a pang of shame at Beth's remark. Of course she was right. Helen was just not having any right now, thank you very much.

"They also said you'd fully recovered from being shot a couple of years ago," Beth went on. "That true?" Beth fiddled for a moment with a dusty box of nails on the table, averting her gaze from Helen. Helen watched her hair fall over her cheeks, dappled gold in the play of sun and shadow. "You really okay now?"

"I've been better. But then, haven't we all?" Helen had to look away from Beth's hands moving across the countertop. She couldn't stop the memory of the way Beth's hands had felt moving across her breasts the last time they'd made love. Damn, why the hell did her mind have to go there right now? She didn't need this. And she knew she was acting like a brat, hiding out here drinking and pouting and thinking evil thoughts about those harmless souls from the church. Instead of taking Beth's hands in her own, Helen took another drink.

Beth interrupted her vaguely lustful reverie. "What are you doing out here? Your aunt's been asking where you were." Helen watched Beth's gaze stray to the bottle of bourbon. "I think she's wearing out. She could use some moral support in there."

"Moral support," Helen snorted. Fuck it, she thought, taking the cap off the bottle again and lifting it to her lips. She drank too quickly, however, and had to choke back a coughing fit. "I seriously doubt anyone in that room would consider my support to be moral."

Beth shook her head and folded her arms. She leaned

against the table next to Helen. "Believe it or not, Helen, I don't think anyone in that room is paying a whole lot of attention to you and your little sins. Right now, your family needs you."

"Thanks for the sermon. I'll keep it in mind every time I overhear their snide little remarks about my evil ways. Oh, that's right — you got to the funeral too late to hear any of them. Want a sample? I can remember most of them word for word." Helen leaned forward, shoved the bottle toward Beth, and felt the mild edges of vertigo that told her she was indeed on her way to getting slightly looped. Good, she thought. That will make sitting here with Beth easier, particularly when I'm behaving so badly.

Beth ignored the bottle. "What's wrong, Helen?"

Helen sat back on the stool and drank some more, this time slowly. She closed her eyes and tilted her head forward, let the cool air that signaled another storm wash over her neck. "Jesus fucking Christ, Beth. I just buried my uncle, the only man in my family who'll still own me, and you have the nerve to ask me what's wrong."

"This isn't grief, Helen." Helen opened her eyes at the barely controlled anger in Beth's low-pitched voice. "This is a tantrum. And what the hell are you doing hiding booze out here?"

"What are you going to do, write me a ticket, Officer? So I wanted a drink away from the Holy Rollers. So fucking what?"

"All I have to do is look at you to know something is eating you alive, Helen." Beth moved closer, and Helen got a good view of her eyes. "Look, I know we haven't talked in a long time, but —"

"That's right, Beth. We haven't. So you don't know a damn thing about my life."

"Then tell me." Beth glanced down at the bottle. "Surely talking about it is better than drinking, isn't it?"

For a moment Helen had a terrible desire to tell Beth

everything. Even though Beth had let her go, as a teenager when they were caught together and Helen was disgraced and thrown out of her own home. Even though when they'd met again five years ago Beth chose to stay behind in Mississippi while Helen went back to California. Even though every time Helen had opened up to Beth it had left a tear-stained trail of pain between them. Beth knew her, better than any other lover she'd ever had. And Beth would understand what Helen feared most — that her life was unraveling like a cheap piece of fabric, slowly unwinding into a thin thread that would snap at the least pressure, that her uncle's death and her return to Mississippi were yet another tug at the fragile weave. That Helen wasn't at all sure there was anything to go back to in California.

Helen's grip on the bottle tightened. She felt a grin stretch her lips. "Did Aunt Edna just appoint you my official baby-sitter? Or did you volunteer for the job?"

Beth moved away, her eyes darkening with hurt. "Come back in the house, Helen. Quit thinking about yourself for a minute. There's a woman in there who really needs you right now."

"What about you, Beth? Do you need me?" Helen watched herself reach out to the tall blonde standing in front of her, observing with a mixture of fascination and disgust as she stroked Beth's soft cheek. It was as if she stood outside herself, Helen thought, letting her hands travel to Beth's throat. Was this really her, making a drunken clumsy pass at a woman who recoiled in disgust? It must be someone else. Helen Black didn't behave this way. Then she heard her voice say, "You used to. Remember?"

"Helen, stop this. Not here, not now." Beth moved further away, and Helen let her hands fall to her side. Beth stood rigidly by the door, her face a stony mask of revulsion. "Maybe you should stay out here after all, Helen. I don't think you'll be much help to Edna right now." Then she was gone.

Helen let herself sit on the stool wallowing in disgust and guilt for a while — she didn't know how long, but it couldn't have been more than a few minutes. Feeling about an inch high she pulled her pantyhose on, buttoned her blouse and stepped out of the shed after secreting the bourbon behind the extension cords. There was indeed another storm on the way. Already the sky to the north was boiling with black clouds, and thunder echoed from far away. A few drops sprinkled her face as she strolled by the waiting wolfhounds. Their huge heads lifted eagerly as she walked by. "Take it easy, guys," she muttered. "You'll get another chance at me one day."

But instead of heading directly back into the trailer, Helen decided to walk around for a moment, maybe dispel some of the effects of alcohol and self-pity before facing her aunt and the others. Silly idea, of course — coffee and a shower would be more helpful. She walked around to the front of the trailer, encountering a couple of the brethren at the side of the house. They watched her as she carefully walked, a smile plastered to her lips, concentrating on each step so she didn't falter in front of them.

Now what? She'd have to go inside, and God knew what she smelled like, between sweat and liquor. This really was terrible. Beth was absolutely right. As she continued her interior monologue of shame, Helen found herself near the edge of the property. Rain was beginning to come down hard by the time she reached the front door, excusing herself as she squeezed through people gathered on the tiny veranda. She ended up standing by the mailbox, waiting for a chance to get inside and look for Aunt Edna. And maybe Beth, to see if she could manage a decent apology.

Without thinking she reached for the mail as she waited, noticing that yet again it was stuffed to overflowing. A few pieces of junk mail announcing sales and deals throughout the county had slipped to the porch. Helen didn't trust her head to withstand leaning over to get them, so she let them stay where they were. Instead she nodded and smiled at the good folks milling about near the door, glancing down now and then at the assortment of bills and cards clutched in her hands.

Besides the phone bill and the electricity bill, the rest of the mail was probably sympathy cards, Helen guessed. But one envelope stood out from the others. It was slightly larger than business size. A clean, clear script marked the return address on the thick vellum of the envelope. Stivers, Stivers, and Hutchison, Helen read. Sounds like lawyers, she decided. What the heck could that be for? It was addressed to her aunt. It wasn't terribly thick, but the weight of the paper seemed to her at that moment to carry the weight of significance.

Helen felt the fog of bourbon lift a bit as she studied the envelope, edging herself through a knot of people toward the edge of the porch where Aunt Edna had hung some kind of leafy fern plants. Everyone else seemed to be intent on crowding into the house, so she had a thin shield of privacy from their gaze for a few moments. She chewed her lip, thinking.

After a quick, internal debate, Helen decided to open the letter. She'd just take a quick look and figure out if it was something big and bad before letting her aunt see it. She read it twice, puzzled, before going into the trailer to find her aunt.

Chapter Three

"Are you sure you've never heard of them before, Aunt Edna?"

"No, honey, I'm sure. I'd remember if some fancy lawyers ever called us."

Helen sighed and rubbed her temples. The coffee wasn't helping her hangover. Once again she'd gone a bit too far with the bourbon, like so many other days in her recent past. The bright sunlight streamed through the squeaky-clean windows of the trailer's tiny kitchen, spilling liquid gold through the yellow gauzy curtains hung at the window over the sink. The letter from Stivers, Stivers, and Hutchison lay on the table amid the jam jars and butter dish and stack of uneaten toast. It was propped up against the stainless-steel percolator, where

Helen had left it after reading it over with her aunt. The small, neat print hurt Helen's eyes, but then everything was hurting Helen's eyes right now. Instead of laying off the booze for the rest of the afternoon yesterday, Helen had sneaked back out to Uncle Loy's workshop for another couple of belts after the brothers and sisters of the church had finally left. It hadn't seemed like a good idea right then to show her aunt the letter, so Helen had put it off until this morning.

Still didn't seem like a good idea. Aunt Edna had puttered around in the kitchen just before dawn, waking Helen from an uneasy sleep in the living room on the foldout sofa. She'd tossed and turned restlessly all night anyhow, so it seemed like a good idea to go ahead and get up to keep Edna company. Big mistake. Her head felt like an overripe melon about to burst, and several aspirin and two cups of coffee later it still felt that way. Bobby hadn't helped, either, lumbering heavy-footed through the trailer at his usual clumsy pace, making the walls shake and all the little knickknacks arranged around the house rattle as he stumbled from room to room. He'd taken a single slice of toast dripping with jam and margarine with him as he'd shuffled outside right after the sun came up.

"Why would Loy have anything to do with them? He was never in trouble with the law, you know that."

"It doesn't sound like it was trouble, Aunt Edna." Helen reached for the letter and read through it again for perhaps the twentieth time. It didn't read any differently, now that she'd sobered up, than it did yesterday afternoon when she'd been half drunk. "It sounds like they have some kind of business to conduct with you that's in some way connected with Uncle Loy. I guess it must be something to do with his pension, since they describe themselves as representing Roberts and Farrell."

"But Loy quit that job almost twenty years ago!"

"Quit? I thought he retired," Helen commented, only mildly puzzled. She put the letter down and squinted through the sunlight to look at her aunt's face. For the first time that morning Helen realized that it wasn't continuing grief twisting her aunt's features. Edna refused to meet Helen's gaze, fidgeted with knives and plates, fussed with her thinning white hair — yes, she looked more nervous than anything else. "I thought you guys were living on his pension plan already."

"No — well, he took a big check — I mean, he left them a long time ago, that's all. I just can't imagine why they'd want to bother with all this now."

Helen gently shook her head. She felt like shit and wasn't sure how fuzzy her mind was right then. "Bother with what?" she asked.

"Did you want anything else, sweetheart? More coffee?" Edna got up quickly, nearly upsetting her coffee all over the letter. Helen rescued the letter from being soaked with cold coffee, glanced once again at the cold eggs and bacon congealing on her plate, then looked away quickly to swallow down the nausea that threatened to overtake her. A shadow fell across the table. Bobby had just passed by the kitchen window. Edna followed Helen's gaze with a sigh.

"He's hardly talked at all today. Do you think he understands about his daddy, Helen?"

Helen focused on the elderly woman sitting across from her, her headache momentarily forgotten. Her aunt seemed to have shrunk, she realized suddenly. And not just because she looked smaller, frailer — it was in her tremulous voice, her shaking hands, the way her eyes would look at things without really seeing them. Now she watched as Aunt Edna's fingers plucked at a tear in the cheap flowered-plastic table covering, picking and fraying the ragged edge of the hole. Like Helen, she hadn't touched any of the food she'd prepared. There was enough breakfast to feed all of them and then some, Helen saw with a sinking heart. It was going to take quite a while for Edna to learn to cook just for two.

"It's okay, Aunt Edna," Helen said softly, covering her

aunt's hands with her own and stilling the frantic motion of her fingers. "I just wanted to make sure. We'll go see them together." Maybe she was afraid those lawyers were going to cancel Loy's retirement, or some such thing. And after what she'd been through in the past month, Aunt Edna had every right to be shaken and afraid. She'd just lost the anchor of her whole life, and now she faced a future of aging while trying to figure out how to care for her mentally incompetent son. The least Helen could do was make sure she tagged along with her aunt, try to keep the aging woman from being intimidated by a bunch of people in suits at a conference table.

"You-you don't mind, honey?" She lifted her face to her niece, and Helen saw tears welling up in her aunt's already red-rimmed eyes. "I wouldn't know what to say to a bunch of lawyers. I never really had to talk to people like that before. I'd sure appreciate it if you're not too busy."

"What would I be too busy with?" Helen asked, forcing herself to smile. "That's why I'm here — to be with you and Bobby for a while."

"Well, as long as you're sure you don't have to go back home."

Helen started to shake her head, stopped when a twinge of pain seared behind her eyes, and kept smiling. "Hey, I'm my own boss these days, remember? I'm in no big hurry to get back to California. We'll just call these folks up this morning and head right over there. Maybe Bobby can stay with one of your friends from church while we're gone. And then I'll take you out for lunch downtown. How does that sound?" she added brightly, hoping to distract both of them from their feelings for a little while.

"Oh, well, maybe not this morning, sweetheart."

"Why not?"

"The ladies from the church are going to come over and go through the house today."

"What are you talking about?" Jesus, nothing was making any sense. Maybe it wasn't too soon for more aspirin. "What ladies?"

Aunt Edna grabbed a napkin and dabbed at her eyes. "You know, to help me pack up Loy's things and take them over to the church. I thought it would be a good idea to do it right away." Her aunt's voice trailed away behind the napkin. She crumpled the paper in her hands and turned a face lined with pain to Helen. "There's four ladies coming over this morning."

"I see." Why did this information infuriate her, Helen wondered. It felt like a violation, somehow. What did these women have to do with her uncle? They didn't need to be invading today. Helen had had more than enough of them yesterday.

Then, seeing her aunt's grief-stricken features, she felt a pang of shame. Once again she was — what did Beth call it? — having a tantrum. This had nothing to do with her. This was something her aunt wanted to do. Helen's presence was probably a lot more like an invasion than the arrival of Aunt Edna's friends from church. Beth had been right — they were just people trying to help, no more and no less. And who the blazes was she to quibble with what her aunt wanted right now? "That's fine, Aunt Edna. Maybe we can just call them and set up an appointment for later this week. How about that?"

So it was Helen who made the call about two hours later. She decided to wait until ten, when the law offices were sure to be open. By that time the quartet of church ladies had already landed like storm troopers, armed with covered dishes and Saran Wrapped plates of food. Bobby, clearly confused, poked his head in once or twice and grabbed some cookies before loping off toward the patch of woods next to the trailer park. Helen had her last glimpse of him that morning as she was straightening up the living room.

"Oh, hello." The ladies smiled and looked curiously at Helen as they passed through the living room just as she was replacing the last cushion on the restored sofa.

"Good morning. Nice to see you again," Helen lied.

"How are you feeling today?" That was the oldest of the group taking the lead. Her sharp little eyes flickered up and down, studying Helen closely. What, Helen felt like asking, is something hanging out of my nose or my butt or something?

Instead, she just answered, "Pretty well, considering, thank you."

The woman, dressed in a cheap thrift-store version of a Chanel suit and a faux designer bag to match, sniffed and smiled a tight little smile. Helen guessed someone had seen her stumble out of the toolshed yesterday and reported back to the church version of the KGB. What was her name? Minson, Minton, something like that. Her entourage looked embarrassed but too cowed by the queen bee before them to say a word beyond murmured greetings.

"Oh, Mrs. Muncie, thank you so much for coming." Aunt Edna, composed and sporting fresh lipstick, came out of the kitchen wiping her hands with a dishtowel. It hurt Helen's heart to see her aunt pathetically grateful to this bitch on heels. Now, now, Helen reminded herself, these are my aunt's friends, and I'm imagining things. She had to tell herself the same thing again as she saw the predatory gleam in Mrs. Muncie's eyes. Why all the excitement? Why did this woman want to head up the hunting party? Because that's exactly what it felt like at that moment to Helen — a bunch of hounds let loose on an unsuspecting deer. Maybe, Helen mused as she plopped down on the sofa next to the phone, they were just hoping to find some kind of treasure trove in her poor uncle's possessions.

The cleanup team had divided their duties, each taking a turn to comfort Edna while the other three disappeared into various corners of the house. Kind of like tag team wrestling,

Helen thought nastily as she settled on the sofa, holding the lawyers' letter. A sliver of shame went through her. Except for the Muncie woman, the others seemed genuinely concerned about her aunt.

Helen opened a window and let the warm breeze, fresher and cooler after yesterday's rains, drift over her face. Her head had finally cleared up a bit. With a conscious effort she shut out the sound of the women's voices as she dialed the number printed on the letter. She had to go through three different people to get to one of the lawyers.

"Yes, we got the letter yesterday. No, my aunt, Edna McCormick, isn't available to come to the phone right now. She just — no, I'm her niece. I came out here for my uncle's funeral. All right, I'll hold." Helen sighed and let her gaze drift toward the yard. There was Bobby, sitting on the one patch of green grass still flourishing next to the driveway. The wolfhounds, ever alert to the presence of a potential meal, sat watching him. What was her cousin holding in his hands? She craned forward, ignoring the resurgence of pain in her head as she leaned forward.

"What? Yes, yes. This is Helen Black. That's right, Edna McCormick's niece," she repeated. Would she have to go through that again? Apparently not. "Okay, tomorrow afternoon. Two-thirty. You're in downtown Tupelo? What's the cross street?" Helen fumbled for a pencil and scratched the time and location on the envelope.

As she hung up the telephone, Helen looked back out at Bobby, who was still sitting on the grass. Something glinted in his hands. He shifted slightly, and Helen finally figured out what he was doing.

"Shit," she muttered. Lawyers and headaches forgotten, she hurried outside. "Bobby, let me see what you've got there."

He turned around, the half-empty bourbon bottle swinging in his hands. Helen saw with relief that the level of liquor wasn't too different from what she remembered leaving there last night. He couldn't have had more than a swallow or two. And, judging by the look on his face, he hadn't liked it much.

"How come you was drinking this yesterday, Helen? It tastes real bad."

Great. All she needed was for Mrs. Muncie and her minions to get a look at this. Helen pried the bottle loose from Bobby's grip. "It's definitely an acquired taste, Bobby."

"What's that mean?"

"It means —" She finally wrested the bottle free. Some of it sloshed out onto the grass. To her left the wolfhounds rustled, alerted by the sudden sounds and motion, maybe even the strong scent. "It means you don't need any more of this."

"But it was in the workshop, Helen. My daddy had it in the workshop. You had it yesterday." Bobby squinted up at her and struggled to his feet. "How come I can't have some too? It was my daddy's. He had it."

"Oh no, Bobby. Please don't cry." Big fat tears coursed down his cheeks and he screwed his face up in preparation for big sobs. "Look, this wasn't your daddy's. This is mine."

"But how come it was in his work shed, Helen? How come it's out there? That was Daddy's place."

Helen shook her head. Nausea came back in waves. She breathed deeply for a moment until the urge to retch passed. This was getting worse and worse. And there was no end in sight. Church ladies inside, Aunt Edna terrified of lawyers, and now Bobby was going to wander around with bourbon on his breath. For a moment Helen desperately longed for her lonely little house in Berkeley. Why the hell had she been whining to herself about the emptiness of her life? Right now it sounded pretty fucking good.

"Hush, Bobby. It's okay. I just put this outside in the work shed for a while."

"What is it, Helen? It tastes bad. I don't like how it tastes." He puzzled for a moment, then his face brightened. "Is it your medicine, Helen? Like what Daddy had to take

40

when he got sick? And Mommy takes medicine, too. For her blood precious."

"Her blood precious. Oh, her blood pressure."

"Uh-huh." He seemed satisfied with his own explanation of medical necessity, and Helen decided she didn't have the energy to come up with anything better. He got to his feet and turned away to the house. Helen, seized with sudden panic, took him by the arm. Maybe it would be better not to let him go back in the house now, smelling faintly of liquor and spouting off god-knows-what in front of Aunt Edna and Mrs. Muncie. Who knew what Bobby would say? She looked down at her cousin, his eyes blearing, his mouth gaping, his plaid shirt buttoned wrong so that the tails hung unevenly over his loose jeans. He picked lazily at his bulging stomach, scratching as he smiled up at her trustingly, all his love and confidence for her shining through his disheveled appearance.

"Idiot, idiot, goddamned idiot," she cursed herself. Acid boiled in her throat as she crossed the backyard. What the hell was she thinking, behaving like this? There was no excuse for it. Just because she was feeling sorry for herself, rolling around in self-pity like a hog in mud, that was no way to help her aunt and her cousin right now. Uncle Loy would have been ashamed of her. And Beth — Helen felt herself flush with humiliation at the memory of how Beth had seen her yesterday. Did she really make that clumsy pass at the woman? Had she really been so mean and nasty in her comments about Edna's friends? She shivered in the heat at the thought of how much she'd been drinking lately. Enough that it may have begun to warp her perceptions. Helen shoved that thought aside and steered Bobby around the side of the house, keeping up a low murmur as they walked. "Let's just put this back in the shed, Bobby," she said. "We'll keep it out there where it belongs."

"Okay. We gonna go back there, Helen? We gonna look at my daddy's stuff?"

"Sure, Bobby. Just you and me. It will be just the two of

us, okay?" Maybe if she made it a game between them, a secret, that would keep him quiet for at least as long as it took Mrs. Muncie and the others to clear out of the house. Periodically, as she led the way, Helen glanced around. There were sounds coming from inside the house, but apparently the team of ladies were busy inside, occupied with whatever they were turning up among the clothes and shoes and papers in the master bedroom. First things first, she thought, stepping quickly around the dead tomato plants. Get this out of sight, and take Bobby into town for lunch or ice cream or something. Get him sobered up. Then, when the coast was clear, she'd get rid of the bourbon — she'd already guiltily decided to do that, anyhow — try to keep Aunt Edna from finding out —

"They was here, Helen. Right here in this drawer." He stood beside her as she carefully wedged the half-empty bottle back behind the extension cords. Later, when everyone was gone, she'd take both bottles out and get rid of them. It would be too risky to try to do that now, not when several sets of curious eyes might be watching from the trailer. She pushed the drawer shut, using both hands, wincing at the faint squeal that sounded from the rusting metal.

But it refused to stay shut. "Shit," she muttered, pushing harder.

"What's wrong, Helen?"

"Nothing, honey. Cousin Helen is just not having her best day today." Again she pushed, and again the drawer slid back open, revealing its contents in the dusty light.

"Did you break it, Helen? Did you break Daddy's stuff?" Bobby leaned over her, reaching down to poke at the drawer. "I can fix it. Watch," and he shoved with such force that the worktable shuddered.

The drawer only stayed closed for a moment. As soon as they'd stood up and started to back away it slid open again. Helen sighed and took the bottles out. This was turning into a farce now, minus the laughs. "Never mind, Bobby. Let's just take the, uh, this stuff out of here and we'll fix it later."

Holding the bottles close to her chest, as if that would somehow keep them out of view, Helen backed away from the worktable. "Let's go to town and get a bite to eat, okay? How would you like that?"

Unfortunately, Bobby didn't seem to care about her suggestion. He stared down at the worktable, and Helen watched with dismay as the telltale signs of frustration appeared. His shoulders tensed, and she could hear his heavy breathing. Even in the dim light she could see the flush of anger spread across his broad flat face, his lips twisting in fury. In any other man of his years, this kind of rage would frighten her as the prelude to violence. In her cousin's case, she knew, it was the result of a lifetime of frustration. Frustration at having at least some dim awareness that he wasn't quite all there, that he was missing something vital, that there were pieces of the puzzle of life he'd never possess. All it took was a small incident like this — an inanimate object that refused to obey his wishes — to set off that deep, uncomprehending agony inside him. She'd seen it all her life. Usually her aunt and uncle had been able to soothe it over. Now Helen, watching his powerful muscles bunch and tremble, had a moment's fear that she wouldn't be able to talk him out of it. "Bobby, it's okay." She began to reach out, to try to touch him, but thought better of it when he turned a bright red face to her. "It isn't anything bad. Let's just go away now, all right?"

Maybe it was pent-up grief over his father's death. Maybe it was the sound of one more complacent adult voice trying to patronize him. Or maybe it was a lifetime of such iniquities visited on him. Whatever it was, Bobby wasn't about to be calmed down. "No," he muttered through clenched teeth. "No!"

"Bobby. Listen to me."

But he was beyond listening. He turned away slowly, lifted both his hands, and pounded on the worktable. "Daddy's broke! Daddy's broke!" The muffled words, spit out in fury, echoed in the tiny chamber. Helen watched, transfixed with both fear and amazement, as his meaty fists cracked the old rotted wood of the table under his repeated blows. The old metal file cabinet slipped forward as the table buckled. At its edge the vise clattered to the floor in a series of dull thuds, and the piece of wood it had held for years shattered into several rough-edged pieces.

Behind her, through the open door, Helen heard footsteps crunching over the lawn. Fluting, birdlike voices lifted through the hot, still air. "Great," she sighed, not bothering to look. Sure enough, the four women from Aunt Edna's church were trotting across the dead grass to witness the sound and the fury coming from the shed. And there was Aunt Edna bringing up the rear. Helen almost smiled when she saw Mrs. Muncie standing at the entrance. The sun beamed down into the woman's hard little eyes as they recorded every detail of the sorry pageant unfolding before them.

Helen, still clutching the bottles, stepped between Mrs. Muncie and Bobby. "I don't think you should be out here," she said firmly.

"He might hurt himself," Mrs. Muncie said, craning her neck to see around Helen. At this point, Bobby was methodically kicking at the offending cabinet. The worktable had split down the center into two neat halves, ends poking up around the caved-in center of the workspace. Bobby landed a well-placed kick that sent the cabinet slamming into the corner, making the entire shed tremble. "He's a danger to himself and to everyone when he's like this."

"Now, Mrs. Muncie, I think Miss Helen has it under control —" The efforts of the other women had no effect on Mrs. Muncie, who stood rooted to the ground, watching in fascination.

The scene got even more confused when Aunt Edna forced herself into the room. "Bobby? Honey? Honey, it's Mommy." She fearlessly reached out and stroked her son's head.

"Mommy? It's all broke. I'm sorry. I broke it. I'm sorry,"

Bobby wailed, instantly brought to his knees in a fit of exhausted grief. Helen closed her eyes for a moment. What the fuck did it matter now? Maybe she should just go ahead and finish the bottle as they stood here, she thought, aware of Mrs. Muncie's mean little smile as she observed what Helen grasped to her bosom. This would probably be a delicious topic of discussion at Mrs. Muncie's next tea party. The other women turned away discreetly and tiptoed back to the house.

"No!" They all turned around to see Bobby push his mother away in petulant anger. He shoved once again at the worktable. This time the old boards of the shed couldn't withstand the pressure, and they gave way. A gaping hole let in light and heat and dust. As they all stood staring, Helen saw a box topple onto the floor, spilling out papers onto the mingled wood chips, dust, and soil.

"What the —" She edged forward and peered up at the edge of the hole. Had there been a shelf, or another drawer? The box seemed to have appeared out of the wall. "Weird," she muttered.

Her comments stopped when she bent over to see what the box had contained. The photographs were old and faded, dog-eared at the corners, taken in black and white that had faded to gray and yellow with time. Helen picked up the nearest picture. Bobby knelt beside her, his rage forgotten as he started sifting through the mess. The scene looked familiar, as though she'd been there many times herself and just couldn't quite place where it was. And the man in the photograph was familiar. Uncle Loy had hair back then, a full, glossy black mass that tumbled provocatively over his eyes. Apparently the woman with him thought so too. She smiled up at him invitingly, leaning into the curve of his arm with her head resting on his shoulder. "Jesus fucking Christ," Helen breathed. The woman was definitely not Aunt Edna.

Chapter Four

Helen stared across the small kitchen table at her aunt. Spread out before them, a small collection of postcards and envelopes surrounded the single photograph Helen had grabbed a couple of hours ago. They'd been alone, the two remaining McCormicks and Helen, for most of that time. The others had departed the scene about half an hour after the debacle in the backyard. Helen had absolutely no doubt that the entire embarrassing episode had been memorized by the cold-eyed leader of the pack for future reference.

The real surprise, Helen realized as she sat in the sweltering little kitchen of the trailer, was that her aunt had not snatched up all the stuff that had come tumbling out of Uncle Loy's secret hiding place and scooped them back into either obscurity or destruction. Instead she'd quietly disappeared into the house while Helen coaxed the bits and pieces from Bobby's grasp and sorted them into the assortment arrayed on the table now. Edna made her entrance just as Helen had arranged everything in a neat row.

Now she sat staring at her niece, keeping her gaze averted from the tabletop. Helen watched her warily. She'd never seen her aunt so silent and still. Usually Edna was a busy and bustling person, fidgeting and fussing with anything her hands touched — a napkin, a pen, a fold in her dress, whatever lay in reach of her fingers. But the woman sitting across from her might as well be dead. Maybe, Helen thought, she was dead in some sense. Certainly Edna McCormick's safe serene little world had completely dissolved into chaos in the past month, particularly in the past forty-eight hours.

"Well?" The single word, spoken by her aunt in a flat toneless voice, conveyed no emotion at all. Her voice, her eyes — she was as faded as the print blouse she wore.

Helen moved her hands to the top of the table, ready to snatch away the evidence of her uncle's crimes should his widow make a move to snatch them away. "Well, what?" She tried to make the words sound less belligerent than would ordinarily be the case and realized that she'd succeeded only in sounding like she wanted to pick a fight. "What would you like me to do with these, Aunt Edna?" she continued quietly.

The older woman shrugged and turned her face to look out the window. Bobby was sitting on the dead, brown grass of the backyard, digging at something in the dirt. "It doesn't matter," she answered, still in monotone. "Everybody's seen them now."

"Everybody? Just a few people from the church."

Edna snorted. "Everybody. You think I don't know what that Mrs. Muncie is like? What she's saying to people right now?" She looked back at her niece. Helen recoiled at the cold hate in her aunt's eyes. She'd never seen that look there before. "Dollars to doughnuts she's on the phone right now spreading the news about my dead husband and his girl-friends." Suddenly a wry smile appeared on her face. Helen shifted nervously in her seat. Another expression she'd never seen on her aunt's features — and not a very nice one, at that. "Go ahead and ask. I know you want to."

Helen looked down at the table, collecting her thoughts. How on earth was she going to ask her aunt questions about her uncle's mistress? Stalling, she reviewed the items on the table.

Three postcards, all generic scenes of Civil War sites in Mississippi, postmarked Biloxi consecutively in the summer months of 1975, sat in the center of the table. Each had a brief, cryptic message: "Everything going well. Can't wait for you to get here. Mum's the word." "Heard from our friend last night. All is well. Only need you here." "Have to leave soon. Spotted you-know-who this morning, and I think he saw me. Please, please hurry." All had been sent to a post office box in Tupelo. Helen had a hard time imagining her Uncle Loy, with his John Deere cap, lurking in the post office downtown waiting for love letters at a secret drop point — but apparently that's what he had done.

Next to the postcards Helen had placed two ticket stubs. Hard to say what color they'd started out, but now both were a uniform gray with faded black print. No date or identifying features were visible on the frayed bits of paperboard. The ink around the borders of the stubs curlicued and weaved in an intricate, baroque pattern that reminded Helen of something she couldn't quite remember. Maybe it would come to her soon if she left it alone. The stubs sported numbers thirty-four and thirty-five. Had Uncle Loy and his ladylove, or whatever the woman was, gone on some kind of ride or to a show or something during their affair? And Uncle Loy had kept every scrap that could constitute a souvenir of this particular event? Another act that was difficult to imagine.

Then there was the seashell. Helen was surprised it had withstood time and the elements and the confines of Uncle

Loy's shed. Its delicate whorls fit in her hand comfortably. When she'd first picked it up something had rattled inside. Upon carefully shaking it, a few bits of sand and dirt, hardened by years of air far removed from the sea, had dropped out into her palm and dissolved into a fine grit. She'd gently shaken the shell again but there was no further sound. Not even the murmur of the waves, Helen thought regretfully as she held the shell to her ear. Since the postcards had come from Biloxi, Helen guessed the shell had also come from some beach on the Gulf of Mexico. Again, most likely some souvenir.

The pile of brochures about the Natchez Trace looked out of place among the other items. They were much more recent and still retained their glossy appearance, despite having been folded away for some time. Each one described a different scenic point of the restored, ancient Native American trail, which cut a diagonal swath across the state to the city of Natchez on the Mississippi River. The rubber band holding them together snapped with a dry, brittle pop when Helen had first picked the brochures up. Had they even been opened up? Helen wondered. Some of them had pages stuck immovably together as if they'd sat there in her uncle's treasure trove for years without being touched. And what were these relative newcomers doing with the pile of aging fragments of a decades-old secret?

That left only the single photograph. Helen picked it up reluctantly, unwilling even now to admit to herself that her much-beloved uncle — good old salt-of-the-earth Loy McCormick, strong and silent hero glued in her memories like a paper doll — had gotten some on the side. If all this had taken place in the mid seventies, then his infidelities coincided with her arrival on the McCormick doorstep after being beaten and thrown away by her own family. Of course, at the time Helen had been far too brokenhearted and self-absorbed to notice much beyond her own bruises, both physical and emotional. Uncle Loy could have danced naked under the full moon and slaughtered a goat or two to Apollo and Helen probably wouldn't have noticed in the midst of her own pain. And what about her poor aunt? Saddled with an unfaithful husband, a permanently less-than-normal son, and now a perverted niece wailing on their doorstep, Aunt Edna must have been at her wit's end trying to hold it all together. All that the drama had needed to make it complete was a black eye and a foundling child on the porch.

If she'd known about her husband, that is. And of course that was the first question Helen had to ask. "Did you know Uncle Loy had these?" Helen asked, hoping that her voice sounded gentle and cautious.

"Does it matter? Never mind, of course it matters to you. The detective." Helen froze at the ice in her aunt's voice. What was that talking? Fear? Anger? Hurt? It wasn't possible Aunt Edna hated her. The older woman went on, "No, I didn't. And to answer your next question, Helen, I don't know who that woman is. And I really don't want to know."

Edna leaned forward, and Helen instinctively jerked in her chair, her hands reaching out protectively over the pieces of her uncle's past. Oh, damn, she cursed herself, that looked awful. Reflex action or not, her aunt wasn't going to appreciate her move to preserve the evidence.

She was right. "Don't worry, Helen. I'm not going to take your stuff away from you. Like I already said, it's too late to hide any of it now." Edna looked out the window again, taking stock of where Bobby was in the yard. He had moved his digging over to the tomato plants, kicking at the frames that held the dead vines in a desultory manner, his bulk looming against the backdrop of the now-gutted shed. "It will be all over the church about your uncle by now. Not to mention your liquor and Bobby getting drunk."

Helen winced, and her headache stabbed through her temples in a recurrence of pain. "I'm sorry about that, Aunt Edna. I know I can't excuse my behavior, but Uncle Loy, I mean, I still feel so awful —"

"Yes, I know, honey. You felt awful and you had to have a

drink." Edna turned a face of stone to her niece. "It couldn't wait for you to get back home, could it?"

Helen started to protest, then stopped, partly from knowing it was futile, partly in shock at the bitterness in her aunt's voice. "I am sorry, Aunt Edna," she said finally. "I know I can't make up for it, but I am sorry."

"Just like you were sorry to Alison and Freida and all the other women you've been with, I suspect. Well, maybe we aren't all educated and sophisticated about the world out here, and maybe we're not very bright either," Edna said as she stood up from the table. "But this isn't a hotel where you can act like you want, Helen. You should respect your uncle's memory better than that. Do what you want with these," she said as she headed for the door leading to the backyard. "I know you're going to no matter what I say, anyhow."

Helen cleared the table with trembling fingers. Was this some weird, surreal nightmare? Had Aunt Edna been taken over by a pod person? Bad joke, bad humor — but Helen knew it was either that or accept that the sweet, kindly woman who'd been her refuge for twenty years and more was not what she had always seemed.

She froze with her hands on the photograph, after sweeping the rest of the stuff back into the shoebox she'd purloined from Bobby's room. Her refuge. Not a real human being, with hopes and dreams and fears, not a woman who had loved and wept and borne a son and watched all her dreams wither like those tomato plants, not an individual full of pain and contradiction and wonder. Just Aunt Edna, source of comfort and cookies. Helen sank back down in her chair, suddenly overwhelmed with a burning desire for a drink. Lurking underneath her thoughts was a sickening look at herself, and she didn't much like what she was seeing.

So instead she looked down at the picture. Anything, even her uncle with a bimbo, was better than an unadorned view of Helen Black just now. Details, study the details — that should help the nausea roiling up her throat. So Helen tried to note facts, grateful for something to think about besides what had just happened at the table. Dog-eared corners — a crease in the center of the photograph — it had been much handled over the years. The ornate building in the background, like some kind of fancy resort hotel somewhere. Biloxi? Maybe, although Helen couldn't recall anything that gaudy from twenty-five years ago in the vicinity. No signs or identifying features visible, just wrought-iron balustrades, Corinthian pillars, and elaborate window frames behind the happy couple. Loy was smiling and surprisingly handsome, an arm flung loosely across the shoulders of his — mistress, girlfriend, fuck buddy, whatever.

And the woman? Helen had to admit that even in this old photograph and in the weird feathery hairdo popular in the seventies — maybe she even sported blue eyeshadow — the woman was beautiful. Huge dark eyes, a shy smile, almost as tall as Loy but also somehow delicately boned and fragile. Yes, someone who was on the verge of shattering. That's how Helen would describe her — except for the fact that she was leaning into Loy with intimate familiarity.

She flipped the picture over. Yes, the back still merely read "Sept. 10, 1975," just like it had a couple of hours ago. Nothing new there. The name of the film developer was very, very faintly etched along the back, but it was illegible. Maybe she could make it out with a little more time or some way of analyzing it —

The crunch of car tires on gravel interrupted her thoughts. Helen slipped the photograph back into the shoebox and hurried to put the box under the sofa. By the time she got to the front window to see who it was, her cousin Blaine Wittman was knocking at the front door.

He seemed surprised to see her. "Helen! Thought you'd be back in California by now." Blaine shouldered his way into the trailer, his gut brushing her side as he edged past her. Helen saw that he was wearing a much more expensive suit than the last time she'd seen him several years ago.

"Didn't see you at the funeral yesterday, Blaine. How's your wife?"

He had the grace to blush — pale rose creeping up over his plump cheeks. A soft, long-fingered hand brushed his thin red hair from his forehead, and he kept his tiny, black eyes from meeting hers in a staring match of mutual dislike. "Carol's fine. Says to tell y'all hello. She's at home with the kids right now."

"Not still at the bank? I thought she was manager now," Helen said. She'd be damned if she offered this windbag a seat or offered to fetch Aunt Edna. If he couldn't be bothered to come to the funeral, fuck him.

"Nope, nope, she quit that job since I got on with Roberts and Farrell."

"Roberts and Farrell? Where Uncle Loy used to work?"

"That's right." He kept prowling restlessly around the tiny living room, obviously not looking in Helen's direction. "They just made me project manager in development."

"Guess they couldn't let an important man like you off for the funeral, Blaine."

He pursed his lips and made another prowling circuit of the room. "Is Edna here?"

Helen leaned her back against the door. "She's out back. Why don't you go on out and pay your respects?"

"Actually, maybe I could just talk to you, Helen. Kind of make it easier that way, I think."

"Make what easier?" Helen definitely didn't like the sound of this, not coming from a greasy worm like Blaine.

"No need to pull Edna into this, not right now. And you being a woman of the world, so to speak, if you know what I mean —"

A woman of the world. That was a new one, Helen had to admit. "Out with it, Blaine. What do you want?"

"Well, the folks over at Roberts and Farrell would really like your aunt to think hard about their offer. I mean, she'd be set up for life if she'd go along with it, you know? And with

Bobby being the way he is and all, it would just be easier for everyone all around. You understand, no pressure, just think about it."

"Their offer," Helen repeated to buy a couple of seconds. What the fuck was this idiot muttering about? And what did it have to do with Roberts and Farrell? "Are you just a high-priced errand boy in a nice new shiny suit, Blaine?" At least that insult was a fairly safe bet, she reasoned. "What is this car you're driving, Blaine? Oh, I see — a Mercedes. They are the devil to pay for, aren't they? Or maybe money doesn't matter now. Not if Carol could quit her job."

The faint flush on her cousin's face had deepened to purplish-red now. Helen was pretty sure she'd hit a bull's-eye with at least one of her smart-ass remarks. "Listen here, Helen, I'm just trying to offer my nearest and dearest a little friendly advice. Edna needs to really think hard about what those lawyers told her and sign what they give her."

The lawyers. Helen had almost forgotten about the proposed visit to the attorneys tomorrow afternoon. Had Blaine, in his usual Blaine style, gotten his wires crossed and thought they'd seen the lawyers today? And why in hell would Roberts and Farrell be concerned in all this? It made just as much sense as did Uncle Loy having an affair with a brunette bombshell in Biloxi. "We haven't seen any lawyers, Blaine," she said calmly, relishing the way his mouth gaped open in an almost perfect O. "Aunt Edna and I are having a meeting with them tomorrow afternoon. Why don't you just give me a little preview, Blaine? What the hell is going on here?"

The unhealthy red in his face had faded back to pink blush, and he had better control of himself. "I think I'll go talk to Edna now. She's out back, I take it?"

Helen moved to block him, gratified to see him quiver slightly as her hand brushed his arm. Either he was scared of something or nervous about letting a dyke touch his good Christian normal self. The end result was the same, in any case. "I have no idea what you're getting so worked up about, Blaine, and I really don't care. But if I find out you're trying to push Aunt Edna into doing one fucking thing she shouldn't, I will personally go to Carol and tell her about how you propositioned me to put on a little lesbian peep show for you and your pals at work."

He actually sputtered in consternation. "Carol would never believe you, you bitch," he managed to say in a choked voice.

"Why not? She's probably already found your stash of porno. Where do you keep it these days, Blaine — the john? The garage?" The reference to her childhood discovery of his sordid little secret brought the red back to his face. "Anyway, do you want to take that chance? As I recall, a lot of those magazines showed little boys and girls doing things I bet Roberts and Farrell wouldn't approve of. Not in its managers, at least."

With a visible effort he calmed himself and stood straight. From the sounds behind her, Helen guessed that Edna and Bobby were coming back inside and heading for the kitchen. Helen was impressed, in spite of herself, at the way Blaine smoothed his ruffled feathers and displayed a calm smile for public view. That acting ability probably helped him climb up in R and F management, she decided. "I'm just telling you for your own good, and hers, too," he whispered. "Listen to what those attorneys tell her and get her to sign. All right? Trust me, Helen, you don't want to fuck with these guys."

"What guys?" she hissed. But he had already pushed himself past her and lumbered into the kitchen. Helen stood in the doorway for a couple of minutes, watching the tender scene of reunion until she thought she'd gag. Aunt Edna was puttering in cabinets and fussing over the coffeemaker as Helen made her exit. On her way out to the front yard she grabbed the shoebox and her car keys.

Only the wolfhounds witnessed Helen stowing the shoebox

in the trunk of her rental car. Once she'd locked the evidence safely in the trunk, Helen went to the glove compartment and rummaged out a pack of cigarettes. It was another small vice she'd pandered to when she'd gone on the pantyhose run. Like a fucking sailor on leave, she mused — all she needed now was a box of candy bars. At least it wasn't booze this time, she reassured herself as she lit one and took a deep, carcinogenic, unfiltered drag. God, that felt good. She had to smile. She was as bad as Blaine with his secret cache of toys — Helen had her own toys hidden away. The smile faded as she remembered yesterday's melodrama and her own role in supplying the forbidden fruit to Bobby. And given how Uncle Loy had died, maybe cigarettes weren't such a good idea, either.

Uncle Loy. She thought of the box in the trunk. Aunt Edna was right. She wasn't going to let it go. Did that make her a world-class bitch? Even if it did, she had to find out what the hell the man had been doing. Not just because she was a snoop by nature — maybe it was more because it caused terrible pain that Uncle Loy had been carrying on like that at the same time she'd been running to him for help. Maybe guilt, at throwing herself and her teenage tornado at the McCormick family when they were already in a crisis over her uncle's affair? Maybe duty, hoping to at least find answers for Aunt Edna — answers she might not want now. Whatever the reason, she wouldn't trouble Aunt Edna with it. She could pursue it quietly, on her own, not making any more trouble than she already had. Besides, everyone in the tiny trailer would probably feel better with Helen out of the way a bit more over the next few weeks. It was awfully close quarters, particularly with things so heated emotionally. Yep, she realized with a grim smile, running away again, aren't we?

She smoked the cigarette down to ash under the hungry stares of the hounds next door. Helen ground the stub under her shoe and smiled sweetly at the animals. "Don't worry, guys, I'm sure I'll get thrown to you in sacrifice before too much longer if things keep going this way," she called out cheerily. They slavered and moaned in longing as they watched her go back inside to play happy family with Blaine and Aunt Edna and Bobby.

Chapter Five

Helen looked out the window of the office onto Pemberton Avenue. From where she was sitting she could see the tarnished statue of some Confederate hero, encrusted with bird droppings and surrounded by crumpled litter from the nearby fast-food haunts, rearing up on his stallion in an eternally arrested attack on the Yankees invading his homeland. A couple of adolescent boys, both wearing baseball caps pulled low over acne-ravaged faces and slouching in jeans several sizes too big for their skinny haunches, slammed into the side of the monument with their skateboards. Hopping off the wheeled platforms onto the asphalt, they leaned against the pedestal that was inscribed with names and dates of the glorious departed sons of the south from Tupelo. One kid handed the other a cigarette. They lit up and started blowing smoke rings into the hot air.

The two men seated across the enormous polished table from her barely glanced up from their official leather folders and stacks of papers. Their droning voices hadn't helped Helen's sleepiness. She knew they had been surprised when she'd entered the office with her aunt, but after her behavior of the past couple of days Helen was determined to be with her aunt every step of the way in adjusting to her new life without Uncle Loy. And Aunt Edna had raised no objections, merely continued in restless silence, prowling around the limited space provided by the trailer.

She felt her aunt move jerkily beside her at the long shiny conference table. Dressed in one of her best outfits, a navy blue dress with a lacy collar, Aunt Edna had sat quiet and motionless since they'd entered the room. Not for the first time, Helen noted with a pang that the elderly woman sitting next to her seemed to have shrunk in the past month. Hadn't she worn that dress last year, when they'd all met in Laughlin? Then it had stretched tight across a plump stomach and wide hips. Now it bunched loosely around her waist, sagging in all the places it would have been straining seams a year ago. Helen glanced down at her aunt's trembling hands, pursed her lips, and forced herself to keep from touching her aging relative. Aunt Edna had barely spoken to her since the debacle yesterday. Less, Helen thought, from anger at the humiliating scenario played out in front of her church friends than because she was simply drained of all energy and emotion. A shell, a husk. And Helen sighed again at the realization that it was partly her fault. Fortunately, nothing said so far in this meeting indicated a need for Helen or Aunt Edna to pay too much attention. No threats of ending Uncle Loy's pension or of reducing the payments or of interfering in any way with Aunt Edna getting the pittance sent to her every month by Roberts and Farrell.

Instead they were being treated to a long and convoluted

explanation of how Aunt Edna and Bobby would now be the recipients of more funds. Helen couldn't quite understand how this had happened. Had Uncle Loy set up additional life insurance or something? And how was it possible, given the medical costs he'd incurred during the last six months of his life, that any benefits he'd had weren't completely exhausted?

One of the lawyers, Alistair Norman, an unctuous, tall man with a resonant voice, was slapping a folder shut and intoning yet another pronouncement. Helen sat up straighter and tried to pay attention. Once again she was clothed in something dreadfully uncomfortable. The lined black slacks were too hot, and the thin navy blue cotton blouse wasn't warm enough for the aggressively air-conditioned conference room. And her feet were killing her. She wasn't used to anything but sneakers and sandals — nothing to dress up for anymore. Except funerals and meetings with lawyers. Who was it that said to be wary of any enterprise that required new clothes? At least the coffee was good, although no one had done more than taste the rich dark brew that sat cooling in delicate china. Only the best for clients of Stivers, Stivers, and Hutchison. Weird, Helen thought. She would have assumed that the young pup, the younger attorney who quietly passed papers to his colleague, was adequate to handle the likes of Edna McCormick. Why roll out the red carpet in the form of this slick well-manicured gentleman?

"So, as you see, there's quite a large sum set aside in trust for you in addition to your late husband's pension fund," the lawyer was saying. "It will be paid out to you monthly through our offices."

Helen cleared her throat. Her mind had wandered all over the damned place since their arrival — she'd been too upset about the past couple of days to concentrate. But since Aunt Edna seemed oblivious to everything and everyone, Helen decided she'd better make some kind of effort, no matter how foolish it made both of them look.

"I don't believe you've actually said a sum, as yet," she

said quietly. "Perhaps you wouldn't mind telling us exactly how much money is involved in this trust fund?"

The younger attorney who'd accompanied Norman, his every move like a trained poodle, glanced up at her and then at his master with an air of aggrieved nervousness. What, Helen wondered, did no one dare to breathe around Norman? Let alone question him?

Norman cleared his throat, gave Edna another dismissive glance, then reopened the folder with an air of exasperated patience. "Seven hundred and fifty thousand dollars."

Edna didn't stir beside her, but Helen had to grip the arms of the richly upholstered, uncomfortable chair to keep herself from jolting up in surprise. She swallowed hard, making sure her voice was flat and calm when she spoke. "And this is on top of his regular pension check? The one his widow now receives every month from Rogers and Farrell?"

"That's correct." He looked up with a smile.

Helen frowned at him. Where had she seen that smile before? It struck her as the man leaned back expansively in his leather chair. Mrs. Muncie's tight little self-satisfied lips yesterday. What was this guy's name again? Norman. Mr. Something Norman. Yes, he had the same, sleek blond hair, the same long nose that seemed to be sniffing the air at something noxious.

He gave her a chance to confirm her suspicions with his next statement. "And I heard from my sister that you'll be staying on at your present address?" he said, glancing down at the pad before him.

"Your sister? Would that be Mrs. Muncie?"

Those cold, little blue eyes stared through her as though she was a dog that had suddenly uttered something intelligible. "Yes, as a matter of fact. I believe she mentioned you, Ms. Black, as well."

Helen barely suppressed a snort. She could just imagine in what terms that icy bitch had described her, given her hangover, Bobby's temper tantrum, and the apocalyptic destruction of Uncle Loy's shed that revealed the dead man's peccadilloes. Tupelo wasn't all that big a town, Helen knew. And if Mrs. Muncie was solidly welded into the local power structure — which seemed likely, given her hot-shit lawyer brother and her own marriage to a man who was no doubt a pillar of the community — the wheels of gossip were already turning on Aunt Edna. Great. What a big help she'd been to her family in their hour of need. For a second Beth Wilks's taut, disapproving face flashed through her mind. She had to try to rein it in, to keep her mouth shut and keep from embarrassing her relatives any further.

The two men sitting across the wide, polished table were looking at her expectantly. What did they want, another humiliating performance? "Yes," Helen said, "I do recall meeting her yesterday at my aunt's home."

"She's married to one of the deacons at the church," Norman went on. His eyes roved quickly over her face and just as quickly dismissed her. Clearly, she wasn't a client, she didn't have any money, and she certainly didn't present a threat. No one to worry about, his disdainful final glance seemed to say. He openly made a show of looking down at his watch before continuing, "As a matter of fact, a representative of Roberts and Farrell was going to attend this meeting with us. I don't know what the delay has been —"

The door to the conference room swung open, stopping Norman's excuse in mid-huff. The first thing Helen noticed about the newcomer was the length of her red hair, thick and glossy, shimmering down her back in a flame of motion as she strode into the room. Its wild, rich color made a vivid contrast to the simple black suit she wore. Helen got a glimpse of something flashing on her ankle against the dark film of black hosiery — an ankle bracelet? No, it was some sort of metal stitched into the stocking near the ankle, in a pattern of glitter spraying around her feet, catching the light as she moved. As she rounded the table she smiled at everyone with a sweeping glance. No makeup distracted her audience from the brilliant blue of her eyes or the smooth pallor of her skin. Not that she needed any makeup, Helen decided. She was striking, rather than beautiful, and she knew it. If drama was her goal, Helen had no doubt that she achieved it without much effort. And was that Chanel floating on the air behind her? Something expensive and tantalizing.

"Good afternoon, everyone," she murmured as she slid into a chair. The young man, who moments ago had been behaving like a trained puppy, visibly stiffened as the new arrival settled next to Norman. Helen stifled a grin — she couldn't decide if he was hot and bothered or annoyed, perhaps both. The redhead ignored him. She removed a file from her briefcase with slim pale fingers. Just as she'd avoided makeup, Helen noted, she also chose not to polish her short-trimmed nails. Interesting.

"So glad you were able to make it," Norman said, stretching his lips in a false smile that barely concealed his dislike. "Mrs. McCormick, Ms., um —"

"Black. Helen Black. I'm Mrs. McCormick's niece." Did she imagine a flicker of interest in the newcomer's eyes at the mention of her name? It was gone too quickly for Helen to be sure.

"Yes, well, this is Terrie Muncie." Norman waved at her vaguely, as if she were a necessary evil of some sort. Terrie ignored his gesture, stood up, and offered her hand first to Aunt Edna, then to Helen. The older woman took it limply, letting it fall almost as soon as she touched it. Helen met Terrie Muncie's eyes as they shook hands. The woman's touch lingered just a second too long for mere professional courtesy, her warm fingers leaving Helen's grasp slowly. And it might have been curiosity in her gaze. Helen hadn't been on the receiving end of a flirtation in quite a while, but if she wasn't completely nuts that was something beyond interest in her smile.

Another Muncie? Helen sat back and regarded the woman curiously. Unbelievable — the whole town was awash with

Muncies, apparently. She hoped her appraisal wasn't too obvious. There was no overt family resemblance in this particular representative of Muncie progeny, unless her blue eyes were testimony of the connection. Was she perhaps married to a Muncie? Helen glanced at her hand. No ring. In fact, no jewelry at all, as far as Helen could see. She looked up again to catch Terrie meeting her stare with a small smile dancing on her lips, amusement in those startling eyes. Helen realized she was actually hoping that Terrie Muncie was single. Was, in fact, not in the least interested in men. Great — that's all she needed, Helen thought — screwing around with the local corporate closet cases, on top of Uncle Loy's recently revealed infidelities and Bobby's new hobby of sneaking a snort when no one was looking. Anyway, she was probably happily married with the requisite two-point-five children kicking a soccer ball into the back of their family van. Probably a big shaggy dog, too.

"Yes, I think my mother mentioned you," Terrie said, continuing to smile at Helen. "She met you yesterday, I think? When she went over to help Mrs. McCormick."

Just fucking terrific. The way they were all looking and smiling, like contented cats with a juicy mouse poised just beneath their claws. Apparently Helen and her family and their shenanigans were the talk of the town, from the church to the lawyers to the big corporate interests. And this Terrie Muncie was not even bothering to apologize for being incredibly late. Either she had a lot more clout than the legal beagles or she didn't care — or need to care.

Helen managed a smile that she hoped was just as complacent as theirs. She laid her hand on her aunt's shoulders and felt the elderly woman trembling beneath her touch. Whether or not Edna was saying anything, she was certainly taking in the news that she was now the subject of gossip and jokes in every echelon of her community. For a split second Helen nearly screamed in frustration and anger. Who the hell were these people to pass judgment on her or on her family? The weight of their stares broke through her resistance. Like it or not, these were people who could make her aunt's life a living hell. Helen knew she'd already done enough damage — better to just keep her mouth shut and make sure Aunt Edna and Cousin Bobby got the money that was their due.

The moment passed swiftly, and they all settled back into their chairs. Terrie paid no attention to the file she'd pulled from her briefcase, content to fold her arms and listen as the lawyers continued talking. Helen found herself drifting off again until one of them — Norman, she thought — said something about signatures.

"Excuse me, would you repeat that, please?" Helen asked. Another glance at Aunt Edna confirmed that she wasn't following this at all.

Terrie Muncie and the two lawyers exchanged glances. For the second time since her entrance, Terrie spoke in response. "It's an additional clause, similar to the one signed initially by Loy McCormick." She flipped open the file and leafed through the papers until she found the one she wanted. The lawyers continued staring at Helen with distaste. Helen guessed they hadn't expected any questions at all — no doubt they hadn't expected her presence today, either.

Terrie offered her a sheet of paper, keeping up the patter as she watched Helen study it. "It's actually a standard form, used frequently in these kinds of cases."

"These kinds of cases," Helen repeated. Damn, she should have been paying better attention, Helen castigated herself. What was the matter with her? "This is a promise not to enter into any legal action of any kind against Roberts and Farrell, right?"

Norman cleared his throat and managed to suppress a glare at Helen. "It is a standard addendum to the kind of financial agreement originally set up by Loy McCormick and Roberts and Farrell. I think if you'll just —"

"But why would you need such an agreement in the first

place?" Helen laid the sheet of paper on the table and glanced again at Aunt Edna. "You're telling me that my uncle, her late husband, entered into some kind of agreement not to sue Roberts and Farrell? And that in order to receive this, what was it, seven hundred thousand dollars?"

"Seven hundred and fifty thousand dollars," the younger man interrupted. "As I said, this is entirely up to your aunt," he went on, nodding at Aunt Edna. "You, Ms. Black, are nowhere named in this agreement."

For the first time since they'd entered the room, the older woman was paying attention to the proceedings. She twisted her hands nervously in her lap and cleared her throat. "If Loy thought it was all right, then it's probably all right," she said in a voice pitched just above a whisper.

"Aunt Edna, I really think we should take a look at this," Helen said, leaning forward and speaking softly. "There might be more to this than meets the eye. I'm sure these gentlemen, and Ms. Muncie, wouldn't object to your thinking this over before you sign anything. Right, folks?"

"Actually, our business is with Edna McCormick, Ms. Black. You are in no way involved with this." The younger lawyer smiled disdainfully at them both, ignoring the way Terrie Muncie and Norman fidgeted. "This is Mrs. McCormick's decision to make. Now, I'm sure, given the fact that this is such a substantial amount of money, there should be no difficulty in accepting the terms of the agreement."

Okay. That was enough. Not only were they being overtly insulting to her, they were hinting at dire circumstances should her aunt decline to sign their little piece of paper. Fuck the Muncies and Normans and all the powers that be, Helen thought. She'd be damned if she'd put up with their threats or allow her family to be subjected to this.

She rose, gently guiding her aunt up with her. "I think my aunt would like to think this over before she signs your agreement. Isn't that right, Aunt Edna?"

The aging woman looked up at Helen with blank eyes. Was

it confusion? No, Helen decided. It was fear. Edna McCormick was terrified of these people. Fighting off a nagging suspicion that she might be stepping into a pile of shit she didn't want to mess with, Helen held on to her aunt more firmly. "We'll be getting back to you on this subject very soon."

"Come now, ladies — surely you can see that this would all be easily resolved if you'd just accept the terms of the agreement." Norman stood up with them. He controlled his scowl, although his face remained flushed with irritation. "This is, as my colleague has tried to explain to you, a very substantial sum. You, Ms. McCormick, and your son would be well provided for, probably for the rest of your lives. I should think," he said, lowering his tone and leaning forward slightly, "that that would be incentive enough for you. All we need" — he held out a pen — "is one signature from you."

Helen took her aunt's hand protectively. "We will be in touch."

"I don't think you understand," Norman went on, a smile creeping over his thin lips. "Perhaps you weren't listening, or perhaps it wasn't put into terms you could understand."

Helen felt herself go cold at his tone. She barely felt her aunt's hand trembling in her grasp. "Oh, we understand perfectly well. You will have an answer tomorrow." She gave Norman an icy smile of her own, ignoring the whispered protests of the woman behind her.

She couldn't, however, ignore the glances traded between Norman and the other lawyer.

"Certainly, Ms. Black. We will expect your call tomorrow. As long as it's perfectly clear this agreement will not be extended indefinitely — isn't that right, Ms. Muncie?"

Terrie, who'd remained seated and silent throughout this hostile exchange, swiveled her chair around until she was looking directly at Helen. "That's correct. Perhaps Ms. McCormick and Ms. Black would like to discuss this further with me? Just to get a different perspective from the one that's been offered thus far."

Norman's lips twisted. He sniffed with distaste. Must be a family trait, that sniffing thing, Helen decided. Although she hadn't seen Terrie Muncie indulge in the habit. Enough, she lectured herself. You don't need to be watching her every little move and gesture. "Perhaps that would be helpful," he said with obvious reluctance.

Terrie turned back to Helen, eyebrows lifted, a smile dancing on her lips. "Would that be convenient?"

"As I said — we'll have a response for you tomorrow." Helen took her aunt by the elbow and steered her out of the conference room, past the potted palms and ferns, striding along the thick carpeting to exit into the hot afternoon.

Helen blinked up at the sun sliding across a blue-white sky. She fumbled for her sunglasses and slipped them on before her headache got a chance to flare up again. The kids had left the monument for parts unknown, and the plaza facing the law offices was empty. Where the hell — oh yes, she'd parked across the plaza, fortunately under some huge tree with spreading branches. "Okay," she said to Aunt Edna. "I think we should talk to another attorney right away, get them to look at this agreement. I don't like the sound of it, but we need expert advice. I'll bet Beth Wilks can recommend someone. I'll call her right away."

They'd reached the car as Helen spoke. She opened the passenger door for her aunt, but the elderly woman stood, fingers nervously playing with the clasp on her purse, staring up at her niece.

"Let's get home and call Beth, Aunt Edna," Helen urged. "No."

Helen stopped, stared, her hand barely touching the hot metal of the car door. "What do you mean? Do you know an attorney you want to talk to? Let's give them a call, then."

"No." Edna drew herself up straight and returned Helen's gaze squarely. "I mean we aren't calling anyone. We will go back tomorrow and I'm going to sign that agreement." She climbed awkwardly into Helen's rental car and stared straight ahead at the plaza, arms folded across her chest.

"What did Blaine say to you, Aunt Edna? No, please look at me. Did he threaten you in some way? Because if he did, I swear I'll —"

"No one said anything to me at all, Helen. I'm perfectly capable of making my own decisions, despite what you might think of me."

Helen closed her eyes briefly, took off her sunglasses and rubbed the bridge of her nose. Had she finally dropped down the rabbit hole? Nothing was making sense anymore, not even good old Aunt Edna, salt-of-the-earth and all that shit. She rounded the car and took her place behind the wheel. The interior of the car registered slightly below sauna temperature. Helen started the engine and got the air conditioner going, letting cool air blow over them both for a couple of minutes before pulling out.

She glanced at her aunt who kept staring, silent and still, out the window. "Aunt Edna," she began.

But the older woman cut her off with a sharp movement of her hands. "No. Helen, I mean it. There's already been enough trouble since your uncle passed, what with the church and Bobby."

"And me, of course," Helen sighed.

Aunt Edna pursed her lips and shook her head. "No use crying about it now. I know there's been talk, and there will be even more talk if I don't just stay quiet and sign what they want me to sign."

Acid churned up from Helen's stomach into her throat. She should have stayed in California. All she'd done was stir the pot. She swallowed and said, "Forget about all that. You have to think of yourself and what you're doing. We don't know what they're asking of you, and I think you should find out."

"You think? You think?" She turned a tear-stained face to

Helen. "You'll be going back to California soon, and Bobby and me have to stay here. Here, Helen." She pointed out the window with a trembling hand. "Where all these people watch us and talk about us. Oh yes, they talk. They already are, about what we found yesterday."

Helen stared silently, letting her talk. It struck her that in all the years she'd been close to Edna and Loy and Bobby she'd never seen her aunt angry. Now her rage was a tangible force, as if bursting out after years of repression. "I didn't want to make more of a scene in front of those lawyers than I had to, so I didn't argue with you about it. Everyone in town already knows about the scene at home yesterday." Helen winced at the memory but stayed quiet. "But I will go back tomorrow and sign that paper whether you like it or not, Helen. And that's final." Edna's lip trembled, but the tears had stopped. Her face, streaked with runny makeup, displayed a resolve and calm Helen hadn't seen since before Loy died.

Helen shivered. The air conditioner had been blasting at them, so she flicked it to a lower level. "Aunt Edna," she said quietly, "I just want what's best for you and Bobby. The way they're setting this up — it's like they have something to hide, and Uncle Loy knew about it. I'm just afraid they'll try to hurt you somehow." She almost spilled the beans about Blaine and his ham-handed attempt at coercion yesterday, but she decided silence was better. Blaine had just been a bit of added insurance for the likes of R and F and the Muncies. Whatever was happening here was big and shadowy and made no sense at all. Helen was very much afraid now, and she didn't know how to get Edna to be afraid as well.

Edna looked out the window, away from her niece. "They couldn't hurt me more than I already am, Helen. Not after seeing my husband with-with —" She couldn't finish the sentence.

Helen pulled away from the curb. A figure crossed the street. Terrie Muncie strode briskly toward the plaza, stopped when she saw Helen's car, and waved at them.

70

"Great. Now what?" Terrie smiled and moved closer as Helen approached, rolling the window down. The woman leaned over, peering into the open window. "Was there something else, Ms. Muncie? We'd really like to get home. My aunt is very tired." Helen put on her best smile and hoped the sunglasses hid the exasperation she felt.

"Just wanted to give you this. It was a pleasure to meet you. And you, Ms. McCormick." She moved away as Helen glanced down at the business card she'd been handed. Her aunt had barely acknowledged the woman's presence with a nod, so she paid no attention as Helen tucked the card into her pocket.

Wait — something was written on the back. At the first stoplight, once she'd made sure Aunt Edna was still looking out the window, Helen turned the card over: *I work late tonight. Give me a call at the office and let's talk.*

Great. Just what she needed. Was Terrie after a quick fuck or was she going to jump on the bandwagon and make vague threats? Still, it might be more fun than going home and staring at the thin trailer walls for a few hours. And maybe she could get a drink out of it. Decision made, Helen drove back to the trailer park, trying not to think about Terrie's red hair.

Chapter Six

"Is this the whole tour? One office?"

Helen watched Terrie Muncie slink — there was no other word for it, even though Helen hated using fifties bombshell words to describe anyone — around the spacious quarters set aside for the Muncie descendant now working for R and F.

"What, you don't like what you see?" Terrie halted in mid-slink, twisting her body so that she looked at Helen over her shoulder and displayed the nice lines of her torso to perfection in the muted lighting.

"No complaints, no complaints." And who would bitch about the huge suite, decorated in better taste than Helen would have guessed? Terrie must have done it herself.

Expensive rugs, probably handwoven in the Middle East somewhere. A couple of modern paintings on the walls reflected the intricate designs in the rugs. A simple sculpture — a stylized woman's head in polished marble. Low-slung chairs and sofas upholstered in plain neutral tones with the fabric interrupted at odd places in bright blue, picking up the tones of the rugs and the paintings. The furniture even looked like it would be comfortable. The polished wood desk, although large, sat in one corner as if making itself unobtrusive. Taking in the presence of two computer monitors and stacks of files on the desk, Helen knew this really had to be a working office, although it was difficult to imagine getting any work done here.

She said as much as she wandered to the bookshelves and pretended to read a few titles, well aware of Terrie's eyes watching her walk, her gestures. "You mean you actually get work done in here?"

Terrie shrugged. "That's what they pay me for." Helen turned in time to see the other woman fiddle with something on the wall. A panel slid aside to show a view of wooded hills beneath an orange-red sky. The tops of pine trees etched a jagged line below the sunset as it darkened into purple, then black.

"Kind of hard to get an ocean view out here."

Helen shook her head, impressed in spite of herself. "This will do in a pinch." She moved toward the window. Terrie's perfume was subtle, spicy, making Helen want to stand closer. Shit. This was big trouble, she could feel it. Already she was aware of exactly where Terrie stood, where she moved, the way she made a little jerk of her head to toss her red hair back over her shoulders.

"Yeah, it is nice. I had to do some fast talking to get them to let me put this window in. I work a lot of late nights, though — I really wanted something to keep me connected to the real world." She took a step closer to Helen and leaned forward slightly. "See that ridge off to the far right? The Muncie family owns that land." She reached out, pointing, her arm lightly brushing Helen's shoulder.

"I see it." Helen kept her voice flat and calm and tried to focus on something besides Terrie. How about her own reflection? Yeah, that was pretty daunting. As the sky darkened Helen could see her own image more and more clearly in the glass. She looked severe, angry, all planes and shadows. Maybe it was just the lighting, or maybe her clothes. Helen hadn't quite known how to dress for this event, or if it even was an event. She'd made an uncomfortable compromise — black silk shirt with short sleeves and V neck, black jeans, and black flats. No makeup. No perfume. She hadn't packed any, and didn't feel like trying to ask Aunt Edna if she could borrow some of her White Shoulders, or whatever equivalent her aunt might have around. Stark, that was it. That was the look she'd achieved.

Unfortunately — or fortunately, depending on one's point of view — staring into the mirrorlike glass also gave her a good view of Terrie Muncie as well. Where Helen was so dark as to be almost sinister in her getup, Terrie shimmered like a flame in a bright blue dress that revealed every line of her body. The blue matched her eyes, and even in the reflection Helen could see the way Terrie studied her. Just as hard as she herself was looking, Helen had to admit. They were almost the same height, although Terrie's heels added a couple of inches. With her shoes off, Terrie's head would perhaps come to Helen's shoulder.

Helen pushed aside the image of Terrie taking off shoes or anything else and moved from the window back to the safety of the books. "I already got the impression that the Muncie name is one to reckon with in these parts."

"The church folks and all that?" Terrie shrugged and stayed by the window. "They think they are, anyhow."

"My aunt is definitely impressed. So much so that you

don't have to put on any kind of show for my sake." Helen took down a book — what was it, poetry? A name she didn't recognize. Interesting that it actually looked like someone had read it. Terrie herself? Even more interesting. "She's going back on her own to the lawyers tomorrow and sign whatever they put in front of her."

"I don't know what you mean by putting on a show." Terrie went still and her voice went flat. If Helen hadn't known better she would have surmised that Terrie was insulted by the remark. "And I don't know what you mean about your aunt. Are you suggesting she's being coerced in some way?"

"Oh, please, Terrie. I know exactly why you invited me up here." Helen slammed the book carelessly back on the shelf. She had to keep up the act for her aunt and the Muncies and all the rest — she'd be damned if she was going to be nice to this little prize bitch as she slutted around in her tight blue dress. "You're the bait sent to hook me into playing along. Well, there's no game to be played. Edna McCormick is her own woman and she makes her own decisions. I'm just passing through. And right now, my aunt concurs with everyone else's opinion of me."

"And what opinion would that be?" Terrie asked, still in a monotone. She moved to the end of the bookcase and faced Helen, her expression hidden in shadow.

For a moment Helen felt a sliver of hurt knife its way into her chest. Fine, so she'd been right. Terrie didn't give a fuck about Helen Black — she was just doing the Muncie thing, the Roberts and Farrell dance to the tune of a lot of money. No come-on, no interest in Helen as a woman. *How fucking stupid could I have been?*

"I'm just the family pervert passing through. I know that's what you've already heard about me. And I have no influence either way with my aunt."

"So you think I invited you to my office to sweet-talk you

into something? Is that it?" Another step closer, another chance to smell her perfume. "Something to do with lawyers, maybe?"

"What other reason would there be? Why would you be talking to me in the safety of your office?" Jesus, when had she unbuttoned the top of her dress? The woman was still legal, but just barely. Helen couldn't tell for sure in the dim light, but she was betting Terrie's breasts were as pale as what she'd already seen.

"You think this is safe here?" Terrie laughed. "You don't think it's just a little bit dangerous?"

"What is this, every time I ask you a question, you get to ask me two of them?" Terrie was so close Helen could feel the warmth of her breath. "Not fair."

"Not fair, she says. I'll tell you what isn't fair." Terrie traced one fingernail across Helen's neck. Helen felt herself flinch as if touched by fire. "It isn't fair to be stuck in this hellhole of a town full of housewives and assholes, to be forced into this birdcage of a job just to keep the money coming. It isn't fair that I have to play straight lady for the corporate crowd and never be myself. And" — her hand strayed just above Helen's breasts, wavered, then fell to her sides — "it isn't fair that the sexiest woman I've seen in years can't bring herself to see past all that and spend an evening with me."

Helen leaned back and peered into Terrie's face. Yes, folks, there were actually tears brimming in those baby blues. Unbelievable. "Brava, a brilliant performance. But not quite good enough."

Terrie pulled back as though Helen had shoved her. Surprise, surprise — the tears dried up. A slow smile broke the sad expression, and Terrie's shoulders shook with silent laughter. "Can't blame a poor little rich girl for trying."

"Save it for someone who will pretend to care."

Terrie blocked her attempt to move away from the bookcase, one hand reaching out to touch Helen's hair. "And that wouldn't be you, I take it?"

"What do you think?" Helen tried to hold her breath, tried to concentrate on how she was going to evade Terrie's arms, her body as it strained against her. Terrie's hair flowed like red silk over Helen's arm.

"I think a part of you cares. A lot." She moved so that her mouth was very near Helen's ear, and Helen felt her hand gently touch the pulse in her throat. "Oh, yeah, there's a couple of spots that are starting to be very, very interested."

Shit. Of course, what else could she expect? Months of celibacy, months of isolation, months of shutting off everything as hard as she could. A gorgeous redhead, looking for a quick fuck and not much more. It could either be an answer to any red-blooded lesbian's prayers or a one-way ticket to a huge mistake. Either way Helen was pretty sure, judging by the way that she was breathing, she was about to take her chances.

"Now, you can't tell me, Helen Black, that you didn't come in here looking for this. Be honest with yourself." Her hand had moved across Helen's collarbone and now lightly grazed her shoulder. "I could feel you looking at me this afternoon in that office, surrounded by all those idiots. You and me — we were the only people alive in there."

"You're awfully quick to pass judgment, Terrie," Helen said as she stepped away from those trailing fingers. "And I'm not sure I agree with you, anyhow. Those good old boys, the very same ones who pay your salary, seemed quite alive to me. Alive and kicking my aunt all around the room, actually."

Terrie folded her arms and leaned against the bookcase. Once again her face was in shadow and Helen couldn't read her expression as she spoke. "I wouldn't call a large cash settlement for your aunt the same as being kicked around."

"Really?" Helen forced more anger into her voice than she really felt. Maybe it would stave off the other feelings threatening to overwhelm her. She sat down on the sofa, facing away from Terrie. "It's just paying her to keep her mouth shut. And it's a hell of a lot of money for silence. What the fuck is it my aunt is supposed to keep quiet about, anyhow?" Helen twisted around on the sofa, risking a glance at the other woman. "And just what is it you do for Roberts and Farrell? Can't quite see you shoveling grain into elevators, or driving a forklift."

"Basically it's public relations." Terrie moved around the sofa and sank gracefully into a chair. "I get trotted out to make the guys feel good. Run interference with lawyers, take head honchos out to dinner, shit like that."

"And fuck the visiting lesbians? Was that part of your agenda for today?"

Terrie smiled. "Not necessarily. Frankly, I thought it was maybe on your calendar."

Helen snorted. "Fuck you," she muttered.

"Is that a serious offer?"

Helen stood up abruptly. "All right, Terrie. I've had the little minitour of your office and the show of your goodies. I've already told you that my aunt will sign anything you give her. Enough for one night, okay?"

Terrie stretched her long legs out so Helen could see her tanned, muscled thighs. Her skirt rode up just enough to make Helen look. "I doubt that it is enough for one night, Helen. I expect you need a hell of a lot more than a look right now."

"You have no idea what I need."

"But I do. I've done a little bit of homework on you."

"What the hell is that supposed to mean?" Helen stopped at the door, intrigued in spite of herself. Roberts and Farrell, in the delicious person of Terrie Muncie, investigating Helen Black. It made just as much sense as buying Edna McCormick's silence at a very high price — which meant no sense at all. Very weird.

"I know you've been alone for a long time. I know you've been wandering around Berkeley trying to get back into the investigation business for over a year now — and I know how you got the money to open up that office again." Terrie was suddenly standing right behind her, and again Helen felt dizzy in the scent of her perfume. "I even know your ex-girlfriend took the cat with her. You have nothing and no one to come home to, once you leave Mississippi."

Hmm. Interesting. Didn't make sense why they'd check her out. Did Helen represent more of a threat than she realized? She filed that fact away for future reference.

"Great. So R and F employs good detectives to do its snooping. You left out the embarrassing drinking, though." But Helen almost choked on her words as Terrie's hands traveled up her back, kneading the tense muscles around her shoulders.

"Then push me away, Helen. Don't let me touch you anymore." Terrie's lips brushed the back of her neck, and Helen found herself leaning back against Terrie, feeling the press of the other woman's breasts against her back. No, Terrie apparently wasn't wearing a bra.

Terrie's hands found Helen's breasts. Her fingers moved lightly at first, then with firmness as she began to tease the nipples beneath the soft fabric. Helen couldn't prevent a small moan escaping from her throat as a warm wet tongue slid across her ear, followed by a sharp bite to her earlobe.

"I'm sure your employers didn't have this in mind when they instructed you to see me," Helen managed to say in spite of her shortness of breath.

"I'm pretty much my own boss. They allow me a lot of autonomy," and she moved so that her hips nestled against Helen's in a teasing pressure.

Helen stood still, letting herself be touched and tantalized. Weird, very weird — that was her only coherent thought, beyond instinctive reaction to the way Terrie was exploring the outer frontiers of her body. Like something in a soft-porn movie, lots of teasing but not much else. And what the hell was it all for? Even as Helen felt herself respond helplessly to the warm feel of a beautiful woman's body next to her own, she also experienced a cold surge of incredulous observation.

This had no more substance than cotton candy — just as sweet but only air and sugar that left a bitter froth on the tongue.

Helen pushed away with a sudden, rough gesture. "Enough already. What the fuck do you want?"

Terrie's face flushed. Anger? Frustration? What? "I think the question is more what you want, Helen. Why did you come up here looking like a femme's wet dream if you didn't want me to respond in kind?"

"I came up here at your invitation. And I knew you were going to pressure me to try to persuade my aunt to sign your papers."

Terrie shrugged. "So? We've already taken care of business. Now we can get down to pleasure." The smile returned to her lips and she sat down on the sofa, crossing her legs so Helen could see those thighs again. "If you like this office, you should see my house. It's back up in those hills." She gestured languidly toward the panoramic view. "There's no one for miles. Really isolated. Really beautiful."

"Yeah. Mood lighting and lava lamps." But Helen remained standing where she was, reluctant to leave. Was it really such an awful thing, to have a one-night stand with her and then move on? No harm done on either side? Her aunt would probably never find out.

Wait. Her aunt. Her poor cousin Bobby. Helen felt a quick stab of anger at herself. This was just as bad as getting drunk in front of the congregation. What was it Aunt Edna had said? That Helen was acting like their lives were her hotel, just a place to pass through and move on from, leaving everyone else to clean up the mess. And she was doing exactly the same thing now.

Before she could say *virtue*, Terrie was next to her again. The woman must have seen Helen's indecisiveness. Her hands slipped around Helen's waist. "Why don't you come check out the decor yourself?" she murmured, her mouth warm against Helen's neck.

To hell with them all. Helen hadn't gotten laid in over a year — time to remedy the situation. Her body was more than happy to oblige, judging by the increasing warmth between her legs. Terrie Muncie was apparently far too closeted to ever reveal their sordid sweaty night of screwing, and Helen certainly wasn't about to broadcast the event in the *Tupelo Times* or whatever the hell the daily rag around here called itself. With a conscious effort Helen willed her brain to quit whining and let her mouth discover Terrie's lips. Their tongues mingled, and Helen felt dizzy in the warm scent of perfume rising from Terrie's breasts. Helen's hands cupped and examined, stroked and squeezed gently.

Terrie tossed her head back, red-gold hair shimmering with the gesture, laughed as Helen kissed her throat hungrily. "Guess we don't need to go to my place, Helen," she chuckled. "At least not yet."

"Sofa looks big enough to me." Helen half pushed, half pulled Terrie toward the sofa, and they stumbled, giggling, on the handwoven rug. "Or the floor. Doesn't matter." For a split second Helen had a glimpse of herself reflected in the glass of the picture window. Was that really her, dragging Terrie over to the sofa for a quickie? The moment of shock was lost as she tumbled on top of the other woman, her hands groping at the thin fabric of Terrie's dress.

Helen tried to lose herself in the soft, smooth warmth of Terrie's skin, the heady scent of her perfume, the noises Terrie made from the back of her throat. The stark image of her own body falling, dimly mirrored back at her from the window, intruded as Helen slowly explored the contours of Terrie's breasts. It was with a strange mixture of frustration and relief that Helen heard the low-pitched buzz announcing someone's arrival.

Before Helen could struggle up to a decently ladylike sitting position, Terrie had moved from the sofa to her desk. Smoothing her hair into place, Terrie pressed some kind of switch or button and leaned over to murmur into a speaker while Helen caught her breath. Yes, she was all buttoned and zippered and relatively presentable. Terrie was too, she noted. In fact, of the two of them, Terrie looked more calm and relaxed. Jesus, Helen thought to herself, I'm acting like a horny teenager with mom and dad gone for the evening. Am I having fun yet?

Terrie walked briskly around the sofa. Helen stood up, uncertain what she ought to do now. "We have company. I didn't expect this for another hour," Terrie said in a matter-of-fact tone as she straightened the dress.

Helen watched Terrie's face and stood still, feeling idiotic. "Should I leave?" she asked.

Terrie turned to look at Helen appraisingly. A smile threatened to slip across her lips. "Up to you, Helen. You might want to stick around. I think the evening is going to get a bit more interesting now."

"You mean it wasn't interesting enough already?" Helen said, lamely trying to summon up a grin. What was going on now?

The door swung open and Beth Wilks strode into the room, a huge grin plastered across her broad, fair face. Her loose work shirt flapped against her worn jeans as she hurried into the room. "Thanks, sweetie," she said to Terrie. "I know I'm a little bit early, but —" The smile and the quick stride froze as she spotted Helen. "What on earth — Helen, this is a surprise." Beth's features wrinkled in puzzlement as she looked first at Helen, then at Terrie, then back to Helen. "You're the last person I thought I'd see here." Helen was sure Beth was struggling to keep her face a neutral mask. She felt her face turn fiery red and prayed that the dim lighting offered her a slim margin of concealment. Now what could she do? She glanced quickly at Terrie, who regarded both of them with detachment. And was that amusement glinting in her eyes? Helen folded her hands together to keep from slapping Terrie's smug, smirking face.

"What brings you here?" Beth pressed on. Helen's

stomach twisted at the way Beth stroked Terrie's arm, a brief intimate gesture that immediately announced them as lovers. Terrie moved closer to Beth, practically snuggling up to her like a kitten who'd just consumed a forbidden bowl of cream.

"Helen wanted to talk about the money R and F will be paying out to her aunt."

"Really?" Beth turned that carefully blank face back to Helen as she reached down to take Terrie's hand. "I wouldn't have thought that was your department, honey."

"Terrie was at the meeting with the attorneys, so I thought it would be at least a place to begin. I don't know anyone else at Roberts and Farrell, and Aunt Edna certainly hasn't been up to talking to a lot of people. She's still kind of in shock, you know," Helen babbled, hoping she didn't sound as much of an idiot as she felt.

Beth continued to stare, continued to hold on to Terrie. Helen fought down a surge of panic. God. First Beth had seen her getting blasted in front of the decent citizens of Tupelo. And no doubt she'd heard all about the fiasco with the church ladies. Given the joy Helen had seen lighting Beth's face when she first entered the room, Beth was no doubt enamored beyond reason with Terrie Muncie and insanely jealous. Now, no matter what she did, Helen was screwed if she ever uttered a word to her about Terrie's ideas on intramural sports. It was a lose-lose situation no matter how she sliced it. And the Aunt Edna story was incredibly thin. Something — she had to think of something.

She leaned down to grab her shoulder bag from the floor and groped for her car keys in one of the front pockets. Her hand brushed against the edge of the photograph she'd rescued from Aunt Edna's clutches, and Helen pulled it out on impulse. Maybe she could use the picture as some kind of excuse. Hell, it was better than milking Aunt Edna's grief any further.

"And —" Helen paused as she held out the photograph. "I also wanted to ask Terrie if there was any way to find out if the woman in this picture used to work here at Roberts and Farrell."

Beth reached for the picture and gingerly held it in her hands, studying it under the pale glow of the lamp. Slowly she looked back up at Helen, amazement registered in her eyes. "This is your uncle," she said, handing the photograph back as if it would bite her.

Helen nodded and handed it to Terrie. "That's right. We found this when we were going through my uncle's things." Maybe, Helen thought, Beth hadn't heard the latest gossip about what took place at the trailer. She went on. "My guess is this picture was taken at the time my uncle worked here, so it seemed like a place to start, at least."

"Edna doesn't recognize her?" Beth asked. Her face was still a frozen mask, unreadable, unapproachable.

Helen shrugged. "If she does, she won't say."

"Then my suggestion is you leave it alone. It's up to Edna whether or not you ever find out who that woman is."

Great. Helen slung her bag over her shoulder and looked away from Beth's disdain. Not only does she think I'm an alcoholic, Helen thought — I'm rude and insensitive and a slut as well. Stupid idea, pretending to "investigate" my uncle's mysterious past.

Terrie held the picture out to Helen. "I'm afraid I can't help you, Helen. Most of the people who would have worked here when your uncle was employed with us would have retired or moved on by now." She smiled sympathetically and leaned into Beth's side. "Besides, our records are strictly confidential. You do understand that, I'm sure."

"Of course." Helen grabbed the photograph and jammed it back into her bag. She nearly stumbled over a low table in her hurry to reach the door. "Thanks for your time, Ms. Muncie. Beth, nice to see you again."

"Actually —" Terrie broke away from Beth and followed Helen to the door. "We were just about to go out for dinner,

Helen. Why don't you join us? Unless you have other plans, that is."

Helen looked into Terrie's eyes, which were alight with cruelty and laughter, then glanced at Beth, who stood uncertainly in the middle of the room. "Maybe some other time."

Beth's body relaxed at Helen's refusal. "Are you sure?" she asked with false brightness. "There's a great steakhouse up the highway a bit. Good food."

"No, not tonight, thanks."

"You be sure to let me know if I can help you any other way while you're here, Helen," Terrie said as she ushered her out the door. The last thing Helen saw before the door closed was Beth, wary and awkward, her eyes dark with confusion, standing alone in the middle of the room.

Chapter Seven

"I'm sorry. There's no one here who can help you right now."

Her braids fell in neat lines toward her shoulders, framing chocolate-dark features that were strained with the effort to be polite. Helen sighed and moved to make way for the gaggle of people waiting in line for information. The Biloxi Tourist Information Center was, for some reason, a busy place today. It was Thursday. Why weren't all these people at work? Or was everyone stuffed into the lobby a tourist? Maybe it was business as usual since all those casinos had been built, Helen decided as she struggled through the lines back to the glass doors that opened out to a view of the strip of white sand edging the Gulf of Mexico.

She could see one of them now, directly across from the tourist center and across the highway. Even at nine-thirty in the morning a flock of gamblers milled around on the faux antebellum veranda just above the gentle waves lapping at the moorings. Helen stared for a moment, flashing on sudden memories of empty beaches stretching for miles along the Gulf Coast. Apparently undeveloped land was as much a part of the past in Mississippi as it was in California.

As she waited for the parking lot exit to clear, Helen studied the map the clerk at the information desk had given her. Tours of old homes? No, the building in the photograph had more the look of a hotel or resort. Maybe trying to drive by some of the hotels listed? But they were dotted all over town, and she had only limited time to try to locate the spot the picture had been taken. Besides, most of those listed in this particular map seemed to be in the category of cheap motels that accommodated tots. And how the heck could she be sure it was a motel or hotel, anyhow?

The sound of a car horn spurred her to concentrate on driving out of the lot and back onto the highway. Helen sat and pondered at a red light. Why was she acting like a ditzy little novice today? She couldn't seem to get her brain to hold on to anything. Maybe because this wasn't just any piece of detective work — this was digging up the dirt on Uncle Loy, despite Aunt Edna's protests. Her aunt hadn't said anything when Helen had left the trailer this morning, but she had to know that Helen was on the prowl. Fuck it, Helen decided. She doesn't have to know about any of it. I'm doing this for myself, right?

Helen glanced at the map, unfolded in her lap, and saw that the library wasn't far from where she sat waiting for the light to turn green. Surely they'd have some old maps and old newspapers sitting around. If Biloxi was proud enough to have its own tourism center, it would surely equip its library with a record of its proud past — maybe even a photo history of the town in a kind of before-and-after series. She found the

87

library easily — a small, squat red-brick structure in the midst of a neighborhood that perhaps had once been upper class but had the definite look of an area slipping quietly into seediness. Which might mean it was slated for gentrification and outrageous rents during the next decade, Helen thought grimly as she got out of the car and felt the midmorning heat slam into her body.

The library opened at ten, and an elderly woman with tight, permed blue hair was just unlocking the doors as Helen hurried up the stone steps. Her shriveled face wrinkled even further as she opened the door just wide enough to let Helen slide in, and Helen bravely smiled under her disapproving stare. Okay, so she was already sweating — not to mention that her T-shirt and scruffy jeans certainly didn't mark her as a properly feminine reader of literature. Just to complete the portrait Helen debated lifting her shirt and showing the old bat the tattoo above her navel. Instead she merely asked where she could find historical documents, even pulling out the photograph.

"There is a permanent display of old historical buildings in the Robert E. Lee Room here at the library," the woman sniffed, her eyes continuing to take Helen's measure with disdain. "But I'm afraid that room is closed today."

Great. Helen went down the list of other possibilities. Old newspapers (they were being put on microfilm and inaccessible to the public until early next year). Histories of the town (tucked away in the mysterious mecca of the Robert E. Lee Room). Even old tourist guides, similar to the ones Helen had in the car (discarded regularly whenever new editions became available from the chamber of commerce). The elderly woman sighed. "Well, it seems we can't help you today." She didn't look a bit sorry.

Helen gave up. "Thank you so much," she said in a voice dripping with saccharine and sarcasm. The librarian smiled with a prissy pursing of her lips and minced away to the reference desk. Slipping the photograph back into its folder, Helen stood and savored the air conditioning for a few seconds before braving the August heat again. Well, she'd head for the newspaper office next. Probably they had permanent archives and an underpaid staff member assigned to cover historical monuments and such — every small Mississippi town had one of those — and —

"She give you a hard time?"

Helen, startled, turned around and bumped painfully into a wheeled metal cart loaded with books. Her jolt managed to dislodge a few paperbacks from the cart, and she bent down to retrieve them. She came eye-to-eye with a young woman as she stood up again. Coal-black hair, straight and glossy, hung down to her shoulders — it was probably dyed, far too black and stark to be natural. Light blue eyes looked out, round and wide, from a pale face whitened even further with careful makeup. Artificially reddened full lips provided stark contrast. The girl was clothed entirely in black — black nylon shirt, black vest, very short black skirt, black tights, black shoes laced up over ankles. Even the tiny nose ring piercing one nostril was some kind of black metal.

"You could say that," Helen stammered. What was this kid doing in the library in Biloxi?

The girl smiled wryly. "Figures. If you don't have big hair and a husband on the chamber of commerce, you don't get anything out of her. Let me see the picture."

Helen handed it over, hoping she had successfully masked her amazement. The younger woman studied it, holding it cautiously under the light in slim pale fingers tipped with — of course — black nail polish. "Helen Black," she murmured, looking over the girl's shoulder. The old woman, her back turned toward the stacks where they stood, was fussing with a bunch of stamps at the reference desk.

"My name's Victoria." She handed the picture back to Helen. "Hmm. Guess the Robert E. Lee Room is your best bet here. Sorry, I don't recognize it."

"You think I could persuade her I had a husband on the city council? Get her to let me into the room today?"

Victoria — such a dignified and old-fashioned name for her — snorted. "Don't even try. She only puts up with me 'cause my dad used to be editor of the local newspaper and because I'm outta here next month."

"College?"

She nodded eagerly. "Berkeley. I can hardly wait."

Helen smiled. She decided it was better not to mention that she was from Berkeley. "Well, the newspaper office is my next stop, Victoria. Thanks anyway." She could feel the girl's eyes following her as she went back outside. She had to laugh at herself. First Terrie Muncie, now a beautiful young woman with a pierced nose? Maybe she was just a change of pace from the usual clientele at the library.

Too bad there wasn't another Victoria at the newspaper office. Instead she got a fluffy brunette with painted talons and too much floral perfume politely fielding all her questions. No, they didn't have an archives room open to the public. Yes, there were a couple of staff members assigned to reporting local history, but they were both out covering the opening of a new shopping mall built on the grounds of what used to be a park. Well, she could go to the local library, to the Robert E. Lee Room — there was a permanent display of Biloxi history there. Not at all, a pleasure, glad to be of service.

Helen debated the value of mentioning Victoria's name, realized she didn't know the girl's last name, and decided to just drive around for a bit. Maybe she could come back tomorrow, or whenever the fucking Robert E. Lee Room was open. She drove away from the newspaper office and headed back for the highway beside the gulf. After supplying herself with a full tank of gas, she found a vacant parking space. She was pissed off. Time to stop for a few minutes and reassess.

The steering wheel had grown hot to the touch in less than fifteen minutes. That's all it had taken to get to and from the convenience store on the corner for some cold drinks. It didn't seem to make any difference, either, whether or not she cracked the windows open. The late morning heat in Biloxi, even this close to the Gulf of Mexico, soaked through every surface. The interior of the car felt like clogged Jell-O, hot and thick and suffocating. Helen switched on the air conditioner again. Too bad if it wasn't good for the car battery.

Helen glanced down at the growing pile of empty soda cans and bottles she'd tried to keep contained in a plastic grocery bag. After a couple of hours of driving around and looking at the exteriors of buildings she'd switched to bottled water. Didn't seem to make any difference, actually. No matter what she consumed she couldn't cool off.

Helen sighed, leaned back against the headrest, and took a long swallow, nearly draining the water bottle. To her left, the Gulf of Mexico boiled blue and restless, frothing in gently cresting waves in occasional gusts of hot wind coming up from the south. Helen remembered coming here as a kid, when the white beaches stretched for miles in a thin swath edging the water. Small ships in the distance, shimmering in heat waves, had been the only sign of human life on the Gulf back then.

Now, however, a fake paddle-wheel boat rested in the water, belched up like an elaborate wedding cake from some unknown depth in the water. The neon lights screamed out DIXIELAND CASINO in brilliant flashes of red alternating with blue, an endlessly repeating cycle that even in bright sunlight reflected like a lifesaving beacon across the gulf. People milled about the boardwalk that led from the beach to the casino. Helen guessed, from the large numbers of sunburned limbs and cameras slung around necks, that most of the people wandering back and forth from sand to casino were tourists. The locals probably wouldn't frequent something like that unless there was a decent floor show scheduled. Gulls wheeled and screamed across a sky bleached white by the sun. Helen squinted against the bright light, slid her sunglasses back against her sweating forehead, and finished off the water.

The photograph lay in her lap, fluttering in the blast from the air conditioner. Each time she looked at it Helen tried to blot out the image of Uncle Loy and focus instead on the building behind them. Of course, beyond the old brochures from Biloxi, Helen had no idea whether or not she was on the right track. But — and this thought made her wince — Biloxi was one of those places where someone looking for illicit activity might feel safe. People passed through rather than stayed on — the water, beaches and hotels, military installations close by in those days — a place one could be anonymous. Unlike most small towns in Mississippi, in that regard. Perfect place for Uncle Loy to conduct an affair, if that's what it was. Apparently that aspect of Biloxi still held true — maybe more than ever, if the casinos were a means of judging the times. The *Dixieland* was only one of many Helen had seen lined up along the water's edge. She shuddered to think what the beaches looked like closer to these new arrivals. Probably no longer the clean white sand she remembered. Instead, they'd be littered with everything from used condoms to fast-food wrappers. With a sigh Helen put the picture back into the box where she'd stowed everything from her uncle's stash and placed it carefully in the backseat.

She started the car, wondering where she ought to go next. She hadn't really learned anything useful in a morning spent touring Biloxi. Hell, the building in the photograph might have since been torn down or blown away in a storm or hurricane. Helen drove past the Jefferson Davis house on her right, leaving the *Dixieland* behind. She slowed the car almost to a stop as a horde of tourists left the memorial to the Confederacy, most of them carrying bags full of loot from the museum store, and trotted across the street. Helen scowled to herself, thinking how many of them might be going straight from this monument across the beach to the casino. One landmark after another, apparently.

She drove by the library — might as well check on the hours that the doors to the Robert E. Lee Room would be open. Victoria was perched on a stoop at the side of the building, smoking and staring out at the highway. She smiled as Helen approached.

"Any luck?" she asked, shielding her eyes from the sun.

"Nope. They sent me back here."

"Figures. Well, the room should be open tomorrow afternoon, from one to five."

"Thanks." Helen turned to leave but stopped when Victoria called her name.

"Look, he'll probably kill me — what the hell. Got a pen or something?" She followed Helen to her car, and Helen handed her a pen and paper from the glove compartment. "Here," Victoria said around her cigarette, scribbling on the paper. "You can probably find my dad at this place. Did you see the Dixieland Casino out by the highway? Well, go a little further up and turn right on this street. The Gulf Breeze Lounge is in the middle of the second block. That's where he generally starts his rounds. Ask for Bill Mason. He used to be an editor at the paper."

Helen took the slip of paper. "Your father will help me?"

Victoria Mason shrugged. "Buy him a couple of drinks, sure, he'll help you."

"The big question, though, is why you are telling me this. What's going on here, Victoria?"

Victoria stared back at the library as she answered. "You're not from around here. Where are you from?"

"Berkeley, California."

Victoria suppressed a smile. "Well, I knew you weren't local. A reporter, right? Digging up the dirt on something here in the heart of Dixie. Right?"

"I'm not a reporter. I'm a private investigator."

"Even better. Look, my dad knows all the dirt in town. If anyone can remember about this building you're looking for, he can. He didn't exactly retire from his job — they said it was his drinking, but that was never a big deal to these fuckers until he started saying negative shit about our heroes in the Persian Gulf." She ground her cigarette out and leaned against Helen's car. "I'm sick to death of Biloxi bitches like the bag in there who give me this shitty job just so they can look down on me and pretend to feel sorry for me at the same time."

Helen, thinking hard, eased herself back into the car. "Thanks, Victoria. I'll — I'll see if I can find him."

"Promise me one thing."

"If I can."

Victoria leaned into the window, and Helen had a brief, intense memory of Terrie Muncie doing the same thing two days ago. "If you find out anything that will get my dad a really good news story, you'll help him."

"It's a deal." Jesus, now what the fuck was she going to do? Helen slowly left the library, giving Victoria a final look as she drove off. The girl was a mixture of naiveté and callous sophistication, with her nose ring and her pleas for help from a stranger. But Helen had no other leads to follow at this point. Might as well give an aging, alcoholic editor a visit. She'd probably end up back at the library tomorrow, anyhow, if nothing else than to try to let Victoria down gently.

As she picked up speed again, Helen glanced down at the clock in the dashboard. Shit, almost noon. She'd promised Aunt Edna she'd be back by dinnertime so they could go to the lawyers for signing papers this evening. She needed to get out of here soon. So why was she wasting her fucking time? This was all pointless. No one wanted to know about her uncle's behavior, least of all Aunt Edna. Might as well call it a bad idea, get a bite to eat, and head back for Tupelo.

Helen turned off the highway to her right, hoping her memory served her well in the search for food. Once off the main drag she was able to slow down and take stock of her surroundings. It was amazing — just a few feet away from the glitz and superficial glamour of the shiny new casinos, next to

94

the carefully preserved mementos of the Civil War, a different world existed. Shabby liquor stores stood side by side with thrift shops and a couple of markets sporting tables of cheap clothing that looked as though they would fall apart if looked at too closely. One block held a variety of fast-food outlets in close proximity, all with drive-through lanes — but the competition didn't seem to be creating any problems, as each one looked filled to overflowing with customers. People moved about with no sign of needing to get anywhere in particular. Most of the faces were white, but there was a definite presence of some darker colors to be seen. And to Helen's relief, there was no one wearing a camera on a strap.

She kept driving until she noticed a preponderance of adult video stores and bars, replete with flashing neon signs. Yes, there it was — the Gulf Breeze Lounge was nestled between a hamburger joint and an auto parts shop. Helen found a parking spot across the street and darted through traffic into the bar, hoping they served food. She was in luck — some of the patrons, all male, hunched over mounds of French fries and hamburgers as they watched a game show on the television set mounted over the beer spigots. Terrific, once again pushing the barriers of white-male territory. Helen leaned against the counter and ordered a hamburger before asking her question.

"Bill Mason? Who wants to know?" The bartender, a skinny man in his late thirties with an incongruous spray of acne across his face, ran a grimy hand through his thinning blond hair and stared at her with hostile, dark eyes.

"My name is Helen Black. Victoria Mason said I might find him here."

"Victoria? You talked to my daughter today? Is she all right?" The man on the stool across the room stood up unsteadily and made his way to Helen. "Is something wrong? Did something happen to her?"

Helen, under the baleful gaze of the bartender, did her best to reassure him as she studied his features for a likeness to the girl she'd met earlier. Yes, he had the same pallor and light blue eyes, although both showed the effects of too many years of cheap booze. His hair was gray but thick and straight. It was long enough to brush the top of a frayed and dirty collar. Even at a distance Helen could smell the liquor on his breath. It wafted off his clothes as well. What had once been a very good, very expensive suit had been exposed to too many hours of smoke and liquor. Helen felt a brief pang of sympathy for Victoria and wondered what Bill had been like before getting shitcanned.

"So she sent you here?" The former editor of the newspaper scratched his cheek absently, puzzling it out.

"Look, Bill, you want me to get rid of her?" The bartender glanced back and forth between them. Helen saw they'd garnered an audience. No one was watching the game show now.

"Why don't we sit in a booth over here, Bill?" Helen took him by the elbow and steered him away from the bar. "What are you drinking?" A few minutes later they both had burgers and fries and drinks placed on their table and the men at the bar had reluctantly gone back to watching television.

Bill drank down his Scotch as if it were water, then focused a bit blearily on the photograph. "That's the old Beauregard Resort," he said.

Helen stared in disbelief. "You can tell, just from that corner of the building?" She watched as a stillness came over him. Something about the picture — about the place — froze him. He gave her a short, sharp glance, then went back to being the shaky alcoholic. It happened so quickly that Helen wasn't even sure she'd seen the shift.

He nodded, took one bite of his very rare hamburger, then reached for the second shot Helen had waiting. "Did a story on it when it burned down. I knew every inch of that building before I was done."

"It burned down?"

"Yeah, back in seventy-five. Arson. Well, they never proved

it, but I'm certain it was done on purpose." Something tight folded up in his face. There was more to this arson thing than he was telling her — something painful seared in his memory. She'd have to wait to find out what it was. "Who are these two?" he asked.

Helen took the picture back from his slightly trembling fingers. "Who did it? Did you ever find out?" she asked, ignoring his question.

Bill shrugged and poked at his French fries. "Never did learn that one. That was before I was editor, back when I was reporting. I got pulled off the story before I had a chance with it. Stands to reason, though, that it was the owners. I mean, it's usually insurance money they're after, right?" He'd finished the second drink and glanced around as if one more might appear from out of nowhere.

"So who owned it?" she asked after signaling the bartender for fresh drinks.

"Didn't get that far. I traced ownership to some big company before they yanked me off. One of those corporations that have a finger in everything — real estate, foreign investments, research and development —"

"Roberts and Farrell? Was that the company?" Worth a shot, anyway.

Bingo. Bill Mason's eyes shifted suddenly to the tabletop, then to his empty glass, then to the bar. "Can't remember. It was a long time ago, you know? My memory isn't what it used to be in the old days."

The hell it wasn't. She'd gotten a glimpse of the reporter buried under gallons of booze when he started talking about the fire, then Mason neatly submerged that personality beneath the mask of gibbering alky one step away from the gutter. He even managed to slur his words effectively at a moment's notice.

"Who's your girlfriend, Bill?" Two men stood beside their booth. One had an enormous beer gut that hung over his belt with graceless abandon. The other looked like he worked out and took steroids. Either one of them, Helen was sure, could have tossed her around the room like a sack of potatoes. And they both smelled like they'd been in the bar as long as Bill Mason had, although Helen would swear they hadn't been there a couple of minutes ago. Where had they come from? She looked at the bartender, who quickly turned away. Had someone made a quick phone call while they were waiting for their food? Helen couldn't prove it, but these two felt like local muscle — but what the hell were they doing here? Was Bill Mason that big a threat to someone? Maybe, if he knew as much as Victoria had promised. Helen couldn't see their expressions clearly but no doubt they weren't pleased at her presence. Someone from out of town pestering the former editor with annoying questions and, worst of all, going on her own into the bar — definitely not a lady.

"Jimbo. Tommy. What do you want?" Bill didn't look surprised to see them, but he didn't look happy, either.

"Nothing, nothing — just saying hello to our visitor, here." Beer gut, also known as Jimbo, slid into the booth next to Helen. Tommy sat down next to Bill and began to consume his French fries, never taking his eyes off Helen. "You don't have people come out to see you too often, Bill. Except for that pretty little daughter of yours. How is she, by the way? Still working over at the library?"

Helen watched Bill freeze up, his face solidify into a pale mask that made him look even more like Victoria. "This lady is just asking about the good old days at the paper, that's all." Even more slurring, more vague clumsy gestures. Maybe old Bill had good reason to be the town drunk if he had pals like these two checking up on him.

"Well, now, isn't that nice? Doing a news story about it, is that it?"

Helen decided not to answer. She had at least a small piece of what she needed, anyhow, and her presence clearly wasn't doing Bill Mason any good. His gaze met her own, his pale blue eyes pleading something. Helen tossed a few bills on the table and made sure her photograph was safely tucked away. "Too bad you couldn't help me, Mr. Mason. Guess I'll have to try somewhere else." Jimbo sat like a lump of lard beside her, ignoring her moves to get out of the booth, while Tommy finished the fries and started on the hamburger. "Excuse me, Jimbo, I'm trying to get out."

"So soon? We haven't made you welcome here? Now, that's not nice." In a sudden flurry of activity, Jimbo slid out of the booth and Tommy took Bill by the arm and steered him toward the back of the bar. Helen peered over Jimbo's shoulder and saw a back door open and shut, bathing the room in a quick flash of bright light from outside. Tommy had taken Bill out into an alley — or worse.

Jimbo moved to block her view. "That your car out there? The little rental across the street? Nice. Better get into it and drive off, lady."

"Sure, sure, just want to make sure the bartender gets his tip." She feinted to her left, then slipped by him to the right, darting past the men lined up on barstools who'd suddenly found the game show to be incredibly interesting. In another second she was out the back door.

Bill was bent over double, coughing and red faced from Tommy's punch to his midsection. Without thinking Helen landed a kick to Tommy's unprotected groin and had the satisfaction of seeing the bodybuilder open his mouth in silent pain as he stumbled back against a Dumpster. She didn't have to turn around to know that the man rushing through the door was Jimbo.

"Fucking cunt!" Something slammed into her back and knocked the wind out of her. Dizzy, her vision clouded with sparks of light, Helen grabbed a beer bottle off the ground and spun to face Jimbo. "You think you can hurt me, little bitch?" He grinned and walked calmly toward them.

Helen smashed the bottle against the wall and saw splinters of glass fly into the air. "Bill, get the fuck out of here," she muttered.

"Victoria —"

"Just do it, all right?" she commanded, almost screaming. She didn't see which direction he shambled off, her attention too taken by Jimbo and Tommy. Still gasping, Tommy pulled himself up and leaned against the Dumpster, his eyes dark with hate. Helen had a brief, irrelevant thought that Tommy hadn't uttered a word since his appearance.

"You really think that little thing will hold us off, cunt?"

Helen felt fear surge up like nausea, burning in her throat. Of course it wouldn't. "Depends," she managed to say. "Which one of you wants scars on his pretty face?"

The next thing she knew she was on the ground looking up at the hot blue sky. Helen flailed out with the bottle, heard a shriek, saw a gush of blood from something. At least she'd cut one of them. Pain hit her head. Jesus, they were kicking her. The last thing she heard before she blacked out was a siren, wailing, coming closer. Then total darkness.

Chapter Eight

"Are you sure you shouldn't get checked out by a doctor?"

Helen tried to swivel in the car seat and was rewarded with pain. "No, I'm fine. Really." They hadn't actually kicked her in the head — she'd just been stunned for a few seconds. And of course Tommy and Jimbo had not been anywhere in sight when she came to in the alley behind the Gulf Breeze Lounge several hours ago. No, it had just been Helen dragged off to the emergency room and then to the police station. Mostly it was just her side that ached now. A pulled muscle, a few bruises, a scrape or two — she'd live. She didn't need a doctor to tell her that much. "They just wanted my wallet, that's all."

"So you said to the Biloxi police. How about telling me the

truth?" Beth Wilks looked pretty spiffy in her state trooper uniform. Helen felt a twinge of guilt at hauling her all the way out here when she had to be on duty almost the moment they got back to Tupelo. But it was almost worth it to get a look at Beth's muscular body clothed in blue and gray, with that stripe running down the leg and the impressive patches on the nicely tailored shirt. Her blond hair, pulled back in a tight ponytail for work, gleamed in the afternoon sun. Helen couldn't see Beth's eyes behind the sunglasses, but she knew she was pissed off.

"Look, it is the truth," Helen lied. "I was down here hoping to find the building in the photograph."

"That picture of your Uncle Loy and the other woman, right?"

"Right. All I did was stop in this place for a drink before going back home, and I guess these guys thought I had some money on me." She'd been incredibly vague to the Biloxi police, too, fearful of Bill Mason somehow having to pay if she said anything about Tommy and Jimbo. Whatever Bill Mason was hiding about the fire could stay hidden a little longer. "So they knocked me around a little bit."

"A little bit? Enough that the local police kept you at the station until you called me to vouch for you, Helen. Enough that I didn't think you should drive yourself home tonight, not with that bruise on your head. You might have a concussion."

"No, I don't. Believe me, I've had them before and know how they feel. And I can't help it that Biloxi's finest thought it was a good plan for you to come all the way out there and pick me up. It wasn't my idea, okay?"

Beth sighed and shook her head. "They all got a good laugh out of it. I'm never going to live this down. Are you aware of that?"

"What do you want me to do, crawl on my knees over flaming coals? It was nothing — a stupid argument that blew out of proportion and got worse when the cops stepped in. That's it."

"That's it."

"Yeah, that's it. Why would I make something up like that? You know me better than that, Beth." Helen prayed it would work. The last thing she wanted was to get into Biloxi tomorrow and find out that Victoria Mason had lost her job, or that her father had ended up in the hospital — or worse. She had a quick memory of Victoria's pale smiling face, her light blue eyes, the crooked smile she'd flashed at Helen in the library. Enough of that, Helen warned herself. You've already got a rich bitch in Tupelo playing some kind of mind-fuck on you, and a sexy state trooper ready to throw you out the window while going sixty-five. Don't need any more dyke drama than I already got, Helen thought with a grimace.

Beth snorted. "I thought I did." Beth shook a cigarette out of the packet on the dashboard and shoved the lighter in place with an angry push. "I'm beginning to think I don't know you at all. I don't know which is worse — that you're sneaking around behind Edna's back to rake up shit on her dead husband, or that you're hanging around dives like the Gulf Breeze Lounge and getting sloshed before lunch time." She lit the cigarette and took a deep drag, turning to glance at Helen. "Not to mention getting your ass beat up by a couple of shitkickers. No, I don't recognize you any more."

"Done preaching now? Or maybe I could have a shot at how you're fucking the biggest closet case in Tupelo. Is she the one who bought you this fancy four-wheel drive, Beth? Or did a state trooper's salary jump up there just enough for you to afford it?" The moment the words spilled out Helen regretted them. Helen was sure Beth was the last person on earth who'd take money from someone like Terrie Muncie.

Then she saw Beth's hands flinch on the steering wheel. The cigarette was burning down to nothing but ashes as Beth sat frozen next to her. Jesus, that must have hit the mark, somehow, Helen realized. Maybe Beth wasn't exactly a kept woman at this point, but in some way she'd accepted financial help from Terrie. This car, perhaps, or loans or something. Whatever it was, Beth wasn't proud of it. Come to think of it, that was an expensive watch Beth was wearing. And the suit she'd had on at the funeral the other day — it certainly wasn't hot off the rack from the local discount warehouse.

Helen stayed silent, digesting the information she'd just gleaned. Beth was already furious at her, and there was no point in making things even worse. Better to keep this to herself, to keep in mind that Beth was all out of stones to throw at anyone. Might be useful later on, although it turned Helen's already queasy stomach to think of her first lover in those terms.

Beth broke the silence. "Does Edna know where you were today?" she asked quietly. "She might be really worried."

Aunt Edna. Oh god. "What time is it?" Helen asked, struggling to sit up straight and see where they were. Shit, almost at Tupelo now.

"Just after five. At least I'll get to report to work on time. Why?" Beth took the next exit off the highway, and Helen could see the small town in the distance.

Terrific. She'd let her aunt down on something really important. Had Edna made it to the meeting with the lawyers without her? Or had Helen by her absence just blown something big, too big to warrant forgiveness? The pain in her side fought her as she struggled to stay calm. "Do you have some kind of cell phone, Beth?"

Beth had taken off her sunglasses in the afternoon light. She looked curiously at Helen. "Under your seat." Helen groped for and found the instrument without bothering to ask permission to use it. Beth plugged and switched, and Helen pushed at numbers frantically. The phone rang twice before Aunt Edna picked it up.

"No, I didn't get to the meeting. But that's all right,

Helen. That nice young lady who was there is here right now, helping me with the papers." The line broke up for a couple of seconds, and when Helen could hear her aunt again she was saying something about fixing dinner for all of them.

"Where's Bobby?" Helen asked, wondering if Terrie Muncie was witnessing her cousin's behavior — then feeling ashamed for worrying about it.

"He's out back, playing with the train set Miss Muncie brought him. You should just see it, Helen, honey! A little city and everything came with it. It's just so darn cute!"

"I'm sure it is. Is she still there?"

"Well, of course! She's staying for dinner. Helen, sweetheart, when are you coming home? I thought you would be here by now."

Helen sighed and closed her eyes. From the sound of her aunt's voice, all Helen's aberrant and evil behavior, from drinking demon rum to grandstanding the lawyers to exposing her uncles peccadilloes, were forgiven or at least conveniently forgotten in the thrill of signing away her independence to Roberts and Farrell. Okay, that wasn't fair. Aunt Edna was right — she did have to provide for herself and Bobby somehow.

"Helen? Sweetheart, are you there? I can barely hear you."

"Yes, Aunt Edna. I'm almost home. I'll be there in just a few minutes." Helen slumped in the seat and watched Tupelo get nearer and nearer. Beth retrieved the car phone and stowed it under her own seat as they took the turnoff for the trailer park on the other side of town.

"Everything okay at home, Helen?" Beth asked in a neutral tone.

Helen looked at her with surprise. Funny, that holier-than-thou note had totally disappeared from Beth's voice. "I think so. Aunt Edna's getting dinner ready." She had a sudden, malignant idea. "Too bad you can't hang around for supper. Do you have any time before your shift starts?" It might be fun to have Beth and Terrie dance around the trailer in some weird minuet of innuendos and double meanings, in a nasty sort of way.

Beth shook her head and kept her gaze fixed on the road. "No, thanks. I'll drop you off, and then I really have to get going."

Just as well, Helen thought, as she stood in front of Aunt Edna's trailer and watched Beth's fresh-minted four-wheel drive spin off over the gravel lane. Now where the hell was Terrie Muncie's car? She saw it parked around the side of the trailer as she slowly and painfully climbed up the steps to the front door.

"There you are, sweetheart!" Aunt Edna, her faded blouse dusted with flour or cornmeal or some other fine substance, greeted her at the door with a smacking kiss on the cheek. "I was just taking the cornbread out of the oven."

Helen returned her hug, grateful that for the moment at least all recriminations were set aside. If she kept her mouth shut about Uncle Loy and let Edna and Bobby settle into a zone of comfort, maybe all this would just blow over like a bad dream. Yeah, a bad dream that kicks and punches, Helen thought, fighting not to show a wince of pain as she stepped back from the older woman's embrace. She looked up to see Terrie leaning against the doorway to the kitchen. Terrie looked just as delicious in tight jeans and close-fitting, ice-blue sleeveless top as she did in the slinky number she'd worn last night. She held an attaché case loosely in her arms.

Helen ignored her greeting. "I take it you got everything squared away with the papers?" she asked as Edna bustled back to something fragrant simmering on the stove.

Terrie nodded and smiled brightly. "All taken care of. Edna and Bobby won't have to worry about money for a long, long time."

Helen walked past her to look outside. Sure enough, Bobby was absorbed in his shiny new train set. It gleamed in the light as he gingerly handled a brightly painted caboose with awe and wonder. "That's very good of you, Terrie. And of Roberts and Farrell."

She felt Terrie standing close behind her. "I like to think we've been able to help. Your cousin is sweet, you know. He seems to love that train set."

"Well, it's not as expensive as a four-wheel drive, but it certainly got the desired result," Helen murmured as she walked into the living room.

She had no clear memory of the dinner that Aunt Edna served at the shaky little table, or of the conversation that went on that evening, beyond the fact that Bobby entertained them all with his excitement over his new toy. If it hadn't been Terrie Muncie sitting across the table from her, Helen would have sworn that it was old times, with Loy and Edna and Bobby and herself enjoying a simple meal in the aging trailer, enjoying each other's presence, taking comfort and healing from mutual affection. Instead it was Terrie she watched, Terrie's eyes and hands and lips that burned their presence into her mind. Helen stayed almost completely silent throughout the dinner and the subsequent television viewing. Her mood continued well after Bobby had trundled off to his room, lasted beyond Aunt Edna excusing herself with a yawn and a final kiss good-night for her niece. Then the ten o'clock news was coming on, and Helen and Terrie were alone in the trailer's living room — Helen seated on the lumpy sofa with its faded upholstery, Terrie cross-legged on the floor near Uncle Loy's creaking La-Z-Boy recliner.

"So, Terrie, what the fuck are you doing here?" Helen asked the moment she heard Edna's bedroom door shut.

Terrie rose from the floor and sat on the sofa, tucking her legs up under her while the news droned on in the background. "I'm here to help your aunt and cousin. Nothing more, nothing less."

"Right. And I'm straight. Tell me another one."

Terrie leaned forward, and Helen was very aware of the way her breasts pressed against the smooth fabric of the blue shirt. "Maybe I'm here to help you, too, Helen," she breathed. Damn, she was even wearing the same perfume as the last night.

"Yeah, well, I've had all the help I need today, thanks."

"So I heard. Beth called me before she went to Biloxi. We were supposed to have dinner tonight, and she had to cancel."

Somehow the fact that Beth had spilled everything to Terrie made it all worse. "Fine, you've made yourself useful. Now why don't you just go home?"

Terrie stretched her legs out until her feet, minus the shoes she'd shed a couple of hours before, rested in Helen's lap. "Relax," she chuckled as Helen squirmed. "We'll hear your relatives if they come out. Besides, nothing is happening here. Not unless you want it to."

"I don't want it. Hell, you're seeing Beth. She's one of the oldest friends I have in the world. I am not going to fuck things up worse than I already have." Helen shoved Terrie's feet off her lap. "Whatever little games you have going on, leave me and my family out of it."

"What makes you think there's any kind of game here, Helen? Why can't it just be that you turn me on and I want you?"

"Just leave, Terrie." Helen got up off the sofa, favoring her sore side and hoping Terrie didn't notice the halting movement. "You got your signatures and my aunt's undying devotion and a pretty good dinner out of it. Enough."

Terrie stayed where she was and cocked her head to one side as she regarded Helen. "Don't you want to know how I'm going to help you?"

"That's the second time you've mentioned that in the space of three minutes. Just tell me what the hell you're talking about and get out, all right?"

Helen couldn't stop herself from watching Terrie as she got up and walked across the room to her attaché case resting on the floor by the television set. Nor could she tear her gaze away from the view as Terrie quite deliberately bent over to retrieve something from the case. Helen turned down the volume on the set as Terrie handed her a sheet of paper.

"A bunch of names," Helen said as she looked it over. "What is this, Terrie? A list of your ex-girlfriends who are out to kill you now?"

Terrie smiled and moved to stand beside her, peering over Helen's shoulder at the list and making sure Helen could feel her body, warm and fragrant and pulsing with energy. "Believe it or not, a list like that wouldn't be so long as this. No, Helen, these are former employees of Roberts and Farrell."

"All women's names." Helen estimated there were about twenty names. She looked up from the list into Terrie's eyes. "These are possible contenders for Uncle Loy's main squeeze, right? That's what you're trying to buy me off with."

Terrie kept her eyes steady as she looked into Helen's face. "I went to quite a bit of trouble to put that together, Helen. All these people were the right age group for the woman in the photograph, and they were all employed at about the time your uncle was."

Helen moved away, staring at Terrie in disbelief. This was absolutely ridiculous. It made a kind of sense that Victoria had given her information earlier today, given her hopes of somehow salvaging her father and dealing a slap at the powers that be in Biloxi at the same time, but Terrie's gesture was less credible. Whether it was cars or toys or trust funds, Terrie Muncie would rarely give anything away, not without wresting some kind of payment.

"And what am I supposed to pay you with for this, Terrie?" Helen said, waving the sheet of paper at her. "I don't deal in your kind of currency."

Terrie stood in the middle of the living room, still as a statue, arms folded demurely across her chest. "Let's just call it insurance, Helen."

"And why the fuck would you need insurance with me, Terrie? Do you think I'm about to tell Beth you made a pass at me? Believe me, she'd just completely write me off if I did that. She already hates me for falling off whatever pedestal I was on in her mind."

"On the contrary, Helen. I think she still loves you."

"I thought that was your department," Helen said, feeling a warm surge of hope in her chest at the thought of Beth still caring for her. Stupid wish, but now that it was there she couldn't fight it off.

Terrie reached out and stroked Helen's face with surprisingly gentle fingers. "I'm throwing the dice here, Helen. I'm betting that you won't be able to leave that list alone — that you'll come back for more from me, that I haven't seen the last of you."

Helen's stomach tightened with a rush of desire, an unwelcome warmth creeping between her legs. Shit. "That's a really lousy bet, Terrie."

"I don't think so. I think, between your need to get laid and your need to find out what your uncle was up to, I'll be seeing an awful lot more of you. An awful lot." Terrie's hands moved to Helen's neck, then her breasts. Helen pushed her hands away, but with less force than she wanted to exhibit.

"Just because you throw out the line it doesn't mean you'll catch your fish. I'm not hooked by you and never will be."

"Beth didn't say what happened to you in Biloxi. Did someone hurt you? That's a cut on your neck." Terrie reached for her again, and this time Helen didn't try to stop her. For one wild second Helen's mind veered dizzily. Was it Beth in her arms? Was that Beth's neck she licked and gently bit? Then she had an image of Victoria, with her crooked dimpled smile, her ivory skin, her light blue eyes that darkened when she talked of her father. No, it was Terrie Muncie in Helen's arms, Terrie's tongue lightly licking Helen's lips, Terrie's hands gently kneading Helen's breasts and teasing her nipples.

"Not hooked, Helen? Is that still what you're trying to tell

110

yourself?" Terrie's breath was hot against Helen's neck as her hand crept between Helen's legs. "You'll have to throw away those jeans, Helen. Or make sure you get your aunt to wash them for you."

The mention of Aunt Edna was like freezing water on hot glass, shattering the moment. Helen pushed Terrie away, none too gently, and managed to find her breath and her voice again. "Fine, Terrie. You've proved to both of us that I'm horny as hell, that I'd like nothing better than a good fuck with anything on two legs. Or maybe we could skip the two legs part, as long as there was a vagina and tits involved. What does that prove? I'm not going to be your dirty little secret. Besides, I should think you've got plenty of those already. Plenty that Beth doesn't know about, anyway."

To her amazement Terrie laughed, a low, sweet sound that turned Helen on even more as she couldn't help wondering how Terrie sounded when she had an orgasm. "Beth doesn't really want to know any of my secrets. Trust me, Helen, she might suspect something, but she'll never ask questions. Anything I don't want to tell her stays that way, and Beth goes along with it."

"Are you really that good a lay? Or is it just that you're available and convenient?" That one stung, and Helen felt a stab of pleasure at seeing Terrie flinch. Too bad. And it was a handy piece of ammunition for future reference — Terrie Muncie didn't like any hint that she might not be as hot a piece of shit as she imagined.

But she recovered nicely, leaning down to pick up her case and striding toward the door. "Actually, Helen, I am the best. I don't think I need to provide you with references — I think you should just check it out yourself." She let herself out, and a couple of minutes later Helen heard her car crunching over the gravel lane.

Helen stood in the center of the room, grasping the list,

trembling with frustrated desire. She knew that wanting to have sex with Terrie Muncie was like asking for a lethal injection — but her body couldn't help it. The woman was nothing but trouble, but the trouble was packaged awfully well. And Helen had been celibate — not by choice, either — for longer than she cared to remember. What next?

Chapter Nine

"Fine, you old cow. Go fuck yourself." Victoria Mason lurched down the stone steps of the Biloxi public library slinging a black leather shoulder bag over her arm. Helen could see the elderly, blue-haired woman barricaded behind the thick glass door, receding into the shadows as Victoria gave her the finger. Helen remained in her car, reluctant to move after the damned bus ride from Tupelo and uncertain if she should get out and speak to the girl or wait out of sight until she left.

Too late. Victoria spotted her and marched over to the car. Today the black clothing she wore was variegated with slashes of red showing through her loose tank top, and bright crimson tipped her fingers. A sinking feeling gathered in Helen's stomach as she rolled the window down. Victoria looked pissed off, and not just at the librarian.

"You decided to come in for the kill?" Victoria spat out as she approached the car. "It wasn't enough you had to get my dad beat up yesterday, you had to get me fired from this shitty job, too."

"Just back up a minute, Victoria. Tell me what the hell happened."

"Fuck you. You already know what happened. You stood there and watched it." Victoria kicked the car in a strangely feminine motion, the weakness of the gesture undermining her rage. Helen slowly opened the door and got out, studying the younger woman's face. That wasn't hate she saw under the black and white makeup — it was fear. Victoria trembled and wiped tears from her cheeks as Helen watched, her fingers shaking as she smeared streaks of eyeliner and mascara on her pale cheeks.

Helen risked touching her, tentatively reaching for her arm. She could feel Victoria shaking under the stiff, cracked leather of her jacket. Jesus, wasn't the girl fried in this heat, wearing that outfit? "Come on, let's get out of this place and go talk somewhere."

"Forget it, you bitch. I'm not going anyplace with you." Victoria broke away as her face crumpled in sobbing. "You fucked up my whole life, you know? I bet these assholes will make sure I don't get that scholarship to Santa Cruz, now — and it's all your fault." She began to stomp off, head bent in an effort to control her tears, kicking at debris that had drifted into the parking lot. Helen sighed and got back in her car. Okay, now what? Actually, there was no real question — she was going to follow the girl, make sure she was all right, try to find out what happened to Bill Mason. And, of course, find out what she could about the Beauregard Resort. It had burned down the same summer her uncle and the mysterious woman had been there, according to the ex-editor. Maybe she'd been watching too much television, but it was at least a place to start. Besides, she had nothing better to do.

Right. That's why she'd taken such care over her appearance this morning, wasn't it? Not because she was even remotely considering meeting an unusual young woman who had a cute crooked smile and seemed more than willing to help her out. Of course that had nothing to do with anything — Helen was just bored. That's why she'd worn a deep red shirt that complemented her skin and hair, that's why she'd dug out a pair of black jeans that fit her snugly and showed off her butt. She must be absolutely insane. As if Beth being pissed at her and Terrie Muncie pursuing her wasn't enough — now she had to be vaguely interested in a girl who wasn't even legal age and no doubt leading around a string of devoted boyfriends by their dicks. Helen rolled her eyes at her reflection in the rearview mirror and drove out of the parking lot in search of Victoria.

She certainly wasn't difficult to spot in the midst of the sunburned tourists sauntering around the path next to the beach. Victoria's black-and-red leather aroused mild interest, then dismissal. Just another disaffected teenager wandering around. Nothing too weird about that. Helen found a parking spot a few blocks from the library, maneuvered the car into place, and risked a couple of honking horns from irritated motorists as she darted across the road to the beach. Victoria was smoking and staring out at the bright blue water when Helen joined her on the wooden bench. They both sat quietly for a moment. Helen looked at the froth of waves breaking under the hot breeze. Hard to tell what Victoria was looking at, with those big opaque sunglasses shielding her face.

Helen waited to speak until Victoria had finished smoking and dropped the butt into the sand. "Talk to me, Victoria. Tell me what the hell happened."

She snorted and shoved her sunglasses further up the bridge of her nose. No more weeping — just a stony white stare, hatred and hurt in equal measure aimed at Helen. "As if you didn't already know."

"Jesus fucking Christ, Victoria, the last I saw of your father he was running out of an alley behind the bar and I was the one getting kicked in the gut. Look." Helen leaned in closer and pointed to the bruise on her cheek. "Where the hell do you think this came from?" Helen kept her voice pitched low and continued to glance at people passing by. Helen could smell the scent of suntan lotion mingled with fast food and the unmistakable odor of salt water. No one was paying them any particular attention, but the sooner they had some privacy the better.

Victoria bit her lip and looked back at the water. "All I know is that my dad is scared shitless. He got home and I could tell someone roughed him up. Not really bad, but enough to make a point. And then all night long the phone was ringing. People — I could hear them on the line but they wouldn't talk, just hang up. Then call right back again." She blew out a sigh and slumped down on the bench, feet splayed carelessly, boots scuffing the sand at the edge of the path. "Then the next thing I know, I'm looking around the Robert E. Lee Room this morning and that old hag calls me in to tell me about the budget cuts. They're forced to get rid of me, she says. Bullshit."

"Look, whatever your father said about yesterday, I probably saved him from getting his ass kicked even worse than it was. No, dammit, listen to me." She grabbed Victoria's arm and pulled her back down onto the bench, earning herself a stare or two from people passing by. "Do you really want to have this conversation right here?"

Victoria relented, and they walked back to Helen's car. She sat sullen and silent while Helen drove through Biloxi. At the edge of town Helen spotted a diner sporting an OPEN sign on a grimy screen door, and Victoria followed her inside. Weak coffee, the color, flavor, and texture of dirty water, arrived at their booth along with two greasy, laminated menus. Helen made an attempt at the coffee while Victoria simply sat and stared out the window.

"I need you to tell me something, Victoria. I need you to tell me why you sent me to talk to your father yesterday."

"And why the hell should I tell you?"

"Because you and your father are in a lot of trouble, that's why. I don't know what's going on, but my guess is your dad lost his position at the paper because he knows an awful lot of secrets. Right? So why tell me? I'm a total stranger. You don't know anything about me."

"I thought —" Victoria shook her head and tossed her sunglasses onto the table. "You were asking these questions, and you aren't from around here. I thought you were a reporter or something like that. I didn't know you were a private investigator."

"But I told you —"

"I know, I know. I just — I didn't care. Not when I saw you had a picture of the Beauregard."

Helen felt a chill despite the gathering heat in the café. The ceiling fans whirred quietly, stirring the muggy air into a soup of dust and humidity and years of stale meals. "You already knew what building I was looking for?"

Victoria nodded, toyed with the menu, and pushed her coffee aside. The waitress, tugging at the apron tied around her plump middle, came up and asked in a tired voice if they were ready to order. "Just coffee, thanks," Helen said. She got treated to a disdainful sneer from the waitress, but it bought them a few more minutes of privacy. "By the way," she went on as soon as they were alone, "I noticed this morning that your scholarship to Berkeley became a scholarship to Santa Cruz overnight. There is no scholarship, is there?"

Victoria shook her head. "I made it up. I just wanted you to take me seriously. I just turned twenty-five, and no one in this damned hellhole ever takes me seriously."

Thus, Helen thought, the severe and dangerous look, cadged from album covers and too many music videos. Did she have any idea how attractive she was, with or without the heavy-metal trappings? Stop right now, Helen Black. Don't even go there. "Why did you lie? What are you trying to do?"

"Get me and my daddy out of here. You saw him — he's going to drink himself to death in a couple more years, Helen. It's real bad now. If only Momma hadn't died in that fire, everything might have been different for us." Victoria looked up at last, her pale blue eyes red-rimmed and frightened. "I don't know what to do anymore. I thought — I thought if you were working on a story or a case and he could help you, you'd help us get out of this place."

Helen took a final sip of the coffee to cover her shock. So Bill Mason's wife had died in the fire. That was the inner pain he'd been hiding yesterday. "Your dad didn't say much about that. Just that he'd always felt something was wrong in the fire, that was why he couldn't let it go."

"I never knew my mom." Victoria planted her elbows on the table and her face in her fists. "Her name was Lorraine. I was just a baby then. She wasn't even supposed to be working at the desk that night. She'd just had me and they needed the money, and so Daddy stayed home to watch me that night. And she died."

"What about Roberts and Farrell? Didn't they have anything to say about the fact someone died?"

"Like what? Who gave a shit? Nobody cared about some poor white trash desk clerk, right? Those guys own everything around here. You name it, R and F has a hand in it. The newspaper, too." She gave Helen a small, wry smile that made her look older than her years. "I've heard people say my dad used to be really cool, you know? Before all this. I've only known him the way he is now."

Helen nodded, watching the girl. No wonder Victoria behaved like a much younger person, like a wayward teenager. How the hell could this kid have had a chance to grow up, to get past the shock-value stage? For a split second, when Victoria looked up and met her gaze, Helen saw herself. She went cold with the recognition. Condemned as irredeemable but still surviving — barely.

Helen could feel the waitress hovering impatiently in the background. Fine. She ordered a salad for herself and the same for Victoria, then poked at wilted lettuce while thinking about how to respond. It was ridiculous — like something out of a bad romance. Even the cheesiest lesbian romance from the tiny presses devoted to dyke soft porn could have come up with something better than this. But then Victoria was pretty outrageous herself. Dressed and made up like a wannabe from the seventies punk scene, sporting a nose ring in mother-fucking Biloxi, for god's sake, and hauling in her wake, the dead weight of an alcoholic father and an unknown mother who died tragically. Not to mention being a hell of a lot softer and more sensitive than she tried to act.

"What? What are you looking at?"

"Just wondering how you landed that job in the library. Especially working for that battle-axe."

Victoria failed to hide her lopsided grin. "Sure as hell wasn't her idea. It's the only place they could hide me, I guess. I mean, in case you haven't noticed, we don't get a terribly literary crowd at that branch. Not so close to the casinos."

"Who's 'they'?"

Victoria shrugged and sprinkled pepper on her salad. Apparently it didn't help much — one bite and she made a face and put the fork down. "I don't know. I guess the same guys who made sure my dad lost his job at the paper about ten years ago."

"Victoria —" Helen leaned forward. "Victoria, look at me. I'm not a reporter. I really am a private eye, and I really just want to find out what happened to the people in that picture you saw yesterday. I swear to you, your dad was scared but okay when I saw him last."

"Was it Jimbo? Who hit you, I mean."

Helen nodded. "And his pal Tommy was there. I kicked Tommy in the nuts, though, before he laid a hand on me."

She grinned again. "And you didn't say anything to the cops?"

"Not a word, I swear. I think the bartender alerted the troops. Skinny guy, bad case of pimples."

"Yeah, I know him. He's always trying to get in my pants." Victoria's eyes teared up again, and she dabbed at her face with a crumpled napkin. "I'm sorry I lied to you."

"You know, you could just leave. Just pack up and go. You don't have to stay here."

"But — but I can't leave him! I mean, I don't have anyone else. No one." She stared at Helen, her face twisted in puzzlement. "I'm not going anyplace without my father."

Helen waved at the waitress and asked for a dessert menu, only to be informed that they didn't have a dessert menu as such — merely a selection of apple pie, or maybe some apple pie. Or they could have apple pie. "Guess I'll have the apple pie, then. You want some?"

Victoria shrugged and nodded. The waitress, assured of at least a small tip now, managed a weak smile after sliding two saucers laden with slabs of runny pie at them. Helen picked at the apple slices and ignored the doughy crust, thinking hard as she watched Victoria dig in. The girl had already lied to her a couple of times. Why the hell should she believe anything Victoria said now? Pretty blue eyes didn't always merit trust. And Helen had to laugh at the idea of herself as some kind of knight in shining armor rescuing the fair damsel and her drunken daddy. Weird, though — the image felt good. She hadn't tried it on in a long time. Maybe this time it would work. And maybe, a sneaking voice said from somewhere deep inside her mind, it wouldn't just be the Masons you save. Maybe it would be your own ass, too.

No, it was more that Bill Mason was the best lead she had so far on what Uncle Loy had been up to with his paramour. And the way to Bill Mason was his daughter Victoria, despite her lies. Cold reality intruded on the heroic image. Even if Helen couldn't believe her, she had to rely on her to get what she wanted. And in payment, what could she do for Victoria? Right now the girl wouldn't accept anything less than a one-way ticket for herself and her father out of Biloxi. Helen didn't know if she was capable of delivering on such a pledge. Maybe something less would do as well. "So you want to go to college in California?"

Victoria's pale blue eyes darkened. She impaled a piece of pie as she answered. "California, Massachusetts, Indiana — anywhere but here. Berkeley sounds good, though."

"What do you want to study?"

She shrugged. "Anything. Well, not library science, I can tell you that." Helen obliged with a laugh, an idea forming in her mind. "But I really do want to go to college. And not just one of those dumb-ass community colleges where you learn how to be a beautician. A real university."

"Tell you what, Victoria. You help me find out about the Beauregard, and we'll figure out how to get you to California." Surely she could get the girl situated in a job and an apartment while they looked at college options.

Victoria stared. Maybe she'd made it too easy. Helen tried again. "I'm not promising anything for sure, okay? I want you to understand that. But we'll definitely talk about this."

Victoria's fork clattered to her plate. She sat back in the booth, stunned. "What about daddy? He has to come, too."

Helen nodded. At the very least she'd find some kind of rehab program for Bill Mason. Not in California if she could help it, since she wasn't too sure she was up to being permanent baby-sitter for the Mason family — but certainly outside of Mississippi. Then maybe some kind of work somewhere. She'd have to use every thin string she had left to pull. And no doubt her solutions would fall far short of Victoria's Hollywood-style dreams. But as long as Helen got her answers, she'd jury-rig something, and —

"What, Helen? You look funny."

"Probably just the food here." Or another inconvenient attack of conscience. Jesus, she was doing it again — acting like the self-centered bitch Beth and Aunt Edna and all her exes had claimed she was. So what if Victoria was lying? Helen wasn't doing much better in the sainthood department at the moment. She'd better be careful not to promise more than she could actually accomplish. "Look, Victoria, I don't want you to imagine I'm going to land you in some spectacular college dorm of your dreams, but I will do what I can to help." Maybe there was a way to grovel in front of Aunt Edna and get a little money out of this. She hadn't been included in any discussion of the cash settlement, but surely she could appeal to her uncle's memory, to how much her uncle loved her and wanted her included in his little nuclear family. And of course that thought churned Helen's stomach even more. Given the way she'd been causing Aunt Edna grief lately about her dead husband, perhaps an appeal to his better nature was not the way to go. Any way Helen looked at this she was going to come out smelling like shit. Terrific — and certainly in line with her rapidly deteriorating status in the eyes of everyone she thought she loved, or who loved her back.

These thoughts continued to plague Helen as she paid the bill and followed Victoria back to the car. Victoria, on the other hand, practically gushed with excitement. "Let's go to my house right now. I bet my dad is still home, since he wasn't feeling so well. Even better if he's gone out — I know where he keeps his files."

"Files?" Helen asked idly, trying to drag her thoughts back to the present situation. Victoria had directed them to a small, two-lane paved road that led off the highway right out into the countryside. They were surrounded by pine-treed, gentle curves. Helen kept glancing in her rearview mirror as Victoria talked. No sign of any other vehicle on this isolated stretch, but she didn't want to be surprised by the likes of Jimbo or Tommy this afternoon, particularly if their destination was the Mason residence. "He kept information from his days at the paper?"

Victoria laughed, the first expression of pleasure she'd had all day so far. Not surprising, considering. "He may be turning into the town drunk, but he's not an idiot. The suits that got him fired, well, they know he knows a lot more than he's telling. And they know he can prove stuff, too."

"Stuff? What kind of stuff?"

Victoria quit laughing and stared out at the road. "Stuff like what you're trying to find out. A lot like that. There's plenty of dirt to dig up on these guys. Who fucks who, who has this drug habit, who embezzled money —"

"And who burned down a hotel for insurance money?"

"Yeah." Victoria visibly shrank into her seat, huddling inside her jacket as if she were chilled. "Stuff."

"So where does he hide this 'stuff' to keep it safe?"

"You'll see."

Great. Was she getting another runaround? Were two more ugly, smelly thugs waiting to beat her up? Not likely, she decided. Besides, she'd just drive off if anything looked wrong. That would show them, right? So there. Yeah. Helen's hand strayed to her cheek, tenderly touching the bruise. She wasn't up for another kung fu act.

Too late now. "Turn here." A dirt lane led through the pines, and Helen turned sharply at Victoria's sudden command, spinning rocks and red dust behind them. The pines gave way to broad-leaved shade trees, and there was a drop in the temperature beneath their long, thick branches. Just beyond the trees she saw a fence overgrown with some kind of flowering vine and some cottages clustered together. Helen rolled down her window and let in the intoxicating scent of pine needles and honeysuckle. Still no sign they were being followed.

"It's not much further." Helen slowed down and saw the lane widen. Her tires crunched over gravel. Then, as if out of nowhere, the house appeared. Not much more than a dilapidated shack, really — brick that looked ready to crumble at the least pressure, a sagging porch, an overflowing garbage can settling into the loam beside the wall. And a yard full of police cars, lights flashing. What the hell was up now?

"Oh, shit!" Victoria dashed out of the car before Helen stopped. Helen ran after her but not fast enough. Victoria managed to thrust her way past two startled police officers flanking the front door. Helen made it to the porch in time to hear Victoria — it had to be her — shriek in pain and fear. She kept shrieking, and Helen tried to take advantage of the police officer's surprise. Suddenly the screaming stopped, as quick as if someone had flipped a switch.

"Dammit, let me go to her!" The hell with caution. Helen shouldered past the two sentries and stumbled through a messy living room heaped with piles of newspapers, books, and shabby furniture. Bright lights shone from the narrow corridor that she assumed led to bedrooms. Helen saw it all with the clarity of a snapshot — the plainclothes detectives wearing surgical gloves, the flashbulbs popping as the crime-scene people took pictures, the blood on the wall, the blank faces staring in stony curiosity at Victoria kneeling on the floor, her head in her hands. Helen knelt beside her. The two women gazed at the corpse of Bill Mason, his brains blown out all over the faded blue bedspread, a shotgun lying beside his cold body.

Chapter Ten

Helen sat in the living room and waited. She was used to this, of course — the lengthy and apparently useless wandering around by police officers, both uniformed and plainclothes. All men, too, she noted, except for one woman in uniform who had the thankless task of "comforting" Victoria. And from her own experience in Berkeley, all those years as a cop, she also knew that what looked like purposeless wandering often was exactly the opposite. Poking, prodding, listing, measuring, watching — these guys were making sure they didn't miss a thing. Particularly when it came to Bill Mason's daughter. After the first few minutes of screaming shock, Victoria had cycled through a full gamut of emotional responses, ranging from silence to more screams to helpless sobbing. Despite the show of concern from the female officer and the deference from a couple of the plainclothes detectives, Helen knew with complete certainty that everyone in the shabby little house was cataloging each flicker of emotion from the dead man's child. Helen didn't let her face show her surprise at the half-assed way they were handling the scene. Allowing her to hang around, along with Victoria — even for a suicide this was incredibly sloppy investigation. Maybe it was just a way to watch the girl's reactions. Or maybe everyone was so relieved that Bill Mason and his embarrassing knowledge were out of the way that they just didn't care to look too closely at how he died. It sure as shit wasn't because these guys didn't know what they were doing. All she had to do was catch them turning hard gleaming eyes on the girl to know that. It was an act, put on for reasons known only to themselves.

Helen's behavior was noted, as well. People stopped to listen as Helen related who she was, where she'd come from, why she was there. It didn't escape her, either, that one of the uniforms had also been present yesterday when she'd called Beth Wilks from the police station in Biloxi. *Great. Now all that shit was going to get dredged up and they'll probably keep me here for hours and hours.* But the man said nothing, merely stared for a few moments then went on to record the contents of the dresser in a notebook, taking dictation from a plainclothes officer kneeling on the worn, dust-covered rug. Helen was led to the sofa to sit and begin the waiting process, her presence neglected except for the occasional interruption of another cop with another set of questions.

So Helen sat and tried to keep her eyes and ears wide open. She was pretty sure that she provided a good alibi for Victoria for the time of death, not to mention that the old bat at the library could verify the girl was being fired from her job at the time Bill Mason was allegedly committing suicide. Helen could hear, from her position in the living room, voices from the front yard drifting in through the open windows on the warm breeze.

"I swear, I always knew this would happen one day. Didn't I tell you, Bob? Didn't I always say he'd do away with all of us one day?"

Whoever Bob might be, Helen couldn't hear a response from him. What she could hear, after she'd quietly and cautiously scooted over the worn sofa cushions closer to the window, was the drone of a cop asking questions. Helen decided against craning her neck so she could look out the window — the movement might get unwelcome attention from the cops in the house — and instead strained to hear what the woman said.

"It was right after the talk show on channel six, the one with that cute couple? That pretty blond pregnant lady and her husband. Well, anyhow, I heard the shotgun go off. That would have been about noon, I guess, wouldn't it, Bob?" This time there was an unintelligible mutter from Bob, apparently an assent. "So I called the police. I mean, after all that yelling and hollering all morning — it was just like the last time he was drunk and started screaming. Usually about everyone out to get him. So, Bob says, he says, 'Doris, you better call the police. Sure as daylight he's killed that girl of his.' So I did."

Bob and Doris — mostly Doris — answered more questions. Helen heard only bits and pieces. How they hadn't seen anyone else around the house that morning, although after hearing the gun go off they'd been too scared to look outside. How there was an established pattern in the Mason household of Bill's drinking followed by Bill's paranoid ranting. How the neighborhood had known he was armed but had never considered him dangerous until today.

The woman's shrill voice amplified as her knowledge of her importance increased. There must be quite an audience gathered by now, Helen guessed, judging by the number of voices raised out on the lawn. Soon even the sharp tones of

Doris got lost in the general noise of a ghoulish crowd, and Helen gave up trying to listen.

Instead she turned her eyes to the house, or at least what she could see of it from where she sat. Worn furniture, stacks of old books and newspapers piled neatly on every available flat surface, threadbare rugs on the unpolished wood floors — but not a single dirty dish, nothing that could be called garbage or waste. The place was a curious mixture of care and neglect, and Helen found herself wondering whether it was Bill or Victoria who'd made at least minimal effort to create a comfortable home in the midst of loss and chaos. Of course the sense of chaos would be permanent now, long after the police presence had departed leaving both material and emotional detritus in their wake.

The activity in the bedroom was much more focused. By the time she and Victoria had arrived, the homicide folks were well under way at their assorted tasks. Helen had already been through several question-and-answer sessions, first by uniformed officers, then by a couple of different men who emerged from the bedroom. Victoria was marched by a female officer into the kitchen, a dingy little galley tucked into a corner of the house that even at midday needed lights switched on. Helen could see her sitting at the table, sullenly refusing water or tea and veering from tears to rage. As far as Helen could tell, Victoria had completely forgotten her presence.

Tearing her attention away from Victoria and the commotion outside, Helen looked around the house. The crumbling doors and windows, some of them sans screens, certainly wouldn't have stopped anyone from getting in. If Doris and Bob were lounging in front of the tube they might easily have missed the arrival of someone at the Mason house. She'd have to find out where the intrepid neighbors lived. Maybe one of those cottages just before the bend in the road that led to the Mason home? If the couple had cowered in the safety of their own house after hearing the shotgun they wouldn't have seen anyone leave, either. In fact, most people in Helen's experience were inclined to avoid confrontation with conflict or domestic disputes, preferring to let it rage itself out without getting involved. So it made perfect sense that they ignored the noise from around the bend, at least until they heard the gun.

And once past the vanguard of the neighbors it was a free-for-all. Bill Mason, the acknowledged town drunk and a raving lunatic with a rebellious and irritating kid — it would make perfect sense to anyone that he'd do away with himself one day. Maybe the brat would leave town now and a local problem would resolve itself to everyone's satisfaction. Unless now Victoria would become some kind of target.

Helen sighed and shifted on the uncomfortable cushions, squinting in a shaft of sunlight that suddenly pierced the gloomy living room. What the hell time was it, anyhow? She squirmed to the other end of the sofa, realizing that some of her discomfort was with her own train of thought. Without any reason to get herself worked up Helen had already arranged a scenario of murder in her mind, when it was just as likely that Bill had done himself in. What did he have to gain by staying alive? Constantly watched by the powers that be, descending in a drunken spiral to utter oblivion, hopeless and jobless and no place to go — death might have seemed welcome.

Except for the girl sitting at the table. Spotlighted under the harsh overhead lamp Victoria ignored the halfhearted attention of the woman officer. Instead she stared out into the living room, into the dust-moted air where Helen sat. Even across the distance between kitchen and living room Helen could see the blank iciness of shock on the girl's features. Helen almost got up, thinking that Victoria might be looking to her for some kind of support.

No, that wasn't it — Helen realized that Victoria was looking beyond the sofa, over Helen's head. It was an intense gaze, burning across the short expanse of the house. What the hell was back there? Helen resisted the urge to turn around. There was the window, through which she'd heard Doris relate the day's events. Next to that a set of shelves with books, magazines, and folders stuffed haphazardly in no apparent order. And beside that a coatrack that stood crookedly against the wall.

Helen looked back toward the kitchen and stared, amazed, at the sudden transformation in Victoria that took place as she watched. Victoria's face crumpled in a paroxysm of grief. The officer sitting in the kitchen flinched in surprise at the metamorphosis from shock and rage to grief-stricken banshee.

"Oh god, I can't believe he's really dead! I can't handle this anymore, I can't take it! My daddy, my daddy!" She flung herself onto the uniformed woman, who looked up in consternation and gingerly patted the girl on the back. Helen listened with admiration as Victoria laid it on thick with the southern accent and moaned piteously. "Now I have no one, I'm all alone in the world." She dissolved in copious tears, finally resting her head on her arms on the table.

The officer kept up the patting process and gestured frantically until a couple of reinforcements broke off from the herd prowling the house and went into the kitchen. In the confusion Helen stood up and quickly scanned the wall behind the sofa. What the hell had she been looking at before creating this little scene? Up until now Victoria had been in grief and shock, certainly, but this kind of outburst seemed forced. It was far too histrionic. Still what did Helen know? She'd only met the girl yesterday, and who could say what the proper reaction was to seeing your father dead in the bedroom? It was just weird, after the calm and the control she'd just seen, that Victoria would shatter in this way. Rage, cursing, lashing out — that she could believe. But an act worthy of a cotillion debutante didn't sit right.

While attention stayed centered on Victoria, who continued to fling herself at the female officer and wail out her fate, Helen looked again at the wall behind the couch.

Now the crowd had knotted up close to the window, pressing up against the yellow tape bordering the scene of the crime. Maybe that was Doris, the skinny woman with unnaturally blond hair and unfortunate blue eye shadow, holding hands with an equally skinny man whose potbelly gave witness to years of beer in front of the tube — Bob, perhaps. Nothing interesting on the coatrack — nothing at all, in fact, just metal hooks gathering dust while they waited for hats and garments. And the shelves. More interesting.

Helen took a step closer to the shelves. Now she could see it. She glanced around the living room again and confirmed her suspicions. Despite the apparent sloppiness of the room, despite the overflow of printed matter piled up on shelves, tables, and even the floor, Bill Mason's collection of literature was neat and organized. Here were stacks of the local paper, edges aligned, most recent edition on the top of the pile. Next to it sat the *New York Times*, also in an orderly pile. A set of paperbacks on foreign affairs, by different authors but arranged according to size, lined up next to these newspapers. And a quick look at other shelves in the living room told the same story — a method to Bill Mason's madness, a careful arrangement of information and resources that made sense to him.

The bulletin board on the wall over the desk was plastered with photographs, clippings, and charts. Helen managed a few steps closer and saw that Lorraine Mason's death was the main topic covered in this information — pictures of the hotel, of the smoking ruins, of Lorraine herself, details of the building, and articles from several different newspapers. Helen shuddered as she thought of Victoria growing up with this reminder of her loss displayed before her daily, always a raw wound that was never given a chance to heal. A uniformed officer hovered nearby, so Helen stepped away from the bulletin board, back to safer terrain in the middle of the room.

The shelves behind the sofa told a different story. Books

were stuffed in upside down, mixing categories of fiction and fact, some even shoved in backward with spines hidden against the wall. Manila folders, crammed in every which way among the bound books, spilled out clippings and photocopies in an array of disorderly carelessness that belied haste and confusion. Not at all in the style of the rest of the room.

Helen looked back toward the kitchen. Was that what Victoria had seen? Of course there was no way at all to ask her since she was now surrounded by nervous police officers. Something had apparently been decided in the few moments Helen had been studying the bookshelves, because Victoria was now being ushered out of the kitchen toward the front door, surrounded by a protective phalanx of cops. Helen could see her shiny black cap of hair gleaming as she was maneuvered from the harsh glow of the kitchen to the dim realm of the living room. And was she leaning against one of the men as she was led away? Helen stepped forward.

"Just a moment, please. Victoria —" Helen inserted herself into the group. It was almost as if she'd been forgotten in the melee, and everyone looked at her with surprise. Everyone but Victoria. Helen couldn't read the expression in Victoria's eyes — might have been anger or impatience flickering across her face, maybe still grief and shock. Whatever it was, Helen wasn't going to let herself get completely shut out of this.

"Officer, I'm sure this young woman shouldn't be exposed to anything further this afternoon. Perhaps we could let her leave?"

Helen met the cold gaze of one of the cops who'd questioned her earlier. "I think we have this under control, ma'am," he said in a flat voice. "I'm sure Miss Mason has someplace to go. Maybe a friend's house, or a relative —"

They'd all reached the front door by now, and they were met by observers and a couple of news teams with cameras at the ready. Helen sized up the surroundings and decided to risk a bit of public exposure. While the police were busy trying to push people aside Helen edged herself in front of Victoria, laying a protective hand firmly on the girl's arm. She made a big show of shielding Victoria from the cameras, shaking her head firmly at the shouts of the reporters.

"Did your father kill himself?" "Who found the body?" "Were you there when he shot himself?"

"We have no comment," Helen called out. Too bad about any hopes for a low profile — now she'd be on the ten o'clock news. But Helen didn't see any other way to make sure she had a chance of keeping her hand in the game. She was betting that it wouldn't serve Victoria's purpose, whatever that might be, to create a scene for the cameras. Not if she wanted to keep up the pretense of being so shattered by grief she could hardly walk.

Victoria leaned in Helen's direction. "Get the fuck away from me, you bitch."

Helen turned a suitably sympathetic face to Victoria and tightened her grip. "I'm not leaving, Victoria. I'm not leaving you, and I'm not leaving until I figure out who killed your father."

Victoria stiffened, her face shifting back for a fleeting moment to the stunned silence Helen had observed before the award-winning performance in the kitchen. Helen felt an uncomfortable twist in her gut. Was that wistful look in her eyes a sign of trust? Did Victoria imagine that Helen really did give a damn about her, would get her out of this mess and into the supposed freedom of a new life in California? Or was it further calculation of the odds of getting away and doing something else? Maybe getting back into the house and looking at whatever secret those shelves held.

In a few more seconds the whole matter began to be sorted out in a manner Helen wasn't sure she liked. Apparently Doris had a bit more steel in her spine than Helen first surmised. Wrong again, Helen said, kicking herself wryly for yet another knee-jerk reaction that made her think the worst of people. She watched Doris go into tigress mode, firmly pushing aside reporters and taking Victoria under her wing, insisting that Victoria stay the night with her neighbors. Bob stood by silently, belching softly but standing guard with a determined jaw while his wife shepherded the girl along. Doris turned to Helen, looked her up and down, and must have decided it was a package deal.

The police looked equally pissed off and relieved to have the whole thing sorted out for the time being. Of course they weren't done yet — but this way both Victoria and Helen would stay nearby while they wrapped things up. And things would be wrapped up as neatly as a pretty Christmas present, Helen thought as she helped form a parade down the gravel road to the group of cottages where she'd suspected Doris and Bob resided. The reporters brought up the rear in a straggling group, leaving a few of their comrades behind at the house where perfectly coifed men and women finished their commentaries for the evening sound bite. Most of the passersby hung out at the Mason house. One or two fell into the uneven procession leading from the Mason house to the residence of Doris and Bob.

By now the afternoon sun was just beginning to touch the tops of the pine trees. Walking across the sparse brown grass, Helen felt a wave of hunger. Or perhaps, just nerves — she knew that stress did weird things to people, although it seemed strange that her body demanded food in spite of the awful image of Bill's head in pieces on the bedspread. She glanced over at Victoria, who was currently making a show of leaning on Doris. The girl avoided Helen's eyes, instead continuing to heave with sobs and small cries of grief. As they reached the stoop of the house Helen heard someone behind her clear his throat. She turned with the rest to face one of the policemen who'd come along with them. A small official cordon lined Doris's front lawn, their faces impassive and watchful. It didn't help their grave expressions to be standing in the midst of several garish garden gnomes gracing Doris's front lawn, but they managed to ignore the little statues.

"We need to talk to Miss Mason further," one of them said.

It was a familiar face, one of the guys who'd been hanging around yesterday when Beth came to pick her up. "And to you, too."

"Understood," Helen said.

"You thinking of moving back to Mississippi, Ms. Black?" This from another man Helen didn't recognize from her visit yesterday — although he'd seemed to be one of the folks in charge of today's affair. He'd been the first to question her, one of the ones watching her closely all afternoon. "You seem to be spending a lot of time in our fair city since your uncle's funeral. Today is Friday. Second day in a row you've been to the Gulf Coast."

"Fair city," Helen repeated, scanning the unfriendly faces lined up before her. Suddenly she was not only hungry, she was exhausted. Enough already. She was more than ready for a bit of hospitality from Doris and Bob. "That remains to be seen."

"Funny how things seem to happen when you show up."

"Yes, isn't it?" She said nothing more, merely folded her arms and waited. They drifted off after one more admonishment to show up at the station tomorrow, and Helen followed Bob and Doris inside their home.

Victoria wasn't having any. Helen entered the house to the sound of the girl's protests. "I just want to lie down, Doris! I really just need to be alone. To mourn my daddy alone for a while. You understand, don't you?" Victoria lifted her sad eyes to the older woman. "I know you understand too, Helen. Just a little while to rest. To think." The glance she leveled at Helen was a flash of anger. Helen had to hand it to her — the girl was good.

Doris looked reluctant to let Helen go, but how could she refuse the pleas of a this poor young woman? She patted Victoria on the back and smiled at Helen. Helen managed a matching smile, agreeing with Doris as she backed out of the house — certainly, Victoria just needed a few hours to compose herself, get some much needed rest, try to put all this horror behind her. Yes, yes, Helen could come back tomorrow. No, no problem at all. Good idea, to let Victoria get some rest.

Helen fought her way back through the crowd of people to her car, pushing aside microphones and ignoring the stares of the other neighbors still huddled in front of the Mason house. Shit. No way she was leaving the place, but she had to hide out somehow for a few hours. She was certain Victoria would manage to get away from Doris and Bob at some point, maybe even run for it. Maybe Victoria thought she herself would be next. Maybe that was the foundation of that cold stare she kept giving Helen. Of course it would be a stupid move, but it might be exactly what the kid was planning.

Kid. Victoria was no kid. She'd been caretaker of an alcoholic father and had built armor every day against the loathing of the community — now she'd seen her father dead, her hopes for the future blown with that blast from the shotgun. Helen chewed her thoughts over and over as she drove slowly away from the scene, further along the gravel drive. Shadows were lengthening under the trees, and Helen felt her hunger surge again. Screw it — she had to stay for a while, to figure out Victoria's next move.

She stopped, turned the car around, peered back down the road. No one in sight. No one following her. Helen decided to go back the way she came, see what was going on at the Mason house. If it was going to be called suicide, the reporters at least would be ready to pack it up pretty quickly, she'd bet. The police — well, she doubted they'd maintain a presence there all night.

Sure enough, by the time she reached the clearing she could see news vans kicking up dust ahead of her. A few police cars still lurked in the gloom around the Mason home. Helen looked closely at the windows of the house where she'd left Victoria to the mercies of Doris. The place was brightly lit, and she was sure the girl was still safely inside.

Helen kept driving, staying a few car-lengths behind the news van that had pulled out ahead of her — no, she realized with a chill that contrasted with the heat still rising off the sunbaked ground. That was an ambulance, carting Bill Mason's remains off to the city morgue, or wherever suicides were taken in these parts. She followed it as far as the outskirts of town, where she spotted a fast-food drive-through. One greasy burger and fries later she was heading back out to the gravel road.

Her assumptions proved correct. Further evidence, she knew, that Bill Mason was basically just a problem solved to the powers that be of Biloxi. No doubt his unfortunate suicide was merely the final chapter to the sorry saga of one man's descent into a black hole. She could see the somber faces on the nightly news now, the serious tones proclaiming one of Biloxi's native sons fallen to demon drink or some such platitudinous two-minute segment between commercial breaks. Would they remember Lorraine Mason, who'd died in the fire? Helen hoped Victoria wasn't going to be forced to watch the news broadcasts. Helen turned off the car's headlights and parked on a grassy stretch of ground beneath a spreading tree. Helen got out and stood still, listening. Nothing but a weak breeze, maybe threading up from as far away as the beach miles away, stirred the leaves and tall grasses.

She stayed on the grass. It muffled her steps as she slowly moved behind the bank of trees toward the houses clustered just before the bend in the road. Helen didn't dare risk being seen in case she'd been wrong in her guess about the absence of the police tonight.

Finally she rounded a clump of shrubs that lined the yards of the houses where she'd left Victoria. That flat square of yellow light beaming out onto the shaggy lawn marked where Doris and Bob lived — Helen could make out the figures of garden gnomes in the shadows. There were matching squares of light from the two other houses. Everyone was probably looking for themselves on the television news over supper.

Just as Helen was wondering if she ought to check out

whether or not the cops were hanging around the Mason property, she saw a shadow move across the lawn. It was darker than the other shadows enveloping the house. And this shadow bumped into the crouching figure of a gnome. It hissed out a curse, too.

Victoria, her sepulchral garb serving her well in this escapade, moved around the statues and made it to the expanse of uneven ground leading to her own house. Helen carefully edged around the clearing and waited. She'd been right, after all — the Mason house was deserted, a blank square ringed with yellow crime-scene tape. Victoria stood and watched, very still and completely soundless. Helen waited, every muscle straining.

Finally, just when Helen thought she would snap with tension, Victoria turned away and walked off in the direction of the trees behind the clearing. What the hell? Helen started after her, torn between marveling at how easily she moved through the tangled undergrowth and amazement at the direction Victoria took. As she stepped cautiously over stones and broken earth, Helen realized that this was a path Victoria must have taken many times. She jammed her toe against a rock and almost yelped out in pain but managed to stifle her howl. The girl was getting away — Helen needed to hurry.

She didn't know how long it took them to get to the stone foundations in the heart of the grove of trees. And she never knew what exactly the blackened walls had once been. Maybe a house that had burned down. Or an old church that had fallen into disrepair generations past and been dismantled for the brick and stone it provided. Impossible to tell how large the original structure had been. In the late afternoon sun, the bleached stone loomed gray and sere like enormous bones from some long-dead prehistoric creature.

Helen hung back and watched as Victoria, eschewing any attempt to remain silent now, heaved and grunted at a corner of the foundation. Something gave under her continued efforts, and she stood with a heavy sigh. After a gesture that might have been wiping sweat from her brow, she leaned over again, this time lifting what looked like something square. Maybe metal, given the way it shone with a dull gleam in the light. Under cover of the noise Victoria made, Helen inched forward until she could have reached out and touched Victoria's back.

Now, Helen thought. "Look like you could use some help, Victoria."

Chapter Eleven

Helen adjusted the bucket of ice more comfortably in the crook of her arm and closed the hotel room door gently behind her. Outside the eighteen-wheelers hauling freight north through Tennessee rumbled by, jarring the windows with rhythmic rattling that threatened to drown out the whine of the air conditioner. In the parking lot outside a couple of empty truck cabs sat on enormous tires, their drivers no doubt occupying the motel units surrounding the one they were in. Helen had been reluctant to check them into the place, grungy as it appeared, but at the time she'd decided to take Victoria up to Tupelo it had seemed like a good idea to pick a place that was near the highway and patronized by the sort of people who only needed a couple of hours at a pop.

Maybe it was a stupid idea, but Helen had thought a place like this provided a much lower profile than the more expensive hotels closer to town. Anyway, Victoria had barely noticed where they were. At least their motel unit had a semiprivate walkway, hidden from view of the other units, offering a slight edge of secrecy to their presence.

The skinny, sweaty old man who'd taken her forty dollars for the night didn't even look at the name she'd scrawled on the registration card. She figured he wouldn't have known Martina Navratilova from Betty Boop, anyhow. All he wanted was the pair of twenties she offered, then she was free to get her ice.

Victoria Mason looked up from the bed where she sat cross-legged, her flared black skirt fanned out across the nubby pink spread. One hand held an empty plastic cup from which she'd removed the plastic shrink-wrapping provided by hotel management. Her other hand clutched a bottle of cheap no-name vodka with a screw-off cap. She'd kicked off her black boots, and her bare feet nudged the edges of the folder Helen had retrieved from Bill Mason's secret stash in the crumbling ruins outside his ramshackle home.

"Thanks," Victoria muttered, taking the bucket of ice and setting it on the bedside table with a rattle. Helen reached for the phone and punched in Aunt Edna's number.

"Not coming home tonight? What's happened, honey?"

Helen turned away so Victoria couldn't see her expression. Now, once she'd signed the papers and gotten Helen to shut up about Uncle Loy, her aunt was all "honey" and "sweetheart" and "dear." And Edna was confused when Helen gave her the name of the motel. "Why are you staying at that place, Helen? It's not a very nice place."

"It's just for one night, Aunt Edna." Maybe, Helen thought with a nasty jolt, she ought to tell her aunt that her wonderful niece was shacked up for the night with a twenty-five-year-old. No, that wasn't fair of her, Helen realized — give the poor old lady a break. "I can't talk about it right now, Aunt Edna," she said, fully aware of Victoria's curious stare. "I'll see you tomorrow. How are you doing?"

In decidedly happy and excited tones the older woman started talking about that nice Terrie Muncie — how she'd visited that day and had just left, how concerned she was for Bobby. "She even talked about a special house up in Memphis where he could spend some time with other kids. You know, kids who are slow just like he is. Make some friends. Some of them even have jobs."

"That's nice." Helen cut the conversation short, putting aside the odd mixture of anger and longing that Terrie's name brought boiling up for her. The red-haired bitch was doing an excellent job of insinuating herself into the lives of Helen's admittedly needy family. Not to mention working her own perverted magic on Helen, who slammed the phone back down on the table in irritation. She just didn't need this right now — this completely irrational and stupid and self-destructive desire for a toxic woman.

"Jesus, break the phone, why don't you?" Victoria cringed against the pillows in mock fear.

Helen took in her red-rimmed eyes shadowed with grief and exhaustion, her trembling fingers, her sullen glare. "You're still sure you don't want to tell the police where you are?" She sat on the corner of the bed and held out the ice. "Doris and Bob are sure to tell them you took off tonight. And you still have to go back to Biloxi in the morning, remember?"

Victoria snorted and grabbed a few ice cubes from the bucket. "Shit, you saw how they acted about my d-dad." She stumbled over the word, but after biting her lip she managed to go on. "All they need from me is their precious statement in the morning. It's none of their goddam business where I spend the night. They'd just as soon see me with a bullet in my head too."

Helen sighed and reached for the bottle. She would have preferred a decent Scotch, but she'd take what she could get tonight. Whatever it took to keep Victoria quiet and get some information out of her. Helen let the vodka burn down her throat and fought back a cough. Jesus, this was terrible shit. Maybe more ice would help. She swallowed hard and her eyes teared up, thankfully blurring the paint peeling from the walls, the ugly yellow lampshade grimed with a thick layer of dust, the cigarette burns and ancient moisture rings on the cheap table next to the bed.

Victoria pushed the file at Helen with her foot. "Here. This is what they shot him for."

Helen reached for the file and lifted it into her lap, clasping at stray pieces of paper that slid out onto the bed. "Victoria, I know you think he was killed, but you're going to have to face the fact that it's possible he —"

"Fuck you." Already her words were slurring. Helen noted the level of vodka remaining in the bottle but said nothing, letting her ramble on. "He would never have killed himself. Not while I was around. You saw that bookcase. I saw you looking at it. Somebody was searching for these files. When they didn't find it they shot him and then put things back on the shelf. And those cops took their time getting to the house so they could clean up after themselves."

Helen couldn't drum up a negative response. More than likely it was what had happened, although from what she'd seen of Bill Mason, suicide wasn't that far-fetched either. Without responding Helen began to sift through the papers, trying to ignore the incessant thud on the wall that signaled amorous activity in the next room, each bump accompanied by a shifting of the cheap print of a hunting scene on the wall over the bed.

"Jesus," Victoria muttered, lying back on the bed. "Sounds like he should be about done by now, don't you think?"

"Sorry, Victoria. I guess I could have taken you to my aunt's place."

But Victoria was dozing off in a stupor produced by alcohol, sorrow, and exhaustion. Helen moved from the bed to the rickety chair, turning lights off and on so that Victoria was at least in deeper shadow, more conducive to sleep, Helen hoped. What the fuck was she supposed to do now? Helen wondered. Out in the ruins Victoria had agreed to let Helen look at Bill Mason's Beauregard Resort file on the condition that Helen get her out of Biloxi and organize her removal to California the moment the police had finished with her. It was either that or nothing. And rather than go through some kind of prolonged negotiation Helen had agreed.

Now here she was in a fleabag motel, a drunken child — yes, despite her years, a child — snoring away on the bed, a nest of angry relatives down the road, and a pair of noisy lovers banging their way to a loud climax just beyond the flimsy wall. And for what? Helen asked herself as she finished the vodka. For a pile of confusing scraps of information about a fire that took place years ago and perhaps had nothing to do with her uncle and her uncle's secret paramour. She kept plowing through the junk, her anger increasing with each page she turned. How much of this was Bill Mason's slow deterioration into some level of madness, and how much of this was at all relevant to anything beyond his own conspiracy theories?

Helen sighed and glanced down at the sleeping girl. For a moment, in the dim yellow glow of the cheap lamp, she had a recurrence of the earlier image that had floated through her brain. How the hell was she going to shelter this injured bird? What would that mean? In sleep, Victoria's face smoothed into peace and beauty and wistful tenderness. Helen shook her head and looked away. No good, no good at all to see her like this.

Finally — silence from the next room after a prolonged moan. Hopefully they were as spent as Victoria, although certainly for very different reasons. Helen, almost ready to toss the whole folder into the trash, studied the girl sleeping in the dim light of the ugly room. If Victoria was right, Bill Mason had been murdered for the information in this file as well as for other nuggets of knowledge he'd accumulated over the years. He'd been haunted by grief and loss for twenty-five years. His daughter should have a chance to put that to rest. She owed it to Victoria at least to take a serious look at this stuff — particularly if, as Helen feared, she'd end up causing further grief and disappointment to her when she couldn't deliver on her vague promise of a trip to the end of the rainbow in California.

Helen bent over the final pages in the folder, determined to make one last effort. That was when she saw her uncle's name scrawled on a sheet of lined paper torn from some kind of school notebook. *Loy McCormick???* Helen read. With a growing sense of panic Helen went back through every item in the file. No, no other mention of her uncle. But perhaps in her tiredness and her irritation with the whole mess she'd overlooked something else. Quietly, with a glance at the sleeping girl — Victoria hadn't moved a muscle since nodding off — Helen took Terrie Muncie's list of names from her own file she'd been carting around for a couple of days. She'd figured it was just a red herring so she hadn't paid much attention to the list, but what the hell. Couldn't hurt to do a little more digging. Not like she had anything else to do.

After another hour, the only other thing Helen came up with was a headache. Despite the demands of the day, she wasn't tired — instead, she was revved up and restless. And, although she hated to admit it to herself, she kept thinking about Terrie Muncie. Why the hell couldn't the woman leave her relatives alone? And if she prodded enough would Terrie give her anything else about these names on the list? Or about her uncle?

Moving as quietly as possible, Helen picked up the phone from the bedside table. Victoria snuffled a bit but didn't wake as Helen stretched the phone cord as far as it would go and succeeded in nearly closing the bathroom door behind her. Instead of the ceiling light, Helen switched on the dimmer lamp over the mirror. Just as well, she thought, seeing her form only vaguely illuminated in the dark mirror — she didn't want to watch herself making the dumb move of calling Terrie.

Terrie answered on the first ring. "I was wondering when you'd get in touch with me."

Helen did her best to ignore the sensations the woman's voice evoked. Maybe if she started with her anger about Terrie's encroachment on Aunt Edna she could keep control of the conversation, Helen thought. "I understand you've become a frequent flyer in the trailer park," she began in what she hoped were icy tones.

"Are you all right, Helen? Edna just called. She's concerned about you."

"Let's leave my relatives out of this. I want to talk about the list you gave me."

"No problem. Why don't you come on over and we'll discuss it?"

Her voice was warm, enticing, holding promises. Helen felt her body, hot and tired though it was, tighten in response to the sensuous sound. "You seem to be spending an awful lot of your spare time with my family," she heard herself say in a flat voice. "Or is it really spare time? Are you still on the job when you visit the trailer park?"

"Maybe I just enjoy your family, Helen. Didn't that ever occur to you? Or are you too ashamed of them and their double-wide trailer, ashamed of Edna and Bobby, to even imagine that I might like their company?"

It took a moment for Helen to gather her wits and respond. The truth of Terrie's accusation stabbed her like a hot needle. "Let's not talk about me right now," she finally managed to get out. "I'm a lot more interested in what the hell you're up to. Especially with this bogus list you've given me."

"What makes you assume it's bogus?"

"Jesus, enough with the twenty-questions deal. You said you've give me some help, and I'm calling your bluff on it."

Terrie's laugh just infuriated Helen more. "Bet you're cute

146

when you're angry. Look, why don't you come over and we can talk about it?"

"You mean right now." Okay, okay, Helen lectured herself, quit with the excitement at this invitation — the bitch is a tease and a liar and potentially a very dangerous woman. She knew, however, she wasn't off to a good start when she found herself agreeing to a rendezvous in half an hour at Terrie's place.

Idiot, idiot, idiot, Helen raged at herself as she stealthily crept around the motel room, gathering up shoes and shoulder bag and the file folder she'd managed to keep intact for the last couple of days. Her last act before taking off was to slip back into the bathroom to write a note for Victoria, in case the girl woke up before she got back. *I'll be back in a couple of hours,* she wrote, hoping it was true. *Just stay put. Don't answer the door or the phone or make any calls.* Enough with the drill sergeant routine, Helen grimaced. *Breakfast is on me in the morning, and I'll get us safely to Biloxi.* She blushed at the lame gesture of solidarity with Victoria in that last sentence — it couldn't have been more shallow and meaningless. How the fuck would a cup of coffee stand up against her desertion of a grieving and helpless young woman in the midst of what might be serious danger? Helen caught a glimpse of herself in the watery mirror over the cheap dresser. It twisted her guts to see herself, but she kept on going, out into the night and away from the dangerous and lovely girl on the bed.

Helen was still giving herself a list of rationalizations as she pulled up in front of Terrie's place. The pep talk to her inner bitch ceased as she stared, puzzled, at the ordinary looking house. No hint of Terrie's undoubted wealth appeared in the average suburban facade that sat in a flat squat in the countryside west of Tupelo. But, Helen reasoned as she slowly got out of her car, just the fact that it stood alone and remote, deep in the rolling landscape set far from the main road, was probably indication enough that Terrie was of the landed gentry. Isolated by thick rows of Mississippi's ubiquitous pine trees, Terrie's nondescript house was nestled in a shallow bowl of verdant growth. Helen glanced at the slip of paper where she'd written Terrie's directions in haste in the motel bathroom — yes, this was the place.

As if responding to her doubts, a porch lamp flared into brightness. Helen saw Terrie's red hair flame out against the black surrounding the house. Helen stepped forward, her shoes crunching on gravel that gleamed white in the diffused light. Terrie didn't speak — merely held the door open and barely stood aside for Helen to enter, forcing Helen to brush across her body as she stepped into the foyer.

"I wasn't sure you were coming," Terrie murmured as she shut the door and switched off the porch light. The two women stood in shadows. Helen wasn't even sure what Terrie was wearing, beyond the same perfume she'd had on the other night. She hardly dared look at Terrie. Some kind of sleeveless blue top and cutoffs, Helen noted before taking a couple of steps into the house. Terrie leaned against the door, her hands folded behind her back, watching Helen prowl around. "Did you have any trouble finding the place?"

"No." Helen focused on the huge living room, its spare furnishings in light-colored wood, the simple handwoven rugs on the polished parquet, the enormous windows that would, in daylight, offer the inhabitant an impressive view of the deep green hills. She had to admit that the place was much more impressive than it looked, and the plain — even austere — decor only served to enhance the natural beauty surrounding the house. If nothing else Terrie seemed to have good taste in interior design.

Still, Terrie's sense of style wasn't the issue tonight. Helen pulled the file out of her cavernous shoulder bag and took out the list. "So. Now I'm here. Start talking to me. What the hell is this damn list all about?"

Stupid, stupid, stupid. Helen cringed at her own bluster — there was no worse giveaway to the state of her nerves and her hormones than that ridiculous opener, evidence of her need to cover her ass with a bark that hid very little bite.

And Terrie knew it. She pushed herself away from the door and walked past Helen into the living room. Helen could see the satisfied smile on her lips. "At least give me a chance to play hostess." She chuckled. "How about a drink? What would you like?"

Feeling foolish, Helen planted her feet firmly on the shiny floor and folded her arms across her chest, still clutching the file with one hand. "I don't want a drink. I want you to talk."

"I'm not going to talk while you stand there like a cigar-store wooden carving, Helen. Why don't you just sit down?" Terrie draped herself across the sofa and smiled up at Helen.

Fine, Helen thought as she sat down beside Terrie. "Okay, I'm sitting down. Now — the list."

Terrie slid across the cushion until her breast grazed Helen's arm. Damn that perfume. "Somehow I don't think you wanted to talk about those names, Helen. That's not why you're here."

"And in all your wisdom, Terrie, why do you think I'm here?" Helen asked, knowing as she did so that the question was a mistake. Helen observed herself leaning forward, taking in the heady scent of Terrie's perfume, longing for the feel of Terrie's breast on her arm again.

"For this." And Terrie pulled her by her shirt into a deep, long, wet kiss. Then somehow Helen hands found Terrie's breasts, braless beneath the thin fabric of her shirt, her nipples hard against Helen's fingers. Helen let her mouth travel to Terrie's ears, to her neck, tasting her skin. There was a persistent warmth and wetness growing between Helen's legs, a need that refused to be ignored, a pulsing of her blood into a heated rhythm that only increased when Terrie's fingers started playing with Helen's breasts.

"Is this where you got shot, Helen?" she murmured as her fingers found the scar snaking around Helen's side. Gently

Terrie probed the ridges of flesh. At first Helen resisted, flinching automatically beneath the unfamiliar sensation. Quickly, however, she relaxed. It didn't hurt, it really didn't hurt after all. With each tentative brush of Terrie's fingers against the tender skin, Helen saw images of Alison flash through her mind. She'd never once allowed her ex-lover to touch her in this way. Not for all those months they'd stayed together while their relationship died, after Helen had been released from the hospital. Somehow, Helen realized, she'd decided that no one was ever going to touch her again. Ever.

"I can't do this," Helen muttered as she pushed and pulled at Terrie's shirt until it was off, floating to the floor in a wave of pale blue.

"Do what?"

"This." Helen's hand fought its way into Terrie's shorts — when did they get unzipped? — and her fingers forced through the mound of curly hairs into the hot slick surface of the other woman's crotch. Terrie shivered, her legs opened wider, and she heaved a deep sigh accompanied by a moan that sounded real to Helen's admittedly overwhelmed senses. Helen's probing fingers found the hard nub of Terrie's clitoris, swollen and slick beneath repeated gentle urgings from Helen. Terrie's hips surged upward, and Helen moved her hand in and up, her fingers spreading inside the other woman, moisture soaking through her shorts.

"Fuck!" Terrie cried as her body jerked. Helen felt the waves of Terrie's orgasm ripple through her body, making her thighs tremble, her breath gasp out in ragged bursts. Helen slid her hand out slowly, savoring the feel of the other woman's body, breathing deep as the smell of sex and satisfaction mingled with Terrie's cologne.

Terrie lay limp on the cushions, her eyes glittering in the muted light. With a sudden movement she was on top of Helen, her tongue thrusting into Helen's mouth, her hands pulling Helen's shirt off. Terrie sucked and teased at Helen's nipples, glancing up to see Helen's reaction.

Helen felt all the anger, the pent-up rage, even the grief at Loy's death, slip away from her as easily as her jeans fell to the floor to make a dark heap beside Terrie's shirt. More than clothing fell off her body as Terrie pressed her own slim, naked form to Helen's skin, teasing her with a little pressure here or a stroke there and maybe a light pinch in this spot. "Jesus fucking Christ, Terrie, just do it," Helen finally moaned. Then Terrie was inside her, fingers circling and pressing and withdrawing just as Helen was about to come in a burst of movement and helplessness and release.

When she did come it was almost painful in its intensity — like a short, sharp burst of fire erupting out of nowhere. Helen heard herself scream, felt her body convulse for just a moment, sensed the rush of wetness pouring out between her legs. She lay flat, staring at Terrie's plain dark ceiling, hardly even aware of the woman lying next to her.

Then there was another round of it, this time almost in anger, as if she and Terrie were beating the frustration out of each other. Helen's thoughts strayed for a few tortured seconds to the image of Beth Wilks's face — of how she might look when Terrie made love to her. Did they go at each other like this? Helen wondered. Was it that raw, that needy, that angry between them? Then the image was gone as Helen climaxed again. It was longer this time, surging through her body in waves of pleasure that bowed her back and sent her into a numb afterglow.

Helen didn't know how long she lay there naked on the floor, with Terrie sleeping beside her. It was still dark as she crept outside to her car, list safely back in file folder, too dazed to be ashamed of herself. Not yet, anyhow. Shame would come soon enough, Helen realized, as she headed the car back to the motel and to Victoria. She gripped the steering wheel so tightly her hands began to ache. "I just fucked Beth's girlfriend," she said aloud in the car, trying it on for size. "I just fucked Beth's lover, and I liked it. I loved every damn minute of it. And I think she did too."

Helen caught a glimpse of her own eyes in the rearview mirror as she drove under one of the sparsely placed floodlights arching over the highway leading back to Tupelo. Dark smudges in a pale, drawn face — that's what her eyes looked like. Did she look like a bitch? Probably. Helen felt her shoulders shrink under the weight of guilt as she drove down the turnoff that would lead to the motel. She devoutly wished she could regret what she'd just done. She just didn't have the energy.

Chapter Twelve

The sun edged over the top of the motel buildings as Helen pulled into the parking lot. Iron gray clouds threatened an early morning storm. Helen switched off the car's headlights, submerging the squat motel units back into shadow not yet penetrated by daylight. She sighed and sank down into the cushions of the seat. Jesus, she was tired. Her body ached for sleep, for curling up beneath blankets in a cool, darkened room and drifting into oblivion. Not surprising, given the fact that she'd just had the most intense fuck of her life. Well, maybe that was exaggerating, Helen thought with a smile as she started to open the car door — she'd been celibate for such a long time that any sex at all would probably have felt like an earthshaking experience. Heaving herself out of the car with a groan of exhaustion, she dug the keys to the room out of her pocket, dropping them in her groggy state. The voice boomed in her ear as she was standing up.

"One move, bitch, and we'll blow your head off."

That had to be Jimbo. She could feel his beer gut prodding her back as she slowly, slowly straightened up. The other shadow breathing heavily to her right must be Tommy. Terrific. She didn't think she was up to Mutt and Jeff this morning, but it looked like she had no choice. Helen made very sure she barely moved, even to breathe, when she felt the poke of something small and hard against her spine. Ten to one it was a gun barrel. Jimbo snickered, jabbing the gun painfully in the small of her back. Helen risked a glance to her right. Tommy expertly ran hands over her body, nudging Jimbo aside to complete the frisk, taking the liberty of squeezing her tits in the process. Helen flinched when his hands fingered briefly at her crotch.

"Nope, she don't got anything on her." Helen realized this was the first time she'd heard Tommy actually speak — his voice came out in a high-pitched whine that had probably gotten him teased and harassed all his life, coming as it did out of such an aggressively pumped-up physique. In fact, his apparent devotion to bodybuilding might actually be a response to a lifetime of ridicule over his sissified voice. Wait a minute, Helen thought, cold with fear. She had a gun stuck in her back and two very unattractive men harboring grave desires to do her harm — she needed to stay focused on survival, not allow panic to distract her into irrelevant thoughts. Anyhow, maybe she could use this nugget of information shortly in maneuvering an escape from these two hired hands.

"Open the door, bitch. Come on, do it." That was Jimbo again, his hot breath smelling of beer and some stale meal reeking in her face. The gun prodded against her back again with a sharp painful stab, and Helen moved to comply with his demand, fighting to control her shaking hands. Her mind raced around in useless circles. What the fuck was she going to do? Of course, they were probably here more for Victoria than for herself. Not that they'd pass up the chance to hurt her as well. And god knows what they had in mind for the daughter of Bill Mason, who was probably privy to all his secrets. If they lived through this, Helen thought, she'd do her damnedest to find out who set them on the warpath this morning. Maybe Terrie, in fact probably Terrie. Forget the fact that she'd not two hours ago listened to Terrie Muncie screaming out in joyous orgasm as they both fucked their brains out. At least Helen had. Terrie could have faked everything, although Helen couldn't bring herself to believe it.

"Stop screwing around, cunt. Open the frigging door."

"I'm trying," Helen said in a low voice, jingling keys in her palm. How did this happen? How did these two goons find her? She hadn't said a word to anyone, certainly not to Terrie — just that phone call to Aunt Edna to tell her —

Jesus fucking Christ. That had to be it. Hadn't Terrie said something about speaking to Edna that evening? Edna must have dropped something in the conversation with Terrie about Helen's whereabouts. Helen's stomach turned as she finally picked out the motel room key from the knot of keys in her hands. No, wait — in that phone call Edna had said something about reporters, right? About someone claiming to be a reporter trying to get an interview. Who knows what she might have let fall, or what someone might have overheard? Especially if a compliant newspaper from Biloxi was a nice, neat package in the pocket of Roberts and Farrell and whoever else might want to keep Helen from digging up dirt on the destruction of the Beauregard Resort. Not to mention that Helen and Victoria might have been followed all the way from Biloxi by these jerks, despite Helen's conviction that she'd eluded discovery during the drive to Tupelo.

Christ, what was wrong with her brain? Terror and afterglow — a lethal combination. And she had to try to warn

155

the girl sleeping inside the motel room that there were beasts outside the door waiting to devour them both. Unable to come up with a better solution, Helen let her body visibly show her fear. She didn't have to go too far to increase her trembling, and she let her breath come out in ragged spurts.

Tommy sighed and pushed her. That motion only helped her feeble, desperate plan. Helen stumbled against the door and noisily dropped the keys onto the gritty pavement, making sure she bumped and kicked on the flimsy door. "Oh my god," she cried out.

Tommy slapped her, in a neat and abbreviated flick of his hand that drew blood out of the corner of her mouth. For the second time that day she heard his whine. "Keep it down or you're dead," he whispered into her ear. "You and the little cunt inside."

She'd have to be careful how she did this, Helen thought, scrabbling for the keys — not enough noise to wake up the other motel patrons but enough to rouse Victoria and at least prepare her for what might lay ahead of them. "I'm sorry, I'm sorry," Helen whimpered in a stage whisper as she leaned against the door, hoping her voice would carry into the motel room. She rattled the keys and scratched them noisily on the door, pretending to fumble at the lock, until the gun stuck in her side once more.

"Open it now," Jimbo said. Helen gave up — she'd have to think of something else now — and swung the door open.

The room was empty. Helen didn't know whether to be glad or afraid. Had Victoria taken off during the night, while she was out boffing Terrie? Or had some sort of Keystone Cops routine just taken place, during which Victoria had hidden in the shower? Either way, the vacancy definitely took Jimbo and Tommy by surprise.

Tommy switched on the lights. The room stood illuminated in its stark ugliness, and in her mixture of frantic fear and physical lassitude Helen saw meaninglessness details as if in vivid bas-relief. The nubby pink bedspread, tossed in a messy heap at the end of the bed, the ugly painting over the bed, the walls painted in cheap bright yellow, the scuffed and scarred fake-wood furniture, the squat old television set rigidly affixed in the wall in the jaws of some ugly metallic antitheft casing. But in the midst of all this mess and seedy reality, no sign of Victoria Mason. And, Helen realized with a jolt, no sign of Bill Mason's file on the arson investigation. Just a heap of clothing and shoes, Victoria's discards, next to Helen's quickly assembled duffel bag.

The door closed quietly behind them. Without looking around Helen tried to assess the geography of the room and the dangers in it. Jimbo was still right behind her, inches away, his gun sticking into her spine. Helen sneaked a look over at Tommy. To her immense relief he didn't appear to be armed, if his tight jeans and clinging T-shirt offered a reliable means of making a judgment call. Probably he was relying on his manly powers of persuasion in the form of fists, letting Jimbo take charge of ordnance. Not that Tommy's fists should be ignored — it was just that Helen needed to get the fucking gun away from Jimbo before anything else was possible.

"She ain't here," Tommy whined. His bland pale face wrinkled in puzzlement, he even picked up a limp, dusty cushion from the room's single easy chair, as if proving that Victoria wasn't lurking beneath the upholstery.

"Duh," Jimbo wheezed at his partner. He prodded Helen again, ignoring the evil look Tommy shot his way. Interesting, Helen decided — maybe a bit of testosterone-enhanced power play between these two men. Could she maneuver them into a pissing contest that would allow her to get away from them? "I think I figured that out, Tommy. Maybe the bitch here could fill us in on where the other one went."

Helen didn't know if it would help to keep playing dumb frail, female but she didn't have a single other card to play just now. "Oh my god," she breathed, dropping to her knees and getting her fragile spine away from Jimbo's gun for a minute. "Victoria's gone! I-I don't know what to do," she moaned.

"Quiet, if you don't want your brains splattered on the floor," Jimbo growled. The two men shuffled around for a moment, glancing at each other and peering into the room's empty corners. A moment was all Helen needed. Crouching down, hoping Jimbo believed that she was cowering in fear and nothing else, Helen quickly surveyed her immediate surroundings. To her left, she saw a few items protruding from Victoria's purse — a jumble of candy wrappers, a well-worn leather wallet, a vial of perfume that looked expensive, a shoe with a sharp spiked heel. Fuck, Helen said to herself. Victoria couldn't be far if she'd left all her shit here like this. Maybe her desperate attempts to make enough noise to alert the girl had worked — but then, where the hell was she hiding? No way she could escape even the half-assed search-and-destroy mission of the two men that hovered over Helen now.

Directly in front of her, at her knees, Helen briefly scanned the spilled-over contents of her own hastily assembled duffel bag. Nothing helpful there — clothes and sneakers, a soft-shell shaving kit bag containing a few harmless toiletries, even a useless paperback she'd picked up at the airport. Victoria's bag held much more in the way of possibilities.

She had to move quickly now — Jimbo and Tommy were apparently coming to some sort of conclusion over her head at this point. Helen caught a couple of significant glances between them as she pretended to fall forward, grabbing Victoria's shoe as she did so.

Then she heard the telltale click of the gun's safety being released. "All right, bitch," Jimbo muttered. "Let's go." He waved the gun at her, and she caught the flicker of mean light in his eyes. He was looking forward to killing her, no doubt about it. He even started to lick his lips, turned on by the prospect. As if in support of her conclusions, Jimbo's hand wandered to his crotch and he fussed at his fly for a moment and grinned. "We're outta here, and you're coming with us."

"But the other one —" Tommy interrupted, confusion smearing his placid features as he struggled to articulate his doubts of Jimbo's assessment of the situation. "She's still gotta be here, Jimbo. Look, her stuff is here." Okay, then — Jimbo must think he was the brains of the operation, but Tommy did have a glimmer or two of intelligence. That made it more difficult, but not impossible, Helen decided. There might be a way to play them off against each other.

Jimbo glared at his comrade. "I said, we're outta here. You gonna hang around all by yourself or you gonna come with us?" He grabbed at Helen's head. She winced at the pain as Jimbo pulled a thick wad of her hair in his hand, jerking her backward. She felt the gun at her throat and tried to keep breathing. Victoria's shoe was clasped firmly in her hand, and she stayed on her knees, despite the shooting pains in her scalp, hiding the shoe behind her haunches as she forced her body to stay in a crouched position. "All right, Victoria. We got your little pussy-lickin' friend here," Jimbo said in a breathy voice that indicated just how much he was enjoying himself. The words came out in a loud, hissing whisper. She managed a quick glance at Tommy. His dull, dead eyes swept the room, alert for any movement, his attention occupied away from Helen. Good. Something flashed in Tommy's hand, and she saw a thin blade pointing at her direction. Not so good. She bit her lip and ignored the fire breaking across her scalp as she shifted the shoe in her hand so that the sharp heel was pointed outward. "Unless you want to see the bull dyke cut up in little pieces, you better come on out."

Jimbo leaned over suddenly, his mouth next to her ear. Helen gagged reflexively as his warm, wet tongue slid over her cheek, leaving a trail of slime on her skin. "Maybe we'll just fuck her up the ass, Victoria. Wanna watch while we ream her out?" That earned a giggle out of Tommy. He juggled the knife like someone who knew what he was doing.

The snigger froze Helen. She had to move, now, or risk god-knows-what at the hands of these two apes. Wherever the fuck Victoria was, Helen had to do something. She let herself relax underneath Jimbo, feeling his paunch like a warm, oily cushion on her back. "You know, there's this one little thing, Jimbo," she said in a calm voice.

He glanced down at her, startled at her apparent calm. "Oh yeah? What's that?"

"You must really be into pain," and she drove the shoe back in the general direction of his groin. He folded over like a limp sheet of paper, a soundless cry forming on his mouth as his lips shaped a big O of surprise and hurt. Helen shoved her elbow hard, lunging deep into his soft gut, then smacking her arm upward so that her fist caught beneath his jaw. Jimbo's big head flailed to the side and now he emitted a sharp yelp of pain. The gun dropped from his hand onto the threadbare rug — by some miracle it didn't go off as it bounced by Helen's knees — and she grabbed it up in a swift scoop, taking it in a two-handed grip. She rose to her feet and turned on the two men.

Jimbo was still leaning forward, retching his breath in heavy gasps. Tommy stood in a slight crouch like a misshapen crab, his eyes still dull but a bit more wakeful with all confusion drained away. Even if he couldn't quite figure out what to do, he at least knew who was holding the gun and would act accordingly. Tommy dropped the knife to the ground and raised his hands, palms facing outward. That was okay for now, Helen decided, although it probably wouldn't last long. Jimbo kept blinking as if fighting off tears, his glance wavering between the gun and Helen.

"Now, then," Helen heard herself say. She eased down onto the bed, still holding the gun firmly in her hands. "Start talking."

The force was taken away from her command as the bed rolled and surged beneath her. Victoria Mason emerged from beneath the bed, her hair tousled and streaked with the remains of dust bunnies, her eyes wild with terror. Helen, fearful of losing her grip and her position of power, stood up. "Jesus, Victoria, your timing sucks."

Victoria didn't speak — merely stood up, blinking in the light, clutching the file to her chest. She moved next to Helen, not taking her gaze off Jimbo and Tommy, and whispered, "I didn't know what else to do. I could hear you outside, and —"

"Enough. We'll talk later," Helen murmured back. Then, aloud, she said, "I mean it, boys. We're not playing cops and robbers here. Someone is going to be in a lot of hurt before I'm done, and I'm betting it's one of you two."

"Don't — don't tell her nothin', Tommy," Jimbo managed to wheeze out. "We're dead if you say anything."

Before Helen could stop her Victoria stepped over to where Jimbo cowered, his hands hovering protectively near his crotch. "Victoria, step back," Helen said. The situation was quickly moving out of her control.

But Victoria, her chest heaving, stared down at Jimbo as if she hadn't heard Helen at all. Even from behind, in the weird shadows cast by the harsh overhead lights, Helen could see the girl trembling with — what, grief? rage? something worse? Her gaze flickering between the two men, Helen stared at Victoria just long enough to see her hand flash out as she slapped Jimbo's face. Once, twice, then a third time, the man's large face swinging back and forth with each blow. "You're the one, aren't you? You're the one who killed him." Victoria's voice was cool and collected, as if she were talking about the latest bargain on the shopping channel.

Helen watched as Tommy flexed his not inconsiderable muscles, his skin shifting beneath the stretched-out shirt. In another couple of moments he'd make his move. "Victoria. We'll deal with it. Step back. Now. I mean it, now."

The relief Helen felt when Victoria moved back to the bed

was so intense she almost moaned with it. Jimbo and Tommy stared back, wary and uncertain. "Okay, boys. Talk to me and make it good, because I'm really tired. And when I get tired my aim is off. I might think I'm going for your arm or your leg and miss. Who knows what I'd hit then?" Of course the last thing Helen wanted to do in the middle of this motel was fire the gun — bringing down god-knows-what on her head — but she was hoping the two men were spooked enough to not be too sure what she was capable of. Besides, a motel like this, clearly a trucker's haven and scene of many a shady encounter, might not be overly picky about their clientele. Helen would be willing to bet they'd seen and heard worse than a pistol or two going off.

"What? What do you want?"

"Tommy, I told you —"

"Shut the fuck up!" Jimbo struggled to kneel upright. Yes, that was fear in his eyes. And it wasn't Helen or the gun he was afraid of. What the hell was going on here?

"Hey, I'm not gonna get my balls shot off for some whore," Tommy said, his voice cracking piteously. He made a gesture toward Jimbo, a motion he quickly checked as he saw Helen's stance shift.

"Fuck," Jimbo muttered, rolling his eyes and leaning on his hands and knees. He shook his head and spat on the carpet. "We're both dead now."

Tommy went on as if his companion hadn't spoken. "Her name's Dixie Mae. She works the strip by the casinos in Biloxi."

"You have to be kidding. No one is named Dixie Mae," Helen muttered. "And who the fuck is she, anyway?" She freed one hand to gently push Victoria down on the bed, then took a couple of steps closer to Tommy.

"A whore." This, surprisingly, from Jimbo. He spared one more disgusted glare for Tommy, then looked up into the gun barrel.

"So you two whipped little boys take orders from a whore? I'm surprised, guys."

"She calls us and tells us what they want."

"What who wants?" The two men glanced at each other without responding to her question. Helen took two steps closer to Tommy and aimed the gun at his temple. She'd decided she would take him out before she did anything to Jimbo — Jimbo was the weaker of the two, and seeing some blood coming from Tommy might keep him quiet. And she wasn't at all sure Tommy would be put off if she hurt his pal Jimbo. *God, please keep me from having to shoot anyone,* Helen prayed. For just a moment she was aware of Victoria sitting on the bed.

"Fuck if I know," Jimbo said. "She calls us, we go out and do the job, Dixie gives us the money after."

"Where? Where do you go to get paid?"

"The strip. Next to the Athenaeum, at the intersection where the parking building is."

"A casino?" Jimbo nodded. "And you're supposed to go meet her tonight, I take it?"

Again, neither one spoke because they might reveal their plans to kill Helen and Victoria or because there wasn't anything else to say, Helen never knew. As Helen was standing still and trying to decide what to do with the two of them, Tommy bolted toward the door. Jimbo fell over, knocking him flat in the process. Tommy lay on his back, staring at the ceiling, while Jimbo crawled away from him toward the door.

Without thinking, Helen clicked the safety back on and slammed the gun against Tommy's head. He grunted, his eyes rolled up, and he went limp. She heard Victoria gasp. "Not now," Helen muttered at her.

"Is he-is he —"

Helen touched his neck. "He's out cold, that's all." She looked up to where Jimbo huddled against the wall. Before she could speak, something bright and hard flashed in front of her eyes. A thin line of brilliant red etched across Jimbo's neck, and his mouth opened and closed silently as thick gouts of blood welled between his greasy fingers clutching at his own sliced flesh. Victoria staggered back from him, dropping Tommy's bloody knife to the carpet.

"Fuck." Helen hurried to Jimbo. His eyes, glazed and terrified, stared up at Helen's face as she forced herself to fight off nausea and probe the wound. "It's just a flesh wound. He'll live, too, but we have to call an ambulance."

"For these pigs?" Victoria hissed. Helen looked up to see tears streaming down her cheeks, blurring the last of the makeup she'd applied so carefully so many hours ago — a whole lifetime and one parent ago, actually. "We should just let them die." With one foot she kicked at Tommy's body, motionless on the floor. "That's what they deserve."

"Maybe so, but not tonight. And definitely not this motel room." Shit, shit, shit. Wired with fear and adrenaline, Helen felt her mind slip back into the same cool clear focus she used to experience as a cop in life-threatening situations. "Okay. Victoria, put that knife in Tommy's hand."

Victoria stood and gaped. "But-"

"Just fucking do what I say and maybe we'll both stay out of jail, all right?" Under her direction, Victoria clasped Tommy's limp fingers around the knife. Helen wiped the gun with her jacket and wrapped it in a washcloth from the bathroom. Jimbo, slipping toward a faint, stumbled out of the room and slid onto the pavement next to their unit. It might be a fleabag, but at least there wasn't anyone wandering around in this sheltered walkway separating their unit from the others.

The sun was starting to bear down with glaring heat as Victoria and Helen dragged Tommy out of the room. Yes, the parking lot was still empty. And that pickup most likely belonged to Jimbo or Tommy — Helen didn't remember seeing it the night before. She gave the gun one final wipe with the washcloth after she emptied the chamber and pocketed the bullets. Jimbo had passed out, but Helen was able to get the gun nestled into his hands. Then, on impulse, she took the gun back and stuffed it into her waistband. Better to get the weapon away from these goons, she thought — she'd figure it out later.

"Now what?" Victoria was docile and subdued — the recent bout of bloodletting seemed to have calmed her in a gruesome way.

Time for psychology later, Helen told herself. "Just help me get them a little bit further into the parking lot. We don't have much time," she said, glancing up at the sun.

When she outlined her plan to Victoria, the girl protested. "Listen to me, idiot," Helen said as she pulled her back into the room. "We have to make sure Jimbo gets to a hospital right away, and we have to get our own asses out of this place. Do you have a better plan?" Helen hesitated, then took the knife back from Tommy. She wiped it on the ground, flipped the switchblade shut, then stashed both weapons in her bag. Let the cops worry about the missing knife for all of ten minutes. Better to steal the toys from the boys for the time being.

Still muttering angrily, Victoria helped Helen gather their few belongings. Helen sent Victoria in to the motel manager's office with the keys and got the car going. When she saw Victoria inside the office, Helen pulled out of the parking lot and drove to the nearest gas station. Her speech seemed to work beautifully — her tale of seeing people in the parking lot and blood and hearing a gun go off got the bored-sounding dispatcher to pay attention. And Helen was certain that this particular motel was the site of many a police visit, if appearances counted for anything.

She spotted Victoria in the rearview mirror just as the ambulance came veering around the corner toward the motel, lights flashing and siren wailing. A black-and-white followed close behind. Helen had tucked her rental car behind the hulk of a rusting van that had settled into rusty decrepitude in the gas station's parking area. Despite Victoria's complaints she waited until she could see Jimbo being lifted onto a gurney into the back of the ambulance — no sheet covering his face, so at least he was alive.

"You think the cops won't find out who was staying here tonight?" Victoria fumed, her calm having seeped away in fear and confusion.

Helen turned to face her. Anger must have shown vividly on her face because Victoria shut up quickly and settled back in the seat. "Listen to me, you little fool. We're lucky to be alive. No one turned up dead from this adventure, and it bought us some time to find this Dixie Mae woman.

"You mean we're going back?" Victoria's mouth gaped open in amazement. "Why?"

Helen sighed, exhaustion taking over. If this was the price for having sex once every other year, she was ready to check into a convent. "Just keep your mouth shut, Victoria. I'm taking you to the cops in Biloxi, and then I'm going looking for Dixie Mae." Great. Helen wasn't sure she wanted to meet a hooker named Dixie Mae, but apparently it was on her agenda. She pointed the car toward Biloxi and they sped along the highway in silence.

Chapter Thirteen

Helen had plenty of time to think about the events of the last twenty-four hours as she sat in the all-too-familiar Biloxi police station waiting for Victoria to emerge from the lieutenant's office. Watching her being led down the corridor by a uniformed officer, Helen felt the iron bands of guilt and responsibility close over her. The parade of police officers, plain-clothes detectives, and men and women in handcuffs being trundled from desk to desk offered no distraction from the instant replay of Jimbo passing out in the parking lot that kept playing in her head. Helen had no illusions that the cops in Tupelo would fail to put together the simple puzzle of who Jimbo and Tommy had been visiting, and who'd contributed to their damaged state. It was a question of hours before she and Victoria got pulled in for questioning about it. Unless the two men were a little bit smarter than they looked and decided not to talk about it. That was possible, if they were scared enough of whoever was paying them.

Helen squirmed on the orange plastic seats — was it a law that furnishings in a place like this had to be ugly, to remind you that you were sitting in a police station? — and glanced at the clock on the wall. An hour had gone by. What the hell was going on in there?

Almost as soon as the question formed in her mind Victoria appeared. She hurried up to Helen, her face drawn and stricken, muttering, "Let's go, let's get the hell out of here."

Helen led her out of the building and waited until they were in the car before asking her anything. "All right, what happened? What did they say to you?"

Victoria's response was garbled and confusing. Apparently they'd asked her very few questions — mainly they'd focused on her father's degenerate behavior, his drinking, his bouts of paranoia that disturbed the peace. The one thing clear from the demoralizing interview was that they were writing him off as a suicide.

Helen sighed and rubbed her eyes. It was already hot enough to fry the proverbial egg on the sidewalk. And she was starving and tired and she hurt everywhere. "What about arrangements for your father?" Helen asked awkwardly, wishing there was a nice way to find out about where his remains were.

Victoria snorted. "Some of his old pals from the paper have offered to take care of it. Nice, huh? Makes them feel a little bit better for acting like a lot of shitheads when he was alive, I guess."

Helen glanced at her from behind the protective covering of her sunglasses. Right now Victoria's face could have been carved in marble, still and serene and smooth in its hate and fury. It was the same face she'd presented to Helen all through the drive from Tupelo, hours and hours of rage burning up the interior of the car. Helen had broken every speeding law on the books to get them to Biloxi close to noon, so she'd been relieved not to have to process anything with Victoria that morning. Now, as the midday sun burned high overhead, Victoria was finally going to let go. "Fuck 'em all," she went on. "They won't even let me bury him. Me, his own daughter."

Helen heard her stomach growl. She needed food — she was sure Victoria did, too — and she still had to find Dixie Mae. "Look, Victoria, I need some food. Maybe we can just get something to go."

"And fuck you, too!" Victoria screamed. Helen almost jumped through the window in surprise but recovered in time to keep from wrecking the car. "All you've done for me is get my life fucked up, you damn bitch! Now what the hell am I going to do?" Rage dissolved into tears as Helen pulled up at a drive-through fast-food joint. At least we won't have to get out of the car, she thought, fighting back the start of a whopping headache. A few minutes later, fortified by yet another fast food meal, they drove back to the highway that flanked the coast, in search of the Athenaeum.

Victoria barely spoke for most of the drive along the Gulf Coast. Her sandwich, chosen by Helen when she'd refused to make a selection, lay untouched on the dashboard, leaving the scent of hot grease drifting across the car's interior. Helen had finished her food very quickly — amazing how sex followed by threats to one's existence could arouse a girl's appetite — and now divided her attention between sipping coffee, watching the road, and stealing glances at the girl sitting mute and sullen beside her.

An attack of guilt so enormous as to render Helen temporarily speechless had overtaken her as soon as they'd hit the road. For the first half of the ride Helen was more than glad to do her part in maintaining silence in the car. It was bad enough that she'd left Victoria alone last night just to give her hormones a cheap thrill. And it really wasn't much more than that, Helen had scolded herself as she stared at the sunbaked gray pavement of the highway. Fuck the list — neither she nor Terrie had cared about it. That had just been the excuse for a good lay. And that wasn't even beginning to look at the nasty little side issue of having screwed around with a friend's lover — particularly when that friend had saved Helen's ass more than once in a matter of days. Hours, even.

But what was even worse at the moment was her direct responsibility for almost getting Victoria killed. Despite the punk look of solid black and ghoulish makeup and fuck-the-world attitude that Victoria presented to the innocent bystander, this was a naive and helpless kid up against some kind of ruthless enemy who didn't give a rat's ass if she died just so they could protect themselves or their interests. What would have happened if Helen had shown up at the motel fifteen minutes later? Would Victoria be dead now, bloody on the cheap bedspread, forgotten in the wake of violence that washed over her world? She should have left the girl at her neighbors' house last night. It might not have been a long-term solution, but it certainly wouldn't have put Jimbo and Tommy on her trail. Worst of all, Victoria had so clearly looked to Helen for help — for escape from the narrow life that had trapped her, not least because of her father's course of nonaction. Granted, he'd cowered in fear for years, and probably thought he was doing the best thing possible for his only child. Apparently, though, Helen's unique methods of action were only making things worse. Something had to give, right away.

To dispel her own tension Helen finally broke the silence. "Victoria, I'm sorry I left last night. I shouldn't have done that." More silence. Helen tried again. "I was trying to get some more information about what happened to your father. There was someone I thought could help me." Well, it was partly true, anyway — Helen was certain that whoever was behind the arson of the Beauregard had been keeping Bill

Mason under his, her, or its collective thumb for years. And even though she was fairly sure now that Terrie's list was just a lure, she was wondering if Roberts and Farrell — the owners of the Beauregard when it was destroyed — had had something to do with the fire. Her uncle's connection to it all was still a complete mystery, but somehow he'd been mixed up in this.

Still no response. Helen looked over at Victoria, dismayed to see the younger woman shaking with silent sobs. "I — I might have ended up just like my dad. Those two guys would have killed me." It came out as a shaky whisper, but the force of the words hit Helen in the gut, hard and painful. "I heard you at the door with them, and I didn't know what was going on."

Without thinking Helen reached out and grasped Victoria's hand in a quick squeeze. Victoria squeezed back and clung to her like a terrified child. "I don't know what to do, Helen. What should I do now?"

Inwardly Helen cringed. She couldn't walk out on Victoria, not again. It was too painful to see her like this. For a split second, after taking in the wrinkled black shirt, tight black skirt, and black tights riddled with runs, Helen longed to see her acting spiteful and angry — not pathetically frightened, grieving for herself and her father. Then it would have been easy to just take Bill Mason's file with her and disappear, carrying on her own investigation and forgetting about the weird little punk-wannabe from Biloxi.

"Wh-what is it now?" Victoria asked as Helen heaved a big sigh.

"Nothing. I just have to take you back to your neighbors right now and go find this woman by myself, that's all."

"No fucking way!" Victoria wiped her face and shook her head. "After everything else that's happened — there's just no way. Besides, you owe it to me. You know you do."

Helen shut out her furious protests all the way to Doris and Bob's place. Maybe Victoria was just too stunned or shaken to open the car door and take off every time they stopped at a red light or stop sign — maybe she was so confused by grief and fear that she didn't feel capable of getting away — or maybe she really didn't believe Helen would take her there. Whatever the reason, Victoria was still in the car when Helen pulled up behind the brown Cadillac parked behind Bob's truck.

"Oh shit," Victoria breathed, her anger momentarily forgotten. "That's my aunt Josephine's car."

"Aunt Josephine? Your father's sister?"

"No, my mother's. Aunt Josephine hated my dad."

Enormous relief washed over Helen. At least she wasn't handing the girl off to strangers. She did have some family to take care of her. "Look, I'll be back in a few hours. I just want to find this woman and talk to her, then I'll come back and we'll go back to Tupelo. I have a place we can go to."

"Another motel? No, thanks," Victoria snorted, staring at the Cadillac as if it were some new kind of monster. "I'd rather stay with Aunt Josephine."

"I promise it won't be long. Just stall them for a few hours and we'll get out of here." Helen was already planning the story she'd give Beth about needing a place for Victoria to stay for a few days. Beth's house was big enough, and surely the Biloxi cops, if they were choosing or being paid to look the other way while someone hurt the girl, wouldn't want to drag a state trooper into their little pile of shit. She'd be safe enough with Beth. And Helen would have time later to justify dragging Beth into this. Especially after what she'd done with Terrie last night. Nope — no time for regrets right now.

Before Victoria could lodge another protest, a huge woman burst out of Doris's house and lunged for the car. "Oh, baby, baby!" she bellowed, arms spread wide. Helen got a glimpse of lots of gold chains bouncing on a generous bosom clad in navy blue silk and orange-blond hair too bright to be natural. The woman barely noticed Helen as she folded Victoria into her embrace. Victoria's dark eyes, huge and circled with dark

172

shadows, looked back forlornly at Helen. Helen backed off fast, still not sure she meant what she said. Should she come back for the girl? Take her up to Beth's place in Tupelo, get her settled somewhere safely, make sure no one else came after her? Or just leave her to the mercies of Aunt Josephine, where she'd at least be out of harm's way?

Maybe there was a middle path here, Helen thought as she headed back toward the Gulf. Maybe she could take Victoria back with her temporarily, keep in touch with Josephine or she could get out of Mississippi, leaving Victoria behind with her relatives. None of it sounded good, of course. Helen put it out of her mind as she looked for the Athenaeum. It was clearly marked on the tourist map, one of the landmarks of the new and improved Biloxi. And it wasn't hard to spot, with its ridiculous Corinthian columns and fake Greek statuary lining the veranda. The parking lot was packed with everything from tour buses to limos to RVs. Helen found a parking space down the street and made her way back as fast as she could on foot. She stopped only long enough to take some cash out of an ATM machine, knowing that she'd get nowhere without some money to pay for information. After a moment's indecision, Helen took Jimbo's gun from under her seat and tucked it into her waistband, tugging her shirt out so it would cover the weapon. What were Mississippi's laws these days on concealed weapons? She didn't know anymore. At any rate it wasn't loaded. She'd just have to be very, very careful. The sun was going down as she approached the casino and headed toward the back of the building. Helen realized she'd spent an awful lot of time driving today — and she was still tired and hurting from all the activity. Hoping she wouldn't have to make like a television private eye and jump over anything, Helen ducked behind the wall flanking the Athenaeum and entered another world.

It wasn't hard to see why Dixie Mae would like to work this spot. Particularly on a busy Saturday night, when the casinos would be full of potential clients. The back of the casino edged a warren of warehouses that were just barely concealed from the Athenaeum's visitors by a stone wall covered with classical friezes. As soon as she stepped behind the wall, Helen saw cars lined up in the dirty alleyway, their drivers all scanning the row of women and boys standing around. The height of the warehouses deepened the afternoon shadows, lending a sense of partial darkness for these customers to hide their vices. Helen was surprised at how openly these wares were being displayed. Usually there was at least a pretense of propriety about these things, and this kind of entertainment would wait for the cover of night. Perhaps it was the close proximity of large amounts of cash changing hands in a never-ending flow of cyclic capitalism that encouraged these particular entrepreneurs in their boldness. And a lot of their customers would come fresh from the slot machines, with just enough cash to blow on a little bit of illicit fun. Whatever the reason, Helen hoped she'd taken out enough cash from the ATM machine to get some answers.

She had, but barely. Helen tried not to notice their youth, not that it would last long in this environment. "Dixie Mae? Don't know the name," they'd generally answer after pocketing a bill or two. The longer it took, the more nervous Helen got in the gathering shadows. Evening would come soon. And the presence of a stranger would most definitely not be welcome by whatever pimps and dealers prowled these warehouses. She had to get out of there quick. Already she'd noticed several people gathering in groups and gesturing her way — not good at all for her low profile. Anyway, no one seemed willing or able to help her. They all became one big empty face in Helen's mind.

Except for one. One older woman, who looked at the money, looked back up at Helen, and shook her head. She was actually quite attractive, Helen realized, tall and dark, statuesque, moving with languid grace. Even her clothes, while revealing, showed more taste and less gauche cheapness than the outfits most of the others wore. This woman walked away without speaking. Helen stared after her as the woman smiled at the drivers passing by. A car stopped — her smile got bigger, more beatific — and she climbed in. The car pulled slowly away, turning onto a side street. Helen quickly walked by on her way out of the warehouse labyrinth. Yes, they'd stopped there in the alley. Whatever was going on was apparently going to be a quick job.

Helen looked around. It was light enough still to get a good look at the alley. All the warehouses were boarded up — lots of flat surfaces without concealing doorways or Dumpsters to hide behind. Okay, this was as good a spot as any. Fortunately this particular hooker was efficient, and Helen didn't have a long wait. The woman got out of the car with a smile, and the car drove off rapidly down the alley.

Helen walked up quickly, the unloaded gun held in front of her so it wasn't visible from the side or from behind. "All finished? Good, let's talk."

The woman said nothing when Helen grabbed her arm and marched her back down the alley. "Don't make a sound, just keep walking," she muttered as they headed for the wall that sheltered the casino. No one paid much attention to them since the streets had filled with potential customers at the approach of night. They reached Helen's car with a minimum of fuss. Helen could hardly believe her luck — something was actually going right, it seemed.

"And just who the fuck are you?" the woman asked in a bored voice. "Someone's wife? Go point that thing at your husband, lady."

Helen kept the gun in her hand while she fished out the now rather dog-eared photograph of Uncle Loy and his paramour. "All I want is an answer."

"What answer?" She didn't seem too fazed at having a gun pointed in her face, but Helen watched as a tremor shot through her body when she saw the photograph. " Why do you want to find this woman?"

"I have a message for Dixie Mae from Jimbo and Tommy."

The woman froze, an instant stillness that startled Helen. Her face was still as blank as one of the Greek statues in front of the Athenaeum, but her whole body tensed with — what, fear? anger? "What's the message?"

"They won't be back for a while. Got into a little trouble."

"From you?" Now it was fear, and her gaze strayed to the gun. "The same trouble you'll give me if I don't help you, I guess."

"No. No, the trouble wasn't from me." Helen sighed and let the gun drop to her lap. "Look, this gun isn't loaded. See?" She showed her the empty barrel. "It belonged to someone else."

"How the hell did you get it?"

"I took it from him when he tried to shoot me this morning."

"Your day sounds a lot more interesting than mine. I guess you aren't from Jimbo or Tommy, then, are you?"

"Then we do have some mutual acquaintances," Helen said, picking up the gun and putting it back in her pocket. No sense letting it sit around. "Just how do you know them?"

Her companion smiled wryly. "Never mind. If you were sent by those assholes I'd already be black and blue. So I guess you're not."

"Why did you think that? Who are they to you, anyway?"

"No one you need to know about. So why do you want to find Dixie Mae?"

In answer Helen held out the photograph. "This is my uncle. I'm trying to find out who the woman is in that picture, and I think Dixie Mae can help me. All I want to do is ask her some questions."

Helen was about to go into a prepared speech. She even had some money ready in her hand. She was about to give it up when it finally struck her. The first thing, of course, was how she'd been an idiot yet again. Dixie Mae still had long dark hair, the same mysterious smile and compelling eyes as in the photograph taken twenty years ago. Her face was lined, her skin not quite as smooth perhaps — but it was her slouched in Helen's car.

Dixie Mae looked down at the photograph and then back up at Helen. "Your uncle. Looks like a nice guy."

"He was."

"Was?" Dixie Mae's fingers froze on the edges of the picture, and she let it fall back into Helen's lap as if she'd been stung by it. "What happened to him?"

"He's dead, that's what happened to him." Helen was on the verge of telling her that Uncle Loy had died of cancer just over a week ago, but she managed to stop herself. The other woman's reaction was interesting. If she'd been somewhat frightened before, she was now terrified.

"Look, I didn't have anything to do with his death. All I did was provide some distraction, that's it. Nothing more." She fumbled at the car door and started to get out. Helen grasped her arm as hard as she could and was rewarded with a gasp of pain from Dixie Mae. Helen tightened her grip and yanked her back in. With her free hand she picked up the gun by the barrel and held it as if to swing at Dixie Mae's pretty face with the handle.

"I know you didn't kill him. I just want to know how you knew him."

"You mean, how a hooker like me knew him. Right? That's what you want to know." Even in her fear Dixie Mae hissed out the words with venom. "Your perfect uncle, salt of the earth, all that bullshit. Probably raised you from knee-high to a grasshopper or some kind of crap like that."

"Close enough." Helen felt her lips move, heard the words come out, but knew she was sitting frozen stiff with anticipation, brittle and ready to crack.

"I got nothing to say to you, whoever the fuck you are. It was a long time ago, and I have a terrible memory." She struggled to get free, but Helen twisted her fingers with energy she didn't know she had. The other woman winced in pain but stayed put. "Look, I can't tell you anything. I was

177

paid to spend time with the guy" — another wince as Helen dug her nails in — "just like they always paid me. Okay? Anything else, take it up with Jimbo."

"Why the picture, then? Why take a picture of yourself with him?"

"How the fuck should I know?" Now, in full darkness broken only by headlights of passing cars, Helen could clearly see age lines around her mouth, crevices circling her eyes under the expertly applied makeup. "Sometimes they did that, they took pictures. Insurance, maybe."

"What are you talking about?"

She rolled her eyes and quit fighting to get loose. "To keep his damn mouth shut, right? I mean, they can prove he was out fucking a whore — whatever they had him do, he'd keep quiet about it. Okay?"

Helen let go at last, her own hand aching with the strain of holding on to Dixie Mae. "Get out. I said, get out! Get the fuck out of my car. Look, here's money. Just get moving," and Helen shoved the last of her recently acquired cash into Dixie Mae's hands.

The woman stared, fumbled again at the car door, and tripped up a bit in climbing out of the car. "Look," she began, her voice fading into a whine, "I didn't do anything. Just tell whoever sent you, I'm not talking about any of it, all right?"

"I said get the fuck out!" That was all Dixie Mae needed. Helen closed her eyes and leaned her forehead against the steering wheel until the sound of the other woman's shoes dimmed in the darkness. She felt empty, light, as if everything cluttered in her head had suddenly blown away like wind across the Gulf. Uncle Loy hiring prostitutes. Having his picture taken with whores. No, wait — that wasn't it. Someone else paid Dixie Mae for her services. A blackmail setup? But why the hell would anyone deliberately set up Uncle Loy that way? What could he possibly have done that he needed to keep secret? It wasn't as if he were able to pay that kind of money, ever.

In spite of the fact that Helen was trying to analyze the situation as if it were any other case, another part of her mind screamed out at the idea, the very idea, of Uncle Loy bedding a whore. It did not make sense. Did not compute. Not at all. And the puzzle made her want to hit something. Or someone. All the way back to Doris and Bob and Aunt Josephine she felt the division in her mind between detective doing a job and loving niece guarding memories like gold. Her thoughts prodded the painful rift, like a tongue that can't help seeking out an aching tooth. Still in a state of shock, she arrived at the neighbors' house and asked for Victoria.

"You mean she's not with you?" That was Josephine, who'd traded a navy blue dress for a purple caftan. New Age evening wear, maybe. "But — but — we thought —"

Helen's patience had finally drained away. Enough already. "Look, I'd just like to talk to her? Please?"

"But you can't. I mean, that's not possible."

Helen sighed. Her head drooped. Somebody was going to get slapped in a minute. "Excuse me?" she asked in a sarcastic voice.

"Victoria isn't here."

Chapter Fourteen

"Helen, we both know there's no way I can do anything until she's been gone for a couple of days. Besides, shouldn't this aunt of hers be the one to file a missing person report? Why the hell are you getting mixed up in this?"

Beth's voice conveyed restraint and patience — hardly surprising, since Helen had tracked her down, after several tries, at Terrie's house. Terrie had prepared dinner for Beth, apparently, before Beth had to go on duty. Candles and wine and mood lighting, no doubt, Helen thought sourly. And no, it wasn't good that Helen was interrupting their romantic evening, probably complete with Beth in butchly uniformed regalia, with her nagging phone calls about a missing young woman.

Across the table from Helen, Aunt Edna and Bobby sat over the remains of a meal of hotdogs and packaged macaroni-and-cheese. Bobby had regaled them over dinner with finger-painted portraits he'd done at the Independent Living Center that morning. It was his first visit there today, courtesy of Roberts and Farrell and their more than generous contribution to the McCormick household. Actually, after hours in the car, Helen had found it a huge relief to sit for an hour on the sofa while Aunt Edna boiled hotdogs and Bobby talked excitedly about the center, his new friends, and the different projects he'd embark on soon. Helen had left Biloxi at four-thirty, again broken traffic laws to get to Tupelo by seven, and found that Aunt Edna had been waiting dinner for her.

"See, Helen, this one is you." Bobby proudly placed a sheet of stiff construction paper on her lap. The portrait was interesting, Helen thought — swirls of red and black around a muddy-looking person with staring eyes and wide open mouth. What exactly had Bobby seen in her lately? Did those whorls of angry color accurately reflect her personality? Not to mention the stunned expression on the indeterminate facial features. "That's really good, Bobby," she said with more brightness than she felt at that moment. "And who's this?"

Stupid question, Helen realized — the pitch-black background and stark white reclining figure bore lines and tubes snaking out into the darkness surrounding it. "That's Daddy," Bobby said in a muted voice as he carefully held this picture by its edges. "That's from when he was sick." His doughy face folded in confused sorrow, then unexpectedly and suddenly lightened with a weak smile. "But tomorrow Miss Nancy said I could draw a pitcher of him in heaven, where he is now."

Helen nodded. "That's good. I would like to see that." And it probably was good — perhaps the best way for someone as tragically stunted as her cousin, whose mind dealt only in tangibles, to come to terms with what had happened to his father. "Where's Aunt Edna?"

"Mommy? Mommy's here." Helen couldn't help a quick glance up from the rosy, angelic portrayal of a smiling, happy woman in a dress spangled with flowers to the actual subject, whose red face bent over a steaming pot in the kitchen of the double-wide trailer sagged with age and sorrow and exhaustion. "See? This is her favorite dress, but I didn't have room for all the flowers on it."

"I think I like this one best of all." Helen listened with only a small portion of her mind to Bobby's happy prattle. For the most part she was wondering how best to approach Beth with the problem of Victoria. And it wasn't until almost eight-thirty, after the hotdogs were eaten and the macaroni scraped out of the pot, that she decided to bite the bullet and see if Beth was hanging out at Terrie's place.

Unfortunately, just because she'd located Beth didn't mean Beth was going to help her, as it turned out. "Come on, Helen, you know there's nothing I can do. At least tell me what happened today."

Helen glanced into the kitchen. Aunt Edna, after refusing Helen's offer of assistance, busied herself with cleaning up the supper remains. Now she bent over the macaroni pot, furiously scrubbing at the dried cheese, but Helen was sure she was listening intently to every word uttered over the phone. "I can't really get into that right now," Helen finally said.

She heard a heavy sigh from the other end, followed by muffled conversation between, presumably, Terrie and Beth. Then, "All right. Terrie says why don't you come over for coffee? I don't have to go on duty until eleven, so we have an hour or two to talk about it."

Helen let her rattle off the directions to Terrie's house

without interruption. After all, Beth certainly didn't need to know she'd already been there, done that — or was it she'd done Terrie? At any rate, Helen drove back over the same route she'd taken the previous night with a nagging sense of discomfort that only increased when she parked in front of the low, rambling, nondescript house. Just like last night, Helen was too disconcerted to take in much beyond the fact that the house was deceptively ordinary from the outside and palatially luxurious inside. Like Terrie Muncie, Helen realized as she stepped for the second time across the threshold, the house "passed" in polite society, hiding its interior successfully behind a facade of everyday normality.

At least the living room was better lit this time around. Helen waited for her cup of coffee on the same cushion where she'd fucked Terrie approximately twenty-four hours ago. Weird to have a perfectly made frothy cappuccino, Helen mused, sitting next to your best friend whom you've betrayed — and on the same piece of furniture where that betrayal took place. She sipped, ruminated on the surreal touch of the situation, and tried to pay better attention to her surroundings. Now she could see the artwork on the walls. No artist she recognized, but they certainly had the look of originals, mostly abstracts in simple, clean lines that mirrored the sparse furnishings and provided an appropriately understated backdrop for the view of the hills behind the house.

Beth was, indeed, garbed in her uniform. Her gun lay on the coffee table, along with her wide-brimmed hat. She plopped down on the sofa next to Helen and tasted her coffee. "That's good, sweetie. Just like I like it." She smiled at Terrie.

Terrie perched on the edge of a chair and grinned at them both. Tonight she was tastefully clad in baggy jeans and simple short-sleeved black shirt decorously buttoned up to the collar. The black set off her fiery red long hair, and Helen had to look away before she started remembering what it was like to run her fingers through those tresses. She cleared her throat and said, "So you don't think there's anything I can do to help Victoria Mason?"

Terrie moved to sit on the floor next to Beth, leaning against her lover's legs, her eyes focused on Helen with an enigmatic stare. Helen paid strict attention to her coffee. She was surprised — she hadn't thought it would be this hard to stay focused on the problem at hand, and she didn't know if it was guilt or excitement getting in the way.

Meanwhile Beth was talking. "If she's not a minor, and there hasn't been enough time elapsed, then I don't see how normal procedures would be of any use. All I could do is try to unofficially keep my eyes and ears open, talk to the other guys on my shift tonight, see if we can come up with anything. I know a couple of the boys who'll be working down that way tonight. I'll ask around. Anyway" — she leaned over to put her empty coffee cup on the table, earning a lingering stroke on her arm from Terrie — "you never did really explain what happened today."

Helen managed to give Beth an edited version of Victoria's visit to the Biloxi police, her unhappy reunion with the ebullient Aunt Josephine, her alternating fits of rage and sorrow. "I'm just worried about her," Helen finished, keeping her attention on Beth and avoiding Terrie's stare. "I'm scared that in her state she'll do something to hurt herself."

Beth cleared her throat. "My god, Helen, you've had a busy week. Beaten up in Biloxi on Thursday, and this is — what now — only Saturday night? I can't imagine what kind of weekend you'll have."

Helen shrugged and tried to smile.

But Beth just stared. "By the way, I heard those two guys the Biloxi cops pulled in along with you were checked into the local hospital early this morning. Right here in Tupelo."

"Really?" Strangely enough it wasn't hard to fake innocent surprise, even when faced with Beth's penetrating gaze.

"Yep. Interesting, isn't it? They're a long way from home.

But they weren't hurt bad, just a few cuts and bruises. Made a lot more fuss than it was worth." Beth's expression, blank and indifferent, no doubt hid an inner conviction that she was involved, Helen knew. Still, they were both playing along nicely for the time being.

"Why were they in the hospital?" Helen asked. The official version seemed to be that they'd both gotten drunk and had had a nasty brawl in the motel. That was straight from the mouths of Jimbo and Tommy, then — Helen breathed an inward sigh of relief that they'd decided not to say anything about Helen and Victoria. Stood to reason, anyhow. Not that she and Victoria were out of danger. Neither man had been seriously injured, and they were probably going to continue their quest at the behest of whoever paid Dixie Mae.

"Truth is stranger than fiction, I guess." On that note Beth stood up and gathered her hat and gun. "Time to go protect and serve, honey."

"Thanks, Beth — I appreciate anything you can do about Victoria Mason." Helen stayed on the sofa as Terrie and Beth sauntered to the foyer. She didn't need to witness the fond farewell between the enamored couple. To distract herself Helen got up from the sofa and wandered around the room. Shelves lined with books took up whatever space wasn't covered with paintings and niches for small sculptures. To cover the unmistakable sound of smooching Helen pulled a volume off the shelves at random. "Hurry up," she muttered to herself, sighing with relief when she heard the door open and close.

She felt rather than saw Terrie come back, quiet as a cat, into the living room. "Finding anything interesting?" Terrie asked.

Helen, book in hand, turned around. Surprise, surprise — the top two, no, three buttons of Terrie's shirt had somehow gotten loose. "I guess it's interesting that you have so many books on genetic engineering."

Terrie shrugged. "All part of the public relations job. Not

that I understand any of it, mind you — it's just necessary to have a feel for the business in order to get more customers."

Helen replaced the book on the shelf and rummaged through a few others, buying herself a few minutes before looking at Terrie again. "So Roberts and Farrell are on the forefront of modern agriculture? Engineered potatoes, patented seeds, things like that?"

Terrie voice was bored when she responded. "Same as every other major agribusiness in the country. Buy our products and you won't have to invest huge sums in pesticides, since we can put the pesticide right in the seed."

Helen turned around and leaned her back against the bookshelf. Terrie's red hair fanned out across the back of the sofa, spilling over her shoulders and reflecting the light in a dazzling display. "Sounds pretty straightforward. I'll bet you have a lot of success selling Roberts and Farrell products to prospective buyers."

"Well" — Terrie got up and slinked over to Helen — "I don't rely on scientific information alone, of course. I am good at what I do. I usually have only satisfied customers." She placed her hands lightly on Helen's shoulders, her fingers teasing across Helen's skin near her throat. Helen could almost taste her as she leaned forward. "Sometimes it's all in the presentation."

"Is that so?" Their kiss was hot and hard and long. Helen pulled away and moved to the center of the room. "There's big money in genetic engineering these days, isn't that right?"

"What is this, high-school biology?" Terrie laughed but there was tension beneath it. Helen wished the lighting in the room were brighter — she would love to see the other woman's expression more clearly.

"Just curious. Unfortunately I can't really stay for your sales pitch tonight, Terrie."

"But it won't be a sales pitch. Not for you, Helen." Terrie stood behind her and circled Helen's waist with her arms. "You're already part of the team, in a manner of speaking."

"No." Helen gently disengaged from Terrie's embrace and moved toward the door. "I've done quite a few shitty things in just a few days, Terrie, and I'm not going to continue this evening."

"What the fuck are you talking about?"

Helen looked back in surprise. The switch from sex kitten to furious spoiled brat was instantaneous and complete. "I've already fucked things up with my relatives, with Victoria, and now with Beth, whether Beth realizes it or not. I'm done."

"And what are you going to do now — run to Beth and tell her everything? Somehow I don't think that's a good idea." Terrie tossed her hair back and a small, tight, satisfied smile appeared on her lips. "For one thing she won't believe you."

"What are you going to do, send Jimbo and Tommy after me again? Tell them to beat up my Aunt Edna?"

"I didn't —"

"Just shut the fuck up, Terrie. I don't really care if you yourself sent those goons to the motel or if you called some other asshole and they handed out the instructions. Doesn't matter anymore." Helen kept moving to the foyer as she spoke, turning her back on Terrie. "As far as I'm concerned the game is over."

"You think so?" Terrie followed her into the foyer, scornful amusement replacing anger in her voice.

"I know so." Helen opened the door, letting it slam against the wall, and stepped out onto the front porch.

"And how is that?" Terrie stood framed in the light coming from the door, her lovely slim body exquisitely posed for full effect on the unwary. "Just what special information do you have that makes you so sure?"

Helen stepped back to the threshold. The tightness that had been growing in her gut for the past hour hardened into something cold and sharp and untouchable. "Because," she said softly, with a smile, "I will rip your pretty little red head off your slender neck if something else happens to someone I care about. Do you understand me? I don't give a fuck about

187

myself anymore," she went on, stepping back into Terrie's house as Terrie withdrew, suddenly wary. "My life has been screwed for some time now, and nothing matters to me. Does that sink into your selfish brain, Terrie? Do you understand? I don't want money, I don't want to fuck you, and I don't care about my safety. What I care about is the truth."

"No matter what that truth is, Helen?" Terrie responded, recovering a bit of her cool surface. "Truth can hurt like hell. Are you sure you're ready for it?"

"Anything is better than this, Terrie. I'm tired of your bullshit and I'm tired of being nice about it." Helen went back outside and headed for her car. Of course Terrie trotted after her. Helen rolled down her window as she started the engine. "What is it? Final words of wisdom?"

"Just some advice, Helen." Terrie gripped the window with both hands. Helen looked up to see that smug smirk on her face again. It took all Helen's will to keep from slapping that smile off Terrie's pretty features. "I'd be careful about doing any more digging around what happened with your uncle."

"Yeah, right. And you're going to give me another list and send me off on another wild-goose chase. Seems like I've heard that one before."

"You really don't know what you're fucking around with, do you?"

Helen didn't wait to hear more. She sped off down Terrie's driveway and headed for the trailer park, trying to sort out what had just happened. Truth was, she still wanted Terrie — wanted the woman's taste on her tongue, wanted the feel of her hair and the scent of her skin, wanted the luxurious melting sense of Terrie's body as it pounded into orgasm. Somehow the fact that Helen hated Terrie Muncie only made it more desirable. Go figure. Helen felt her hands shaking on the steering wheel and forced herself to breathe, to reach for some kind of calm, to slow the fuck down before she got a ticket from Beth or one of Beth's comrades in arms. By the time she reached Aunt Edna's place Helen had managed a semblance of peace. At least she wasn't trembling with mingled rage and desire when she parked in front of the trailer.

Just as well she had herself under some kind of control, since there were a couple of state trooper vehicles parked next to Uncle Loy's dilapidated green pickup. Lights flashed red and blue across Edna's scraggly flower beds. The wolfhounds in the next yard stood sentinel in their usual silent stance of alert hunger, ready to become predators at the first hint of blood. Not to mention the curtains flickering open and shut on the trailers all around the park as Aunt Edna's neighbors noted yet another exciting drama unfolding at the McCormick place.

Helen didn't know whether she should be relieved or worried that Beth Wilks stood in the middle of the living room, notebook open and pen ready. Helen wove a path between the officers to take her place by Edna's side. Bobby stood in the corridor, bobbing in confusion, eyes bleary with interrupted sleep and mouth working in a buildup to some kind of outburst.

"Beth, I know you'll tell me what is going on," Helen said, standing next to the sofa with arms folded. Aunt Edna, her face bearing the countenance of someone to whom nothing else could astonish, looked at her niece like she was an exotic zoo animal.

Beth cleared her throat and looked back at her fellow troopers. Somehow that seemed to signal something to the others, and with murmured apologies they all moved outside, the thin flooring shuddering under their heavy boots and the knickknacks rattling on the flimsy shelves that lined the sitting room.

"Helen, honey — they were asking where you were. I don't understand —"

"Mommy, I'm scared!" Bobby finally broke out in the expected moan of confused frustration, one meaty fist pounding on the wall in a repeated thud that echoed

189

throughout the trailer. "Why are they here? Mommy, they have guns!"

Edna hurried to try to pacify her son, ignoring Beth's apology. "Helen, let's go outside for a minute."

Helen managed to contain herself until they were standing on the gravel drive flanked by the other officers. Beth exchanged a few words with them in a low voice, and two of the men got into a patrol car and backed away. Beth's partner stood leaning against their car, muttering into his radio. Helen waited while Beth flipped through a few pages in her notebook.

"All right," Helen finally said through gritted teeth. "You win, the suspense is killing me. What the hell is going on? Why are you here?"

Beth kept her gaze fixed on the notebook as she spoke. "Trooper just outside Tupelo found a body by the highway about five hours ago. A woman, age roughly forty-five, long dark hair, five feet eight inches tall, one hundred twenty-five pounds. Anything sounding familiar to you?"

Helen felt her stomach drop. Thank god it was dark and they were standing outside the circle of light coming from the porch. "What's your point, Beth?"

"She's been identified as Clara Collins, also known as Dixie Mae. Known as a prostitute in Biloxi. She was beaten to death sometime after four this afternoon, according to the medical examiner."

Helen stood very still and hoped her face and breathing also presented a calm front to Beth and to her partner. "Why did you come out here to tell me this?"

Beth looked up. "She had no identification, no purse found with the body. They did the ID from her fingerprints. However, they did find some money in her pockets, which leads us to conclude that robbery was not the motive for her death."

"That doesn't explain why you're here." Did her voice sound as fake to Beth as it did to her? "Talk to me, Beth.

You've scared the hell out of Bobby and Aunt Edna — it better be for a good reason."

"Along with the cash was an ATM receipt. In cases where a death is involved, it doesn't take a lot of prodding to get a judge to issue warrants. The bank was very happy to comply, even at this late hour, with a request for the videotape showing people pulling cash out of the machine."

Helen swallowed hard and felt her body go into deep freeze. *Shit, the ATM receipt must have been in the wad of bills I shoved into her hand.* "I guess the Biloxi cops are getting familiar with my face by now."

"Helen, you're not under arrest yet. Just because she had your receipt doesn't mean you killed her — at least, not yet. But you're running out of time, fast." Beth's partner had joined them. His eyes were cold and dark and calculating, and his gaze never left Helen's face. "What is your connection to this woman?"

Helen shrugged and told them a condensed version that was partially true — how she'd heard this woman could help her in her search for the truth about her uncle. Leaving out Jimbo and Tommy — not to mention identifying Dixie Mae as the woman in the photograph — made for a much simpler story, Helen found. "So I gave her some money, thinking she'd talk to me if I offered some cash."

"Did she tell you anything useful?" the partner asked — first time he'd spoken to Helen directly.

"Nope. No one down there did. Go ahead, ask around — I talked to a lot of people at the Athenaeum this afternoon."

"Okay. Thanks for your help, Helen." Beth flipped her notepad shut and headed for the patrol car.

"That's it? You aren't going to warn me not to leave town?"

"No. Not yet. Just try to stay out of trouble."

"I always do."

"Then try harder." They were gone.

Of course neither Beth nor her partner were satisfied with

the story, but there was not much else they could do about it. Not yet, anyway. As she watched them drive off Helen knew Beth was right. She had only a few hours before they'd try to bring her in with whatever they could.

Helen stood for a long time by the fence separating her from the wolfhounds. Her side ached with exhaustion, all the healed muscles jerking painfully with each step. In a few more hours the sun would come up. Beth was right — there wasn't a whole lot to do right now, and given her own exhaustion maybe Helen should just sit the weekend out. The dogs drooled and panted while she ruminated. They moved in bursts of jerky energy and expectation as Helen finally pushed away from the fence and started for the trailer.

"Relax, guys, you have to wait in line," Helen told them as she went inside to face Aunt Edna.

Chapter Fifteen

The ancient librarian scowled at Helen from across a pile of books with cracked bindings and loose sheets. "No, I haven't seen her. What makes you think I would?"

Helen stared back. The librarian was right. Why the hell would Victoria Mason come back to this place where she'd been barely tolerated? Helen had been stupid to come here and get noticed. Sure as shit, the biddy was just waiting for her to get out of earshot before she notified the police that the weird out-of-towner who'd caused so much trouble already was back and asking questions.

Helen decided to give it another try. After a restless Sunday cooling her heels and fretting over Victoria, which left her feeling like a wrung-out washrag, she'd made for Biloxi early Monday morning — more than anything to get out of the trailer, where she feared that any minute a solemn-faced Beth Wilks would arrive with a nice new set of handcuffs that had Helen's name on them. Even worse than waiting for her own arrest was the cold silence emanating from Aunt Edna. Helen simply couldn't get over the change in a woman she'd always considered to be warm and generous and affectionate. Had any of that been real, all those years? Had her dear devoted Aunt Edna been taken over by the pod people, perhaps? Of course, dear devoted Aunt Edna had been through a lot lately — Helen couldn't really blame her for keeping her distance from the family pariah. Especially since that family pariah might still fuck up her chance to get her money from Roberts and Farrell. Wait a minute, Helen warned herself as she gathered her wits for another go-around with the librarian — that wasn't fair.

Not hard to believe that the shriveled old bitch guarding the date stamps was a pod person. Her bright red lipstick, far too dark for her faded skin, cracked around the edges of her mouth as she pursed her lips in disapproval. "It's just that I'm very worried about her," Helen said, smiling, putting what she hoped was a feminine note of pleading in her voice. "What with her father passing away like that, and losing her job and all — I just hoped maybe you'd have some idea of where she might have gone. Didn't she have any friends? People that used to visit her here at the library? Maybe a boyfriend she talked about."

The librarian sniffed and then spiked a stack of overdue slips on a metal rod. "All I heard that girl do was complain about everything. Too bad-natured to have friends, you ask me." She turned her mean glare back at Helen. "And if she did have a boyfriend he was probably no good, just like her."

Helen shook her head in dismay. Maybe by appealing to the witch's malice she'd make some headway. "Kids today," she sighed, appalled at how genuine her lament sounded, even to her. "They run around without any respect for anyone. But if you think about how she was brought up, well —" She shook her head again, inviting comment from the other woman.

"I think she may have some relatives from New Orleans, or some such place. Her mother's people. She wasn't from here originally, you know."

That must mean Aunt Josephine of the gold chains and the big bosom. Last night she'd been mystified but not terribly excited about her niece's disappearance. "Oh," Josephine had said airily with a wave of her beringed hand, "she probably went off to be with her friends. You know — spend some time with them before she comes back to New Orleans with me." After that remark it was right back to cake and coffee with Doris and Bob. Doris at least had insisted on calling the Biloxi police, who had of course told her the same thing Beth had later. But Doris seemed a bit overwhelmed by Josephine. After all, kids will be kids, right? Seething, Helen had left them and gone back to Tupelo.

And Helen hadn't been able to arouse anyone to any further interest in the subject. Surely this librarian, sour old puss though she might be, felt something about the girl — particularly in light of the terrible tragedy she'd just experienced. "Maybe Victoria just needs a little bit of help and comfort. I mean, needing her mother and all. I take it her parents were divorced?" Helen went on, hoping to light a fire under the old girl somehow.

Unable to resist the bait, the librarian glanced around the room. They were still alone — the literati of Biloxi having apparently decided to sleep in. She leaned forward and Helen got a whiff of her sour breath when she said, "Her mother died in that awful fire, you know, and that's when Bill Mason started drinking. She should have been at home with that baby, minding her own business and taking care of her husband and child. It was just a question of time before he did himself in, you ask me."

Helen let her eyes widen in conspiratorial interest. "Suicide? Her father killed himself, then?"

"That's what everyone is saying." She leaned back with a satisfied expression on her prim face, pleased to impart the tragic news to a stranger. "Like I said, just a matter of time. Probably the girl will come to nothing good, too."

That was it. Helen drew back, hoping the old woman didn't see her revulsion. She wasn't any help, anyway. "Thank you," Helen murmured. She wandered off through the empty stacks, trying to decide what to do next. Where would a girl like Victoria go? It seemed that, except for the all-too-present Aunt Josephine from New Orleans, she really was alone in the world. No wonder she'd latched on to Helen as a way out of this little slice of hell. It must have seemed like her only hope.

Helen froze in the middle of the biographies, surrounded by dusty copies of lives that had mattered to someone, somewhere, once upon a time. Maybe Victoria and Helen were a lot alike — maybe Helen had clung to the image of her perfect aunt and uncle all these years in the same way Victoria had harbored hopes of leaving Biloxi for the golden paradise of California. Had Helen's image of Edna and Loy and Bobby been just as false, just as overblown as Victoria's gaudier dreams of escape under Helen's protection? Was the trailer on the edge of Tupelo the same kind of fantasy that Berkeley represented for Victoria? Then perhaps Aunt Edna's behavior — so cold, so remote, so formal — wasn't so strange and mysterious after all. Quite possibly Helen had never seen, really seen, the woman that was Edna McCormick. She'd only seen a source of comfort for herself, a place she could run when she wanted strokes and warm, fuzzy feelings.

Helen plopped down on a metal stool that lurched under her weight, skidding over from the biographies to fiction. She stared at the rows of novels without seeing the titles. Maybe

Aunt Edna hated her. Maybe she would have preferred to mourn her husband's death without her needy, whining, self-absorbed niece taking center stage in all her drunken melodrama. Maybe she just wanted a bit of peace and quiet for herself in her final years, and some stability and security for Bobby. Maybe she just wished Helen would go away and didn't know how to ask for what she wished.

Helen leaned against the cold, hard metal of the shelves, some thin, sharp volume wedging an uncomfortable ridge in her spine. As soon as she was allowed by the powers that be, Helen would take herself back to California. She'd do her best to keep looking for Victoria, but from a distance. Might hire local investigators, perhaps Beth could recommend someone there. And she'd never breathe another word about Uncle Loy's shenanigans to anyone. Didn't matter if she never understood the circumstances of his whoring around. Loy and Dixie Mae were both dead, and there were no answers. Edna didn't want them, and Helen refused to keep digging at the wound any more. Fine. She'd take Terrie's advice and leave well enough alone.

"Shit." That book was gouging her in the back. Helen stood up, rubbed the sore spot on her shoulder blades, and peered down the dark corridor. Ironically enough, the room just ahead of her was the fabled Robert E. Lee Room. And damned if it wasn't wide open for visitors, after she'd kicked up all that fuss.

As she stood amidst the books, tired and dispirited, Helen heard the unmistakable rumble of thunder sounding outside, followed by a hard gush of rain hitting the library roof. "Whatever," she muttered, walking toward the display. She wasn't in a hurry to get back to Tupelo, and she didn't want to drive along the Gulf in a thunderstorm.

It wasn't all that exciting, really — hardly worth all the effort she'd expended to see it over the past couple of days. BILOXI: PAST, PRESENT, AND FUTURE proclaimed the placard propped on an easel just inside the door. Sure enough, there was a whole series of faded newsprint pictures of historic sites around Biloxi, along with small replicas of some of the old mansions as they'd stood at the turn of the century. Faces, mostly white and whiskered, a few females, even fewer black ones, dotted the display of Biloxi's prominent citizenry through the generations of civic pride. There was even a small tribute to the local paper and its panoply of awards for meritorious public service. And was that a picture of Bill Mason in his salad days? Jesus, that must have been terrible for Victoria to see every day — an evil reminder of what she and her father had lost.

Helen turned away from that display case only to come upon a series of photographs of the Beauregard Resort Hotel. Not that it mattered any longer. She glanced idly at the row of pictures and the captions beneath them. Only the final set of articles mentioned the fire that had destroyed this landmark of Biloxi. There was even a paragraph describing how Lorraine Mason had died while helping others to safety. Apparently she'd been the one and only victim. The final caption read, BILOXI LOSES HISTORIC HOTEL. *The crown jewel of Biloxi's historical landmarks, the Beauregard Resort, will be only a memory, said a spokesman for the Mayor at a press conference held today,* the article began. There were a few further sentences about the remorse over Lorraine Mason's death, and the decision to forego rebuilding the historic site given the tragic loss of her life.

Tragically, Lorraine Mason lost her life seeking to save the lives of others, the article bemoaned. The photograph of Victoria's mother was faded and fuzzy, giving only hints of the dark eyes Victoria inherited. Long, dark hair hung about a smiling face, but beyond the shy smile and the dark eyes Helen could tell nothing from the face. Did she realize what was happening, Helen wondered, as the smoke overcame her ability to breathe? As flames leaped around her? Did she have thoughts of her husband and her baby daughter as her consciousness faded into death?

Helen stared, transfixed, at the picture of the ruins left after the fire. Most of the article bemoaned the fact that Biloxi had lost one of its finest pieces of architecture in the flames, but a nearby article mentioned how R and F would be locating their new research and development department up in Tupelo.

Research and development. That's what Terrie kept talking about last night — how she went around to all the fat cats in the world of agribusiness and persuaded them to buy into the wonderful new engineered seeds that Roberts and Farrell offered. Helen stared grimly at the article, the words printed there blurring as her anger increased. Must have been some kind of delayed reaction, but suddenly Helen felt an enormous rage boil up inside her. She'd been too exhausted and too worried about Victoria's disappearance to let herself get mad yesterday.

Well, it was a different day now. Helen marched out of the Robert E. Lee Room, away from the dusty remnants of a murky past, and went back to the old woman hovering like a shriveled insect over the information desk. Turning on her last bit of polite charm, Helen managed to talk her way into the use of a viewing machine that allowed her to peruse roll after roll of microfilm containing back issues of the Tupelo and Biloxi newspapers. All the while her grim determination increased — she had to get something on Terrie Muncie, on Roberts and Farrell. It might be the only way to cover her own ass, what with the murder of Dixie Mae and the way Victoria had so conveniently vanished.

It took her several hours, but Helen barely noticed the passage of time. It seemed she was completely alone in the library. The only sounds were the clattering of the librarian through the stacks, trundling her creaking wheeled metal cart loaded with books and magazines, and the drumming of rain on the roof interspersed with the odd burst of thunder. By the time Helen had gathered what she needed, the sun was out and her stomach rumbled with hunger. She sat there, surrounded by notes scribbled on an odd assortment of scraps, staring at the titles before her without really seeing them. It was all there, right in front of her — she'd just been so blinded by her concern about Uncle Loy's feet of clay that she hadn't noticed where truth lay hidden.

Not that it completely made sense, yet — at least not her uncle's involvement. What was clear, however, was that the Roberts and Farrell research and development department, the center of their gradual entry into the world of genetically engineered food, appeared after the fire at the Beauregard Resort. After the receipt of an enormous amount of insurance money, after a decision by the board of directors not to rebuild this historic site, after having any investigation into the cause of the fire stifled in a maze of red tape and deliberate ignorance, R and F had been able to forge ahead with getting a toehold on the new age of high-tech agribusiness.

Stock prices for R and F had been steadily plummeting for months prior to the fire. A few months after the fire, though, that trend had reversed. Helen was no financial wizard, but anyone with eyes who took the time to squint at the Dow Jones figures and read between some of the lines in the financial sections could discern a shift in the company's fortunes. Big money — that's what this was all about. Nothing new there, and nothing terribly ingenious about her discovery. Anyone could have seen it. Bill Mason most certainly had. So why hadn't people said anything at the time?

Helen leaned back in her chair and looked out the window on the wall opposite. Through its streaked glass she could see the sun shining brightly. Two birds, some kind of large, seafaring predators, soared like black slashes against the backdrop of gray and white from sun and storm, wheeling out to the Gulf, cawing at one another or at the sky or water. She followed their wavering path as far as her eyes could see, wishing her thoughts had as much sense of direction as the birds did. All right. Forget about Uncle Loy for a minute — she might never know what the hell his part was in this, anyhow — just think about R and F and what they're up to, she lectured herself.

The insurance money from the fire had financed the company's start in a whole new direction of technology, a brand of technology that was, while perhaps morally questionable, certainly profitable. Bill Mason had not had to look too hard to figure it out, if Helen herself could see the connection. It stood to reason that plenty of other people could see it, too — from insurance investigators to police to R and F employees. So why the hell hadn't anyone said a damn thing about it?

Money. If Roberts and Farrell folded up and left town, or left the state of Mississippi, huge segments of society would be affected. Employees by the hundreds or perhaps thousands laid off. Comfy CEOs suddenly pushed out of their big suburban houses and their fancy cars. Potential customers, from small family farmers to cooperatives to larger corporate agricultural concerns, all moving off to other companies. This way, though, with the influx of cash, everybody was a winner. People stayed on their jobs at R and F — including Uncle Loy. The suits at the top would, among a select few, pocket tidy sums in specially earmarked "bonuses" while keeping their nice jobs and nice houses and nice reputations. And with the release of newly engineered cash crops, folks down on the farm would be neatly hogtied to a brave new world of controlled sowing and reaping. Contracts for seed, patented production of food, more and more control of the land, and the food supply in the hands of fewer and fewer people. And only a handful of loonies no one took seriously — the organic farmers, the tofu eaters, the commies and conspiracy nuts — would ever complain. Just a few big, noisy mouths served up for laughs on the nightly news.

Why bitch about it, then? Who was going to complain when everyone came out ahead? Just Bill Mason, who at the time of the arson was in a position to make some trouble. Bill Mason, with his convenient drinking problem and his

201

irritating kid and his dead wife. Easy to take care of him, wasn't it? And it had worked, all those years. Years of the ace reporter corkscrewing deeper and deeper into alcohol and paranoia, dragging Victoria down with him. Shut him up and everyone makes a little money and no one gets hurt. It was an accident, right? They hadn't meant to kill anyone. Whoever set it had done so in a way that allowed a bit of time for people to get out with their lives, if not their possessions. All except one person. Helen had checked that first, in the sequence of events as related in the Biloxi paper. No other deaths, just some minor burns, cuts, and scrapes, and a bit of smoke inhalation. At the very least, a great deal of care had gone into the arson itself.

That fact alone set an uneasy stirring in her stomach. Helen was beginning to get a better picture of what had taken place, but she didn't like the way it was shaping up. To distract herself from the idea that was beginning to take shape in her mind, Helen stood up, knocking a couple of rolls of microfilm off the rickety table with her quick motion. The wrinkled prune shambled over, still pushing her noisy cart. Kind of like Marley clanking his chains, Helen mused as she scooped up her papers into a semblance of a neat pile. Wonder if she'll end up in the hereafter roaming the earth with that cart and its squeaky wheels, like Scrooge's partner did.

"Did you find what you were looking for?" The old woman looked down her nose at Helen. Her little eyes gleamed hard and maliciously, and her talonlike fingers tightened on the cart's handles. "You sure needed to look at a lot of microfilm." Her glance disapprovingly took in the small square boxes that sat open on the table.

"Don't worry, I'll put them all right back where you showed me." Helen managed one more bright smile and was rewarded with the sight of the cart and the librarian moving slowly back through the stacks, which echoed the squeaky wheels. The old bat's interruption was actually a welcome relief to Helen — she needed to sit and stare at nothing and think for a while, she knew. Away from everyone and everything. As she shoved the microfilm rolls back into their respective boxes and carried them in a stack back to the drawers where they had lain untouched for years, Helen saw out of the corner of her eye that a couple of other people had entered the library now. Perhaps, like Helen herself, they'd looked for a refuge from the storm. Better to leave now, she thought, shutting the drawers. Bad enough she'd had to ingratiate herself to that shriveled witch — she didn't want anyone else paying attention to her presence. Helen hadn't forgotten that Jimbo and Tommy were still out and about and that the woman known as Dixie Mae had turned up dead last night. Surely the librarian would spread the word as soon as she got over her pleasure at sharing gossip with a sympathetic stranger. And Helen had the feeling she wouldn't be very welcome any longer if she made a repeat visit to the Biloxi police for so much as a parking ticket.

She noticed a couple of teenagers leafing through some magazines near the information desk. Her pal, the old witch, was nowhere to be seen. That surprised Helen, who would have expected her to keep a close eye on the youngsters. An elderly man snoozed over the *New York Times*, snoring gently and riffling the pages with each breath. Another person was moving somewhere at the far end of the stacks where Helen had just closed the last drawer on the newspaper records, but the shelves were tall and the shadows deep. She couldn't see who it was.

Helen squeezed past the metal cart — had the old biddy gone to lunch? — and was immediately reminded of the first time she'd seen Victoria. The girl had been standing by the cart and staring with great interest at Helen's exchange with her curmudgeonly boss. Helen grimaced at the pain this thought gave her. For just a moment it was as if she could see Victoria herself, huddled against the piles of nondescript books and papers rotting with neglect, forgotten for years.

Helen blinked. Jesus — it really was her. Her clothes, the

usual somber display of gray and black with no color to break the dark monotony, bore signs of dirt and discomfort, clinging with wrinkles and streaks of dust to her slender frame. Helen hurried down the aisle after a quick glance over her shoulder. Still no sign of the librarian, and the other patrons seemed to be absorbed in reading materials.

"Victoria!" Helen hissed at her without meaning to, worry and relief battling with anger at the concern Victoria had caused. She grabbed her by the arm and led them both out of sight behind the shelves, surrounded by yellowing, musty county records no one cared about. Victoria was trembling beneath her grip, and Helen saw fresh tears glimmering in her eyes beneath the harsh light. She let go but blocked the girl's path so she couldn't take off again. She sighed and tried again, aiming for a softer tone. "Do you know how worried I've been? Why didn't you tell me you were leaving?"

"But — but I didn't leave. Not really." Victoria wiped her face, all vestiges of heavy makeup now gone. She hugged herself as if she were cold, and Helen saw that she was still trembling. Her glance darted around the library. "I don't think anyone saw me come in."

"Maybe not. Come on, we have to get out of here. Now." Without waiting for the girl to compose herself Helen took her by the hand — fuck decorum, she'd take hold of Victoria if she wanted to, dammit — and snaked a path back around the edges of the stacks, avoiding the trio of readers grouped near the information desk. Their luck held. The old librarian must have gone to the rest room or some such errand. Whatever the reason, the two women made it out the front door and into the parking lot.

The sun had burned away the last traces of the storm, and in its intense heat Victoria seemed to relax. Just being outside helped. She took deep breaths of the humid air as they got into Helen's car.

"Okay. You're going to be fine, Victoria," Helen said as she steered out to the highway fronting the Gulf. "Whatever you're running from, you don't have to worry. I'll get this sorted out. First," she went on, in high organizational gear, "we have to let Aunt Josephine know you're okay. I mean, she didn't have a clue what happened to you. And then I'll call Beth. We can stay with Aunt Edna —"

"Helen." Victoria's flat voice stopped her cold. Helen looked over at the girl, who stared blankly out the window at the blue-green water breaking on the white sand. "Helen, stop talking for one fucking minute and listen to me. Just listen to me."

Chastened, sorry she'd babbled in her relief like a damn scout troop leader, Helen shut up. She knew she wasn't going to like what she was about to hear.

"I saw them last night."

"Saw who?" And Helen knew the answer almost as soon as the words were out of her mouth.

"Jimbo and Tommy. Helen, they-they killed her."

Chapter Sixteen

Helen tried not to allow herself to get distracted by Beth's house while listening to Victoria talk about what had happened to her in the past forty-eight hours. It had seemed like a good idea to go to her ex-lover's place as a refuge from whatever the hell was after the girl, but despite the seriousness of the situation Helen found that she kept wondering if Terrie and Beth had fucked in every room of the house. It wasn't all that big a place, actually — one cramped bedroom, a small study that was not much bigger than a broom closet where Beth had her computer and some books, a living room that bled into a dining alcove, a galleylike kitchen. Wouldn't have taken them long to initiate each room with sex, Helen thought. Surely they'd screwed on this very sofa. She shifted uncomfortably on the cushions and wished she could get Terrie out of her head. Did Terrie like the faux southwestern décor of the house? The terra-cotta and sand motif? Maybe she couldn't care less. Certainly the understated luxury, the quiet comfort, owed something to her influence. Helen remembered Beth as cluttered and messy, ignoring her surroundings. Hell, if Terrie could whip Beth into shape maybe she could get the trains to run on time. Stop that, Helen warned herself. That was nasty, and Beth was going out of her way to be accommodating.

As she squirmed on the sofa, Helen stole a glance at Beth. Most of what Victoria was saying now was repeating what Helen had already heard in the drive back from Biloxi, although in the second recital the girl's thoughts and words were less garbled. It still sounded insane, worse than most conspiracy theories Helen had seen proclaimed from the tabloids in the supermarket. Beth slouched in an armchair facing the sofa, leaning her head on her hand, regarding Victoria over a steaming cup of coffee. Helen had a sudden flash of memory, this time of Beth instead of Terrie — Beth kissing her breasts, Beth tossing her head and moaning in orgasm, Beth stroking her thighs as she parted them with both hands.

And that was another train of thought Helen didn't need right now. If Victoria's story was true, then all of them were in grave danger. Helen needed to get her mind out of her crotch and pay attention to what was said and done here.

Especially since Victoria, quivering with shock and terror, huddled at the other end of the sofa in a big soft blanket provided by Beth, who had the night off. While Beth hadn't said so, Helen was certain she'd cancelled some prior arrangement with Terrie for the evening. The way she sat, her carefully controlled smile, the cautiously worded questions and comments — all pointed to Beth's irritation. Please, Helen said in silent plea, hoping her expression conveyed her feelings to Beth, please just give the girl a hearing — don't write her off because you're pissed off at me. She looked again at Victoria's pale, haunted face. Couldn't Beth see how serious this was? Whatever had really happened, Victoria believed her life was in danger. Even if Beth couldn't care less anymore about Helen — a thought that made Helen's heart twist in pain — maybe she'd care about this lonely kid. As far as Helen could see, she might be the girl's only chance, melodramatic as that sounded.

There was a brief silence as Victoria finished. Beth stood up and stretched and began to prowl around the room, giving them both a good look at her fit, muscular body. Even out of uniform she looked terrific, Helen thought with a pang. "All right, let me ask you a few questions."

Victoria glanced at Helen, then looked back at Beth. Helen had no idea what was going through Victoria's mind — she still looked scared out of her wits. Helen hoped Beth wouldn't go into state-trooper mode too deeply. Given the experiences of the past few days, it would render Victoria mute and helpless, making things sound even more ridiculous.

Beth leaned against the mantel and folded her arms. "You went back to your father's hideout on Saturday night, the burned-out building near Bob and Doris's house, looking for the rest of his files," she said.

Victoria nodded vigorously. "That's right. And when I got there, Jimbo and Tommy were already waiting for me. Like they knew I'd come."

"Okay. And they had all your father's files?"

"I don't know. The files were just gone, and they said they'd taken them — but I didn't see any papers or anything." Victoria's voice trembled. "Now I don't have anything left. He's dead, and all his work he was hiding is gone. There's nothing left now. All the stuff about my mom — it's gone. I don't even have any of those papers now." She shivered under the blanket and wiped fresh tears from her cheeks.

"You say they told you they'd killed Dixie Mae? Why are you still alive?"

"I don't know! I already told you!" She almost yelled in her fear and frustration. "Why won't you believe me? They told me they'd kill me too, if I ever said anything to anyone about all this. They just stood there, laughing at me. And Tommy — he took his knife and waved it at me — and I got so scared." Her voice faded into a whisper and she shut her eyes tight, as if to block out the visual memory of his threat. "And the other one, Jimbo, he kept trying to grab me. I just started running. I don't even know where I was going. I just had to get away from them. All day Sunday they kept me with them —"

"Where? Where did they take you?"

"I don't know! I can't remember how we got there! Just some old house out in the country!" Helen winced. Victoria wasn't lying very well right now. Okay, so Mutt and Jeff had taken her with them somewhere — then just let her go? This was all wrong, all wrong.

"And then you managed to run away late Sunday night?" Beth's face, a mask of indifference, told Helen she didn't believe a word of it either.

Victoria wiped her eyes and nodded. "They got drunk and passed out in front of the television set. I hitched back to Biloxi. It took hours and hours . . ." Her voice faded. Surely even Victoria realized how lame this all sounded. Helen wouldn't meet Beth's eyes. Terrific.

"Why didn't you go back to your Aunt Josephine?" Beth's voice had chilled another degree. Her face was stony and unyielding as she fixed her gaze on Victoria. Great, Helen thought, her stomach sinking in disappointment. If Beth refused her refuge, Victoria really had nowhere to go. Helen was afraid to take her to Aunt Edna's, but that might be her last resort. What else could she do? Okay, okay, figure out how to get her to Berkeley. Helen let her mind drift as Beth continued her interrogation. What the hell was she thinking — that she and Victoria could set up house? That she'd sponsor the kid through school, somehow, and save her from drowning in the morass where she'd been abandoned? Helen closed her eyes for a moment, wishing Beth had offered her a drink.

"Because Aunt Josephine hated my dad and would never, ever believe me. Just like you're doing." Victoria threw off the blanket and glared at Helen, her eyes flashing with anger. "I thought you said we'd be safe here, Helen," she said. "I thought you said your friend here would be able to help us. Well, she's just like all the rest. Just like Bob and Doris and Aunt Josephine. No one believes anything I say, and no one cares if I live or die."

"Look" — Beth moved away from the mantel and sat between Helen and Victoria — "Don't misunderstand me. You and Helen are more than welcome to stay here. It's just — well, what you're saying really doesn't make a lot of sense. I'm not doubting that you feel threatened, and of course losing your father has been a terrible, terrible event." Beth even reached out to pat the girl on the shoulder. Helen winced. The switch from mean cop to nice cop had been a bit too fast, and her gesture of comfort would probably just feel patronizing to Victoria.

But to Helen's surprise it seemed to calm her instead. She must be desperate, to let herself be deceived by this false gesture — and maybe the girl was just that desperate. Beth uttered a few more soothing phrases as she led Victoria to the bedroom. Helen stayed behind, not sure what her best move would be now. As she watched from the living room, she saw Victoria glance over her shoulder with a strange look in her eyes. Confusion? Longing? No, forget that one. Helen had to remind herself that she was merely Victoria's ticket out of Mississippi, nothing more. Not a pleasant reminder, but necessary. Fuck the knight-in-shining-armor crap. This was the real world, folks, and people did what they had to in order to survive.

Still, Helen found herself drawn into the bedroom after them. "Listen," Beth was saying, still in soothing maternal tones, "I think you're very tired and understandably distressed. Why don't you just lie down for a while — try to get some sleep, see if we can't get this all sorted out in the morning?"

"But Jimbo and Tommy! They might have followed us here, they might know where we are." Despite her protests, Helen could see that Victoria was weakening. The bed looked soft and inviting, no doubt. And even if it was in the home of a stranger, Beth's place was probably much more comfortable and calming than anything Doris and Bob or Aunt Josephine had to offer. It certainly beat the hell out of Aunt Edna's cramped trailer.

"Even if they did, they're not going to get past us. Right, Helen?" Beth turned to her for confirmation. Helen thought of the gun in Beth's holster, tucked discreetly behind the chair where she'd slung her uniform jacket. Then she thought of the gun she'd taken from Jimbo. Beth didn't know about that, and Victoria might have forgotten. It was stashed at the bottom of Helen's shoulder bag, beneath the papers that had spilled out of Bill Mason's file. "Right," Helen finally agreed. "I think between the two of us we can keep them from becoming a problem."

Victoria didn't respond. She wiped a shaky hand across her face, like a small child fighting off sleep, and lay back on the pillows after kicking her shoes off. "I just want to talk to her alone for a minute," Helen said to Beth.

"No problem." Beth closed the door quietly behind her and Helen was alone in the bedroom with Victoria.

"You're homos, right?"

Helen had to smile in surprise. In all this time, running up and down the state of Mississippi, chasing after this kid, chasing down illusions about her uncle, even chasing Terrie Muncie's ass, this was the first time the taboo topic had come up with Victoria. Helen on the edge of the bed, well aware that she was cloistered with a lovely young damsel in distress, maybe even a virgin, who was looking to her for some kind of comfort or help or presence. Too bad Victoria was so young. Then Helen rounded on herself with a flash of anger at her own irresponsible thoughts, looking away from those big dark eyes that seemed to be imploring something, anything, in the way of contact. Wishful thinking. Stupid thinking, more like it.

"Does it matter if we are?" Helen asked at last, unable to come up with witty repartee.

Victoria shrugged and snuggled down deep into the pillows. "I guess not. I just never met one before. Not a woman. A lesbian, I mean."

"Even if we are, that doesn't matter right now," Helen said, hoping they could put this discussion off for a while. She cleared her throat and pulled up her legs so she sat cross-legged on Beth's bed. "What does matter is sorting out what to do and where to go."

"Can't we just go to California? Can't we leave right now?" Excitement at the idea blossomed in Victoria's tired face and she sat up eagerly. "Get out of Mississippi forever?"

"I don't think we should make plans about going anywhere until you tell me the truth about Jimbo and Tommy and your father's files."

"What are you talking about?" Victoria moved back to the other end of the bed, all enthusiasm drained from her voice. She stared at Helen, her expression hurt. "You don't believe me, either, do you? Well, it happened just like I said it did. They were there, they threatened me, and I thought they were going to kill me, too!" She pounded a small fist on the pillow to emphasize each phrase. "Why did you try to find me, anyhow? Why not just let them do it? Get rid of me like they did my dad? And that other woman, the whore?"

"I'm not doubting that they are a threat, Victoria. You just shouldn't have lied about Tommy's knife." Helen spoke calmly, hoping that Beth wasn't listening intently, that their voices hadn't carried into the living room. "Remember? Obviously you don't. I was there when you cut Jimbo's neck

212

with his knife. I made sure there were no weapons for the police to find. I still have that knife, Victoria."

The girl had the grace to look ashamed. She curled up so her knees were gathered just below her chin, and she refused to meet Helen's serious stare. "I'm sorry," she said in a high, soft voice. "I just wanted to make sure y'all took me seriously. I mean, if I didn't make it sound scary and all you wouldn't believe me." Big fat tears squeezed out of her eyes and dripped onto the bedspread. "And now you don't believe me, anyway."

Now was no time to get all soft, Helen realized reluctantly. Now was no time to give in to the desire to take Victoria into her arms — not to make love, but to offer a kind of comfort, a human closeness in the midst of all the confusion and tragedy she'd been buried in for so long. Besides, sex wasn't what either of them was really looking for. "What about the rest of it?" Helen asked gently. "Is the rest of it exaggerated for dramatic effect, Victoria?"

"Look, I know what you're thinking, Helen. But I swear, they were there and they said they'd kill me. I believe them. You saw how they were, how they meant it when they came to the motel room!"

"Yes, I did. I also know you'll do or say anything to get out of here. No, let me finish." Helen deliberately lowered her voice and moved closer on the bed to Victoria. Beth had to know some kind of argument was taking place, and Helen didn't want to prolong this. "We are going to leave, and I am aware we have to watch out for these guys. Just get a little rest while I get things organized here, all right?"

"Then you believe me?"

Helen forced a smile. "I believe you're scared and you need to go. I'm going to try to help you do that. Okay?"

"Promise?" Helen felt Victoria's fingers creep into her hands, tentatively, light as insect wings fluttering with fragile fear across her palm. Oh lord. It would be so easy to let her hand close around the other one, to stroke this young woman into submission based on fear and sorrow and plain old exhaustion. To indulge in the fantasy that it was desire for Helen glowing in those dark eyes, and not the desire to get away.

It was fortunate for them both, Helen knew, that she heard Terrie Muncie's voice at that moment in the living room. The silence between Helen and Victoria was broken by soft murmurs from Beth and Terrie, deep in their own intense discussion. The two women sitting on the bed let go of one another, the moment of potential wrinkled away like old paper. Victoria looked at Helen with uncertainty. Maybe she wasn't aware of what had just happened, Helen thought. Or maybe she could hear the new voice in the other room.

"Just get some rest, okay? I'll get us both out of here in a few hours." Helen left the bedroom before Victoria could protest. In her haste to find out what the hell was going on she bumped right into Terrie, who stood near the bedroom door. Beth stood just beyond, her face dark with frustration. "What a nice, uh, surprise," Helen said with a falsely bright smile. "Funny — I don't remember inviting you to the party. Did our mutual friend here give you a call just now, tell you to come scurrying over and join the fun?"

Terrie kept her face calm and smooth. Helen had absolutely no idea what was going through her mind. "Actually, Beth called me right after you called and invited yourself over here," Terrie said, sauntering into the living room. Damn if she wasn't wearing that gorgeous deep shade of blue again, Helen thought, the one that made her eyes look like blazing emerald. "Beth was worried about you, not sure what to do. She's concerned you're going to make a fool of yourself, chasing this child all over the state and thinking she's somehow tied up with your uncle."

"Is that so, Beth?" Helen brazenly sat down next to Terrie. They both looked up at Beth, who stood in the middle of the room with anger on her face. "You call and Terrie comes running?"

"Knock it off, Helen. That's not it at all, and you know it. I just think you've gone over the deep end with this damn quest to smear your uncle's name. You're pulling this girl into your fantasy." Beth sat down in the armchair, her concern overriding her anger. "You're making yourself a pain in the ass to a lot of people. Roberts and Farrell among them."

Maybe Beth was being patronizing, maybe she wasn't. Helen was far too pissed off at this display of wise concern to care. She lounged back on the cushions and smiled at both women. "Yes, Terrie, what exactly is your interest in Victoria Mason? What brings you here? Surely not sympathy for her poor orphaned plight?"

Terrie shrugged, matching Helen's careless smile with one of her own. "I don't really have any interest per se, Helen. Beth called me because she needed some help. Help she knew I'd gladly give."

"And just what help would that be, Terrie?"

"I thought I'd help this young woman find a place to stay. Give her a job, maybe, help her get an apartment." She reached out to Beth, who snuggled in beside her. Helen tried not to gag at the sight of their arms entwining each other, the loving look Beth gave Terrie as she leaned her head on Terrie's shoulder. "Victoria Mason — that is her name, Victoria? — She seems to be all alone in the world, maybe close to a breakdown. Not surprising, given the circumstances Beth told me." Here Terrie gave Helen a show of affection in the way she smoothed Beth's hair and kissed her brow. "Poor thing, she's been through hell, I understand. I'm only too glad to be of help if I can." With that she turned an innocent gaze back to Helen, granting her another beatific smile. Beth smiled, too.

Helen stood up, unable to take another syrupy moment. "Yes, Terrie, you're such a helpful kind of person. Interesting, isn't it, how all of a sudden you're feeling concern for Victoria Mason."

"I don't know why you're being like this, Helen —"

Helen cut Terrie off. "Interesting, too, that her mother died in the fire at the Beauregard Resort. The only victim."

"Helen, I have no idea what you're driving at." Terrie leaned back into the cushions and rubbed gently with thumb and forefinger at the bridge of her nose. "What does a fire that took place twenty-odd years ago have to do with anything at all? Especially with Victoria?"

Beth glanced from Terrie to Helen and back again. She said nothing, but her expression was clear — she didn't like what was going on.

Terrie fixed her bright green eyes on Helen's face, something dark and unreadable shadowing her features. Helen looked down at her and kept talking, despite the knot growing in her own stomach. "I think the fact that Victoria's mother died in it may have some bearing on what's happening right now, don't you? And twenty-five years doesn't really make any difference when it comes to murder. There's no statute of limitations on that particular crime, Terrie."

Beth stood up, her face darkening to brick red. "Helen," she said through gritted teeth, "I think you'd better shut the fuck up right now. Both Terrie and I have gone out of our way to be helpful here —"

"Helpful to people like Jimbo and Tommy, too, aren't you?"

"Now wait just a damn minute, Helen!" Beth stepped away from the sofa. "You don't honestly believe any of that bullshit the kid was trying to feed us, do you? I grant you, she's hurt and confused, and she'll probably say anything, but —"

Helen ignored Beth's indignant speech and focused all her attention on Terrie. "I just bet you want to be helpful. Help Victoria right into something even worse than she's mixed up in now."

Terrie waved away Beth's furious protests. "No, sweetie,

let her talk. Let her rave. What did I tell you about her? She's really gone right over the edge." Terrie took Beth's hand and pulled her back down on the sofa. "Just let her rant. You had to see it for yourself, darling. I tried to tell you, but you needed to see her when she's like this."

Helen shook her head. "That's right, Terrie. You've got a really terrific con going on with Beth. Listen, Beth — I know what Terrie means when she offers to 'help' someone. From firsthand experience."

"What the hell are you talking about?" A flicker of confusion wrinkled Beth's brow, and she pulled slightly away from Terrie.

"Don't listen to her, sweetheart. She'll say anything to get you to pay attention."

"Even you don't really believe that, do you, Beth? No, I can see you don't. I got a sample of Terrie's 'help' just the other night, on that lovely expensive sofa. Got 'helped' pretty thoroughly, as a matter of fact. I can see why you go to her for assistance on a regular basis."

"Get the fuck out of my house." Beth moved closer to Helen until their faces were just inches apart. Anger and hurt seethed in her eyes, and she gritted her teeth in the effort to maintain self-control. For just a moment Helen thought Beth would slug her — then she realized that her fists were staying at her sides, balled up to contain her fury but not to lash out. "Get out, and take that insane girl with you. I don't ever want to see you again, Helen."

"No, Beth, no." Terrie was at her side, pleading and conciliatory. "Let's see what we can do for Victoria, okay? Helen — we don't need you now. We can take care of Victoria without you."

Helen looked from one to the other. "Okay. I'll get out. But I'm taking Victoria with me. I'll never let her get sucked into your games, Terrie." Great, she thought. Here I am putting on the armor after all. And tilting at windmills, too.

"Helen" — Beth's hand rose as if to strike her — "I'm warning you. One more word out of that filthy mouth and you won't be talking for a while."

"Don't worry, Beth. You won't see me or hear from me again. Thanks a lot for your hospitality." Helen went for the bedroom, but Victoria was already in the living room. Helen had no idea how much Victoria had heard, but right now that didn't matter. "Come on, we're out of here."

"Right." Victoria had somehow gained a calm strength — perhaps galvanized by hearing Helen fight for her? — and she moved quickly, gathering coats and shoes and bags. "I'm ready, Helen."

"Me too." Helen picked up her shoulder bag, aware of the weight of the gun inside. She turned around for one last look at the happy lovers. "You two deserve each other, Beth. It's been a real slice of life, Terrie."

"And where the hell are you going to run now, Helen?" Terrie left Beth standing in the living room and followed Helen and Victoria to the front door. "Back to your Aunt Edna, who's sick of the sight of you? Back to Biloxi and these imaginary hoodlums you plan to fight off with angry looks? There's no place for you to act tough now, Helen. Why don't you just go get drunk? That's what you do best when the pressure is on."

Helen couldn't stop herself. As if she were watching a movie of something that happened a long time ago, Helen watched her hand rise up and slap Terrie across that smirking mouth. She was rewarded with a look of utter amazement followed by red fury. Terrie made no move against Helen, however. She simply stood and stared. Beth was too stunned to do much but watch with her mouth hanging open.

"Come on." Helen grabbed Victoria by the arm and hurried out into the night before Beth could recover herself and come after them. Together they walked across Beth's lawn to Helen's car, the night dark and silent and oddly chill around them.

"Where are we going, Helen?"

Helen started the engine, gripped the steering wheel, and stared out into the night while the engine idled. "I have no idea."

Chapter Seventeen

Victoria Mason stood in the center of the small room, hands on hips, scowling at Helen. "I can't believe you brought me here," she muttered, kicking at her duffel bag with one Doc Martened foot. "First that awful motel, now this place."

Helen, lying flat on one of the twin beds, opened her eyes to offer Victoria a baleful glance. "They won't look for us here. I can just about guarantee you that."

"Of course. We're in the middle of nowhere, you haven't even told me what this place is, or why we aren't going right now to the airport to get out of here. Hell, you haven't even tried to talk to this aunt of yours and tell her what's happening. Thought you were so worried about them."

"Speaking of aunts, did you get hold of Josephine at the gas station?"

"Yeah. I don't even think she noticed I was gone, anyhow."

Helen closed her eyes again. Jesus, her head was splitting. She'd taken aspirin on their arrival a few minutes ago. She'd swallowed the pills by draining a can of too-sweet soda, hoping the sugar and medication would take over quickly, but the pain reliever hadn't kicked in yet. She didn't know if she could muster up the appetite to go after any of the bread and cold cuts they'd picked up at an all-night market on the way, but she knew she ought to try. "No point in calling Aunt Edna," Helen managed to get out. "She'd only try to find out where I was, and then Terrie Muncie would get in touch with her, all concerned and worried. Then that would be that. We'd have company before you know it."

"But where the hell are we?" Victoria plopped down on the other bed. Even with her eyes shut Helen could imagine the pout on her lips, the angry suspicion in her dark eyes.

"We're in a safe house. That's all you need to know for now."

"Yeah, really safe. Juvies and drug addicts and god-knows-what sleeping in the next room."

Helen opened her mouth to protest, then changed her mind. Given the circumstances — and Helen's suspicions about Victoria — the less said the better. It had been a stroke of luck that the supervisor in charge at the Warren County Step-Up Program, a halfway house for teens in recovery and rehab programs, remembered Helen as the woman who'd donated this building for their use. When Helen had inherited the house from an elderly relative, she'd never had any intention of using it herself. Better to let the place be used for community service. Especially since it had been originally built by her progenitors in part to cover up a murder.

The committees in charge of maintaining the Step-Up programs had done a lot with the place during the intervening years. Helen's late great-aunt would never have recognized her old house. Walls knocked out, new rooms where formerly the ancient lady had held court on crumbling furniture, additions taking up some of the old yard space. When she'd ushered Victoria inside, after a grueling drive from Tupelo toward the outskirts of Vicksburg, Helen had been concerned that old ghosts would haunt her and make it impossible for her to stay the night. But nothing had surfaced during the tense half-hour of waiting for the young, nervous woman at the front desk to get hold of her supervisor — no old ghosts, no painful memories, no wisps of long-dead lies floating through her mind. For all her fears, Helen hadn't picked up bad vibes — just a nasty tension headache.

"Why won't they let us even watch television or something? That skinny little bitch at the desk said I wasn't allowed to use the living room at this hour."

"Victoria, give it a rest. It's the rules of the house, okay? The kids here are really strictly supervised, especially when they first get into the program. If one of them saw a new arrival breaking the rules it might cause trouble."

"Well, I'm not one of their druggies, remember?" Something smacked down onto the floor — probably Victoria shoving things off her bed in a snit of temper — Helen didn't bother opening her eyes to survey the damage. "I'm not in their little goody-two-fucking-shoes program."

"Enough." Helen opened her eyes and turned on her side to look at Victoria. The aspirin was finally working. Her head didn't feel like someone had her brains in a sausage grinder, and she could look at her companion without grimacing. "We're damn lucky I thought of spending the night here. And damn lucky we're allowed to stay at all. This gives us a night to sort out our next step, and no one will think of looking for us here."

"Wherever the fuck 'here' is. I mean, I know we're near the state line, but where?"

"Why the hell is that so important? And who is it you need to call?"

Victoria started to untie her shoes, keeping her face turned away from Helen. "Just wanted to say good-bye to Aunt Josephine. I might not ever see her again, you know?"

"I see." Helen sat up. Sandwiches were starting to sound good. Victoria puttered away on the bed without speaking as Helen made a meal from sliced bread and ham and cheese. "Want one of these? You must be as hungry as I am by now."

"No, thanks."

Helen took a huge bite — god, that was good — and sat down on her own bed, watching Victoria as she chewed. "You sure? We got a long drive ahead in the morning."

"You think you might tell me where we're going? I mean, if it's not too much trouble or anything."

Helen finished off her sandwich in a few more big bites. She stashed the sandwich ingredients back in the grocery bag in readiness for taking down to the pantry. "I'll tell you my plans if you tell me the truth about Jimbo and Tommy."

Victoria dramatically rolled her eyes and fell back on the bed in exaggerated boredom. "For god's sake, Helen, just admit you don't believe anything I said. How many times do I have to go through this? They followed me out to the hiding place, they threatened me — oh, never mind. Why am I doing this?" She rolled to her side, her back to Helen. "Just forget it."

Helen went to the bed and jerked Victoria by the shoulder, forcing the other woman to face her. Victoria brushed her coal-black hair off her forehead and looked up at Helen with frightened eyes. "What, are you going to kill me, too? Might as well have everyone in on it, I guess," she said with a nervous attempt at laughter.

"Victoria." Helen let go of her and sat down on the bed beside her. "Jimbo and Tommy aren't the kind of guys who would not hurt you if they had the chance. Not if you were all alone out there in the dark, in a completely deserted place. They're both stupid enough and violent enough to try to take us out in that motel — you think I'm going to believe they'd leave you unharmed in that old ruin by your house? At the very least they would have raped you and beaten you, if not killed you outright." Helen listened to her stomach rumble. What the hell was the matter with her? Given everything that had taken place in the past couple of days she shouldn't be so hungry. Maybe it was a sign that she'd finally reached the saturation point with worry and fear. She moved off the bed and made herself another sandwich, aware of how odd this all would seem to anyone else. But she was just too worn out to care about that.

"But — but they threatened me. They said they'd kill me, just like they did Dixie Mae."

Helen snorted a laugh. This time she'd gone for roast beef. A little too dry, but still good. "It's not that I don't believe they killed Dixie Mae, probably on their own initiative this time. I mean, the woman hadn't given me any information. She was too smart and too experienced for that. But after fucking things up with us, they probably felt they had to prove they were still players in the game."

"I don't know what you mean." Victoria pulled the bedcover around her as if she were cold. Against the white sheets she looked small and dark and vulnerable. "What game?"

"Come on, Victoria. The same game and the same players that have been behind the whole sick story all along. The same setup that got my uncle involved, that got your father killed, that killed your mother, that pays off scum like Jimbo and Tommy to do their dirty work, that feeds off people like Dixie Mae, that pay women like Terrie Muncie enormous salaries." Helen pawed through her bag, wishing she'd picked up some Scotch or something from the market. Oh, well — she'd probably manage to sleep tonight, in spite of everything else. Her hands found the gun and the knife, still safe and sound and hidden from sight. That made her feel a little better. "Someone — apparently Roberts and Farrell — stood to make a lot of money from that fire at the Beauregard, the one that killed your mother and destroyed your father. They took the money, started a very profitable research and development department with it. R and F were able to pull themselves out of a downward spiral and make themselves players in a very, very big game. My uncle got dragged into it with that prostitute, and your parents got ground up like dog meat in the process. Nothing new here, folks — capitalism on parade as usual. Everyone makes money and no one important got hurt. Just one person who didn't matter a whole lot — your mother."

Victoria shook her head. Her eyes gleamed bright with tears, and her hands trembled on the sheets. "You make it sound like some big conspiracy, Helen. Like those people who go around talking about JFK and the grassy knoll. Or aliens in the government." She giggled. "Kind of like my dad used to talk." The laugh didn't match the expression on her face, though, and she gulped into silence, her wary gaze fixed on Helen. "Why would they do that, anyhow? Whatever my father knew he stopped talking about a long, long time ago when he started drinking himself to death. Even with all that stuff he used to say about my mom, no one would ever listen to him. Hell, I didn't even listen to him."

"Why? Is that what you're asking me?" Helen sat on the bed near Victoria. The girl cringed backward, putting as much space as possible between them. "Easy, Victoria. Profits. R and F financed themselves into a powerful position from the ashes of that hotel fire all those years ago. Libraries are wonderful places, Victoria — even the little excuse for one that you worked for until recently. It's all there, in the public record. How a little bit of arson, and the insurance money from it, dealt them a winning hand. And how they've managed to keep that quiet all these years. Particularly since your father was so easily scared of being steamrollered. The only

225

problem, of course, was that someone died. Your mother. That makes it murder. Which makes it worthwhile to cover things up as completely as possible. And your father — well, he wasn't much of a threat, was he?"

Victoria's face darkened into an angry red. "You shut up about my father. You — you never knew him, you never saw him like he really was."

Without thinking Helen touched Victoria, taking her by the hand in a sudden urge of sympathy. "I realize that. I know he had to be a threat to them because of his integrity and his honesty. Not to mention your father had the best motive in the world for being afraid of what these people would do. He knew exactly what they'd done, and why."

"What motive?" Victoria, still glaring, didn't try to pull away from Helen.

"You." Oh god, this was exactly the wrong thing to do, Helen told herself as her fingers caressed Victoria's palm. "Your father was trying to protect you, no matter what it might cost him as a reporter or as a man. I'm certain he buried himself in Biloxi because he was terrified of losing you, somehow. It's the one reason I can imagine that made him act the way he did. That made him swallow all that pain and keep going as best he could, hoping for a chance to get it all out in the open one day."

Victoria sat very still, her hand resting in Helen's grasp, her stare never leaving Helen's face. "But you still don't believe me?"

Helen shrugged and turned away, dropping Victoria's hand. She stayed on the end of the bed and picked at the fraying threads in the cover. "I think they came to see you at Bob and Doris's house last night. I think they offered you something — maybe money, maybe a ticket out of Biloxi, maybe a cushy job at R and F — if you would lead them to me."

She glanced over her shoulder at Victoria, who'd frozen into statuelike stillness. All anger had drained from her face, and the flush of rage paled into ghostly white. Damn, Helen thought with a sinking feeling in her chest. She'd hit the mark. If it hadn't gone down the way Helen had just described it must have come awfully close. She closed her eyes for a couple of seconds, feeling her armor crumble into dust around her. "Right? Isn't that what happened?" Helen continued, pressing Victoria for some kind of response. "You were supposed to find me and talk me into going someplace with you, or maybe take a chance that you could call them with solid information on where I was going and what I was finding out about them and their paymasters."

"You're crazier than they are," Victoria said with a false laugh. "After what they did to my father? And that whore? You think I want to make deals with people like that?"

Helen smiled and shook her head. "That won't wash with me. Look, you were ready to trust me, a total stranger, just on the off chance you could use me to get out of town. Why wouldn't you work something out with these guys if it would give you a ride to California, or wherever?"

"But — but my father —"

"I have no doubt they threatened you with god-knows-what, Victoria. It's perfectly understandable you'd go along with their plans if it meant your own safety. But to be honest with ourselves, we have to admit that it's entirely possible your father did in fact commit suicide. We'll probably never know. It just doesn't seem their style, staging a suicide like that. Beating a helpless woman to death — that sounds more like the Jimbo and Tommy we know. Even trying to beat your father in an alley, like what nearly happened when I stepped in."

Helen winced inside at the way her words seemed to slash Victoria like barbed wire. Maybe her harsh talk would break through the thin veneer the girl was trying to keep up; maybe Victoria would give in and be honest with her. That's the only way they had a chance. The only way she'd really be able to save Victoria. Maybe herself, too.

Victoria huddled in misery under the sheets. "Then why are you even talking to me?" she finally said in a voice barely above a whisper. "Why didn't you just leave me out there by the library, or tell all this to Beth or that woman Terrie?"

"Because I don't think you did any of this out of malice, Victoria. No, listen to me." Helen, unable to resist her feelings any longer, reached out to stroke her long black hair. "You've been terrorized. I understand that. You've experienced a terrible loss, you have no home now and no one to turn to, and your own life has been threatened. Who wouldn't try to save themselves in a situation like that?"

"Then — then you don't hate me now?"

Helen shook her head. With a sudden swift motion Victoria wrestled her way from beneath the sheets and sat next to Helen, leaning against her. Helen could feel her heart pounding, hear her quick warm breath, feel the soft skin of her arms. "I swear, I just wanted them to go away. I would have said anything, any lie at all, that would make them leave me alone. I never wanted to hurt you or anyone else." Her voice broke momentarily in a sob, and she wiped at her nose and eyes. "It was like you said — I'm not even sure anymore what I did tell them, just that I agreed to everything."

"This was at the burned-out house? The one behind your father's property?"

Victoria nodded. Her brief confession seemed to have calmed her, and she went on quietly. "Right. They took all his stuff and burned it, right in front of my eyes. There's nothing left of his files now — just what we have here. Nothing about my mom. Between them and the cops, I don't even have a picture of her. And — and you were right, Helen. I thought they wanted to rape me." Here her words shrank back into a whisper, and she shut her eyes tight as if to blot out the image of the two men in the darkness. "I ran back to the house. Aunt Josephine was watching television with Doris and Bob. I don't think they'd even noticed I was gone. I grabbed some stuff and walked back to Biloxi."

"All the way back to town? Jesus, why?"

Victoria smiled wanly. "Nowhere else to go. I ended up at the library, thinking maybe the witch in there would go ahead and give me my final paycheck on the spot so I could get a bus ticket or something" — she turned to Helen again, her eyes alight with hope — "and then I saw your car. I knew you were in there. You were my last chance, Helen."

"Not your last chance, Victoria — not by a long shot."

"Why do you want to help me? I don't understand." Her face, although youthful, showed signs of the kind of disappointment and pain that usually comes with years, Helen realized. Why should Victoria believe Helen wanted to do anything but take from her, use her, and leave her wasted in the dust? The girl had known very little in her short life besides lies, pain, and desertion.

Helen hid the pain in her heart by wiping the last of the tears from Victoria's cheeks. "I know you don't get it, Victoria. You'll just have to try to trust me for a while, okay? Maybe I can save both our asses. I've been in worse places." With those words Helen knew she was trying to convince herself as well as Victoria. Hell, it might even be true — and maybe if she could do something for this girl she might persuade herself that her own life could be salvaged. By some miracle, of course. It was too much of a mess right now to imagine getting things in her own fucked-up world straightened out ever again.

And it wasn't helping matters that Victoria leaned her face against Helen's hands, pressing gently and nuzzling her palms, even brushing her fingers with those soft full lips. Victoria sighed and leaned forward, kissing Helen on the cheek with soft, innocent, chaste lips.

Helen wasn't capable just then of pushing Victoria away. It took all her will power to keep from taking the girl into her arms, tasting the skin over her delicate ears, and weighing her breasts in her hands. "No, honey, don't do this," Helen whispered as Victoria kissed her throat and ears with quick touches from her lips. "Please. You're tired, you're scared, you just need a good friend right now. You don't really need this."

"How do you know what I need, Helen?" Victoria moved away enough for Helen to catch her breath and gather her wits a bit. "How do you know this isn't exactly right? For both of us?"

"Not here. Not like this. And you — Jesus, Victoria, you're so young, so untried." Helen got off the bed and prowled restlessly around the room, refusing to let herself look at the other woman.

"You think I'm just a child. Is that it?"

"That's not it at all. Certainly you're very mature in many ways, Victoria." Helen stopped and rummaged in her bag. Yes, thank god she had stowed a pack of cigarettes and some matches in there. Fuck the rules of the house; she needed a smoke right this minute. She paused in her prowling long enough to light up, then continued pacing as she blew gray smoke toward the ceiling.

"I'm not a virgin, you know. Haven't been for a long time," Victoria said in a sullen voice.

Helen almost choked as she took a deep drag. Somehow that claim sounded hilarious just now. "That's not the point. It's not just about sex."

"Then what is it? You do like girls, don't you? I mean, those friends of yours — that Beth — you're a lesbian, right?"

"Okay. Look." Helen sat down on the other bed and faced Victoria squarely. "All I'm saying is that we need a little bit of time. We need to get out of Mississippi, figure out what to do for you, give you a chance to sort things out. I'm not saying go away, I'm just saying let's take it easy. Fair enough?"

In response Victoria began to cry again. "Shit," Helen muttered, dropping her cigarette into the empty soda can by her bed. Words weren't going to help anyone now. Helen took Victoria into her arms, letting her own body absorb the shuddering sobs heaving from the girl's chest, stroking her head until the trembling stopped and her breathing came in steady regular rhythm.

When she'd stopped crying, Helen leaned back enough to look into Victoria's face. "Sure you don't want some food?"

"Maybe later." Victoria looked away, blushing with shame or embarrassment. "Sure you don't hate me yet?" She clung to Helen's hand like a child, like a lover, like someone starving and grasping at crumbs.

"Come on, let's try to sleep." They lay down together on Victoria's bed. Fully clothed, Helen was fairly certain no real damage would be done. They were both exhausted, uncertain, baffled by circumstances. They could sort it all out in the morning. For now, they slept.

Chapter Eighteen

Helen picked her way through an enormous maze of boxes and stacks of packing materials. "When did you decide to move, Aunt Edna?"

"Oh, honey, I've been thinking about it since before Loy passed," her aunt replied, bustling with armloads of linens and towels through the narrow corridors of the trailer. She'd been scurrying around since Helen and Victoria had arrived half an hour ago, avoiding facing Helen directly by staying in perpetual motion. After a drive of several hours from Vicksburg, starting just after dawn and a hurried cup of coffee at the halfway house, neither Helen nor Victoria were in any shape to help much with the packing. Helen was still in a state of shock as it was. What the hell had happened since the last time she'd been there?

"And that sweet Terrie Muncie helped find me a little house just outside Memphis. People have just been so kind — and all the ladies at the church will be over tomorrow to help with the packing. Could you hand me that box, honey?" Helen passed the required box over and watched as Aunt Edna sat down beside her on the old sofa and started piling towels into it. "It's small, but bigger than the trailer, and there's a cute little yard where I could plant my garden, and Bobby could play without those awful dogs next door barking at him."

"Aunt Edna." Helen took the towels from her, hoping to get her to stop babbling long enough to get some sense out of her. "I'm going to be going to Memphis in just a little while. I came here to say good-bye, but I certainly didn't expect this. What made you do this so suddenly?"

Edna got up and began fussing with the knickknacks on the shelves near the television. First an ugly porcelain angel got wrapped in newspaper, then a shiny, grinning gnome went into the nearest box. "You'll be going with that girl out there?" she asked, her back stiff with disapproval.

"Her name is Victoria Mason. She's the one I was telling you about, whose father died a few days ago." Helen moved to stand beside her aunt. She could see the barren backyard, where Victoria played halfheartedly with an excited Bobby. He was jubilant at having a new person to play with, and for now all Victoria had to do was watch while he carefully explained the workings of the various toys he'd brought outside with him. From time to time Victoria glanced toward the trailer, as if longing for some excuse to escape. She'd been too tired, from a restless night and a long dull drive, to protest when Helen asked her to go outside with her cousin so she could talk alone to Edna.

"And no, in answer to your unspoken question, she's not my lover. Victoria is just a young woman in trouble who needs a little help."

"If you say so, Helen."

"Aunt Edna, I'm here to apologize as much as to say good-bye." Helen went back to the sofa. Jesus fucking Christ, she was exhausted. It was only Tuesday, and she felt like she'd been in Mississippi for five years at least. She hadn't slept any better last night than Victoria, fearing that every little creaking noise in the halfway house outside Vicksburg was Jimbo or Tommy creeping up the stairs to attack them in bed. And the drive up to Tupelo had been long, hot, and dull. It hadn't helped that Victoria had done nothing but express her fears when she hadn't been sleeping. Helen collected her weary thoughts and went on, "I know I've been a real pain the whole time I've been here. I have no way to make up for it other than to tell you that next time will be very, very different."

"You're planning to come back soon?"

The underlying worry in her aunt's tone of voice jolted Helen wide awake. "That sounds like you don't want me to come back."

"Well, not until Bobby and me get settled, sweetheart. There's going to be so much to do, what with the move and all." Aunt Edna went next to the bookcase containing mostly Reader's Digest condensed versions of popular novels as well as a few bodice busters from a romance book club and some pamphlets printed by the church. She picked up a few volumes, put them back, fiddled with a pile of magazines, all the while keeping her back to her niece. "I'll let you know once we get settled in, and then you can visit us," she said brightly.

Helen closed her eyes and leaned back on the sofa. A spring popped deep within the cushions as her weight shifted. "If you don't want to see me again, Aunt Edna, all you have to do is say so."

Her aunt froze in front of the television set. "It isn't that, Helen. Honestly it isn't. It's just that, well, your cousin and I have a chance at a new life, a chance we never had all those years." Suddenly she turned around. Helen watched as the aging woman in the faded print housedress and stained apron twisted her gnarled hands together, her lined face dark with worry. "All those years, when we could have been able to take care of Bobby, to have a nice life for your uncle and me, and he wouldn't do it. He just wouldn't do it."

"He wouldn't do it?" Helen repeated. "What do you mean?" But Edna had already bustled into the kitchen, muttering something about Bobby's dinner. Helen followed close behind. "You're talking about Uncle Loy, right? He wouldn't let you have the nice life you wanted? The life you're going to have now?"

"Helen, your uncle was a good man and now he's gone. I have to take care of me and Bobby. There's no one else who can do it now." Aunt Edna dropped the bread knife she'd been using. Mustard from the knife splattered the linoleum, and her hands trembled over the bread and bologna. "Let's talk about something nice, honey. Is this girl Victoria going to go to college now? What about her own family?"

Helen gently took her aunt by the wrists, forcing her to look up at her niece. "Uncle Loy burned that hotel down, didn't he? Then he refused the money they were going to pay him for it."

Aunt Edna stopped struggling. Helen let go, and the old woman fell into a chair at the kitchen table. She sighed deeply, and to Helen's surprise some of the anxiety seemed to drain away from her. Maybe it was just the relief of confession, of not having to hide the awful secret anymore. The story spilled out in a flat monotone, without blame or pointed fingers or stones cast. How Loy had been desperate for money to get medical help for his ailing son — and no money was to be found. No bank would give them a loan, no relative willing or able to provide funds, no savings from their meager income. Desperate, he'd gone to his boss at R and F to hit him up for a salary advance.

"When they said they just needed him to do them a favor

and he could have the money — well, how could he say no? And it was so much money, Helen." Her voice grew animated for a moment at the memory of the offer, the tense discussions she must have had with her husband about it. "We could have taken care of Bobby, maybe even tried out some new treatments so he could be normal." Her voice faded again as she described how her own hopes had faded. All she knew, she told Helen, was that one weekend more than twenty years ago, Loy had gone away. He'd told his wife not to worry, not to look for him, and above all not to ask him questions. "When he came back he wouldn't talk. I mean, not a single word. Not for weeks. I tried everything, but he didn't speak. Not even to me."

Tears welled up in the old woman's eyes as she relived her husband's rejection. She broke off for a moment, digging in her apron pockets for a tissue. Helen thought about her Uncle Loy in the sudden silence. When had his contacts given him the copy of the photograph of Dixie Mae leaning on his shoulder? Right after the fire, probably, in order to buy his silence. So Uncle Loy had kept this secret all those years, hiding the picture but not destroying it — maybe to remind himself that at any moment his life could be shattered by the same people who'd offered him a way out of borderline poverty, a way to improve the lot of his mentally stunted only child. Had he told Edna anything about the prostitute? Her aunt had probably recognized the facade of the Beauregard from the picture, even if she'd known nothing about the woman.

And Uncle Loy had refused the money. That much was solid. Or, perhaps more likely, arranged for it to be invested and held in trust until his own death. Given his smoking habits, he must have been fairly sure he'd die before either his wife or child did. Whatever the scenario, he hadn't wanted to touch it. The threat to expose his alleged fling with a hooker, combined with his own guilt, had apparently been more than enough to buy his silence. The fact that Lorraine Mason had died in the fire had sealed his fate — and the fate of his wife and son for years to come. No way the Uncle Loy Helen knew would ever touch blood money. Unlike his niece, Helen realized with a cold sinking sensation.

So why had her uncle saved those bits and pieces from Biloxi? The shell, the ticket stubs, the brochures? Maybe he had briefly imagined another life for himself. A life of motion and excitement, of beautiful women. No more Edna wringing her hands and muttering platitudes — the only way she knew how to get through day after dreary day. No more half-wit son who would never mature past childhood. Was that box of trinkets his one chance at happiness? Was that why he'd kept it all those years, taking it out and looking at the history of his sins? Both pleasure and pain, all in one package.

Or a way to remind himself of how he'd participated in a crime that ended in tragic death for an innocent woman. A way to keep himself from bending, from relaxing his own rules, from taking that money from R and F and benefiting from Lorraine Mason's death.

Helen recalled her own arrival on their doorstep when she was a teenager. The fire must have taken place right before she'd been kicked out of her home by her father. And she could only recall Uncle Loy as being the strong, silent type — never laughing or smiling, never joking with her, always quiet and watching. But it was never a good idea to trust childhood memories. Had he always been that way? Or had he burned away a large part of himself with that criminal act so long ago?

"When he finally talked to me, he told me to never ask him about it. Never to ask about the money or where he'd been or what had happened." Edna wiped her eyes and face. Calm returned, and she cleared her throat, staring off across the table as if into a great distance. "He just promised me that if I never asked him anything then after he died everything would be fine for me and Bobby." Suddenly she turned to face Helen, her face set like granite. "And that's exactly what he did. He took care of us, just like he promised."

"Aunt Edna" — Helen got up to stand beside her as she finished making her son's dinner — "I've learned a lot of things about Uncle Loy in the past few days. It's clear that you don't want to know what I've found out. But I still love him and I love you and Bobby."

"If you love us, Helen, please go away." Edna put down the knife and took Helen's hands. Her eyes, pleading and still brimming with tears, searched Helen's face. "Not forever, honey — just for a while. Please, please just let me and Bobby get settled in our new home. Our new life."

A new life built on a lie. On a crime. On murder, no matter how unintentional Lorraine Mason's death had been. On silence about wrongdoing and going along with an agenda set by suits sitting around a table. Kind of like what Helen herself had done not so very long ago, wasn't it?

Helen could still see herself reaching out a hand to take the check with all those zeros from a rich man who'd bought her silence with a promise of financial support as she started up her agency again. She could still see herself biting back the taste of bile in her mouth as she cashed the check, used every penny to buy her way back into the detective business. The nightmares, the hours of therapy, the loss of Alison months ago — she and Loy were much more alike than anyone would suspect.

With a sense of loss worse than she'd felt at her uncle's grave, Helen leaned over and kissed her aunt's cheek. "I will, Aunt Edna. I'm going back to California today. And I'll wait there to hear from you."

Her aunt's face spasmed once in pain — or was it release? — and she hugged her niece with more warmth than she'd expressed toward Helen in days. "Thank you, honey. Things will get a lot better now, for everyone. I just know it."

She pulled away just as the sound of tires crunching on gravel could be heard from the front yard. "That'll be Terrie."

"Terrie?" Helen let go of her aunt. Rage threatened to boil up inside her. Now she had to deal with that red-headed bitch as well as everything else. Aunt Edna herded Terrie inside with excited advice on avoiding the boxes tumbled across the floor of the trailer. Terrie didn't seem to be surprised to see Helen standing there in the kitchen. With a bright smile she greeted Helen. Terrie and Edna sat down together on the sofa and chatted while Helen perched on the arm of Uncle Loy's easy chair.

"Well, I better go get dinner finished. Bobby gets so excited when people come over, he just plain forgets to eat!" With a final nervous glance at Helen, Edna left the living room. Helen could hear her rattling and banging and making lots of noise in the kitchen so she wouldn't hear what the other women were saying.

"Didn't you bring Jimbo and Tommy with you today?" Helen asked. "Or this time are you going to beat us up with those pretty little hands?"

"Those two!" She actually laughed out loud, tossing back that flaming red hair in an appealing, girlish gesture. "I never deal with them. And you can never prove it, either."

"I'm sure I couldn't." Helen moved to the sofa, wondering how she could ever have fucked Terrie Muncie. And enjoyed it so much. "It's just a question of making a phone call or two, right? You call up someone, say, head of R and F security, and then they make another call, and another one gets made — and then somewhere down the line local muscle like Mutt and Jeff get in on it. For a small sum."

Terrie shrugged and playfully touched Helen's leg with her sandaled foot. "Sounds like a good method. As long as it works."

Helen moved her leg out of reach. "And those lovely manicured nails won't get dirtied in the process. Kind of like bombers dropping their payloads over villages in an unimportant county, isn't it? Don't see any victims, don't hear any screaming, don't stick around to watch the devastation you leave behind. God knows you never had to deal with Lorraine Mason. All took place before your time. Your job is just to keep the place tidy."

"Don't get all high and mighty on me, Helen. You're out of mud to sling, remember?" Terrie went to the shelves and began examining the knickknacks one by one. "No pedestals around here. Just human beings."

"Human beings who don't mind using and hurting each other. Human beings who don't mind if people are dead."

"That's right." Terrie put the ceramic turtle back on the shelf and turned around to look at Helen. "That's what human beings do. Haven't you learned anything, in all that digging up of people's lives? We're just animals with big brains. It's eat or be eaten."

"So it's perfectly all right that the big fish in the pond do everything they can to gobble up little fish. Or at least make sure the little fish are either bought off or terrorized into submission. If not burned alive."

Terrie rolled her eyes and laughed. "That's nice, coming from you, Helen." She moved closer, almost whispering to make sure Edna couldn't hear. Helen could smell the same perfume she'd used the other night, but now it almost made her gag with nausea. "I don't recall that you complained the other night."

"I'm not trying to make excuses for myself," Helen hissed. "There's a big, big difference between refusing responsibility for my actions and pointing out that maybe there is some need for questioning what's going on."

"Look, this is getting boring. Your aunt and your poor cousin are going to be comfortable for the rest of their lives. No one got hurt — just scared a little bit. What the hell is the big damn deal, huh?" Terrie asked, still smiling, her finger tracing a line on Helen's cheek. "So what if someone died in the fire? It was an accident. It was probably the bitch's fault for not getting her ass out quicker. Some kind of hero act, I guess, trying to make sure all the old farts were out of the building."

Helen slapped her hand away, not caring if her aunt heard. "No one got hurt? What about Dixie Mae dead by the highway? What about Victoria and Bill Mason, let alone Lorraine?"

"In Dixie Mae's line of work people die all the time. Occupational hazard. And the other one was an accident."

"And Bill Mason?"

Terrie's smile slipped a bit at that. Her gaze faltered, and she went back to the sofa. "Either that was a big mistake or it was suicide. No one will ever know, for sure."

"And no one will care. That's the whole point, isn't it?" Helen pushed her way through the kitchen, past a startled Aunt Edna, and slammed open the screen door.

"Where are you going?" Terrie rushed after her. "Helen, what are you doing?"

"Victoria —" Victoria was already heading around the side of the trailer to Helen's rental car, not needing any further encouragement. "Bobby, sweetheart, we have to go now."

"But Vicky and me was just lookin' at my pictures!" Bobby's fair round face was amazed and puzzled. "We was gonna have bologna for dinner. Don't you want to play with me?"

Helen pulled him to his feet and wrapped his bulky body in a hug. "Bobby, I'm going to go back to California and get a present for you. How would that be? Something fun for you to put up in your new bedroom."

"What are you gonna send, Helen? What are you gonna send me?"

"It's going to be a big, big surprise. Tell you what" — she held Bobby's face in her hands, knowing she wouldn't see him again for a very, very long time — "you write me a letter, telling me what you'd like. How about that? And you can tell me all about your new school and your new friends."

That seemed to satisfy Bobby, and he happily walked off to the kitchen for his sandwich. Aunt Edna clasped her niece in a swift hug, but turned away quickly to hide her face. Helen stood for a moment in the kitchen doorway, knowing that neither of them were about to look back one more time. Then she turned to go, only to find Terrie blocking her way.

"Now what?" Helen shoved her aside roughly, gratified at the surprise on her face as she stumbled to retain her footing. "I don't really have time, Terrie. We're going." Victoria was in the car, buckled in and ready to go.

"Just wanted to let you know that a couple of your old friends are in town. You know, the ones you partied with a couple of nights ago at that motel?"

Helen froze. Behind her the wolfhounds panted and drooled, still longing for a taste. "What are you hinting at, Terrie? That you're setting me up for a beating? Or a murder? Which one is more convenient to you at the moment, I wonder?"

Terrie stood inches from Helen, her eyes alight with amusement. "Like I said, I don't really know what those guys do in their spare time. In fact, I don't even know them. In fact, I have no idea what you're talking about."

"Is that so?" Without thinking, Helen felt her hand clench into a fist and lift, as if with a mind of its own, smashing into that smiling mouth. She heard a muffled shriek and watched Terrie fall back on her cute ass to the oil-stained gravel. The dogs jumped and strained against the chain-link fence, their muscled chests heaving in desperate longing for blood. Terrie had fallen close to the fence, and she scrambled to her feet most ungracefully. Her perfect face was already swelling from the blow, and a nasty welt formed next to her mouth. She spat out blood, and the dogs went wild.

"Hurting me won't stop a thing," Terrie managed to say. "Everything will go on just as it has."

"I'm sure it will." Helen stood next to the car, wishing she could feel a lot better about what she'd just done. Seeing Terrie bruised and bleeding should have warmed the cockles of her heart, but instead it just left her feeling drained. Disgusted with herself. Terrie was right. It didn't change a thing. "Things will go on. Roberts and Farrell will continue to put pesticide in the DNA of food crops, and farmers will continue to buy their products. People like Jimbo and Tommy — who may very well be following us — will continue to be hired by big corporations for security reasons. Poor souls like my Aunt Edna and my Uncle Loy will get dragged into your games just so they can survive. And kids like Victoria will get caught in the crossfire. No one will give a fuck."

"Except for saints like Helen Black, is that it?" Terrie staggered to the car. Helen backed away, thinking Terrie might lash out at her. "You're the one who can judge everyone else because you do no wrong, isn't that right? A real champion of justice."

Victoria got out of the car and stood uncertainly by the passenger door. "Helen? What's happening?" she asked in a trembling voice.

"Get back in the car. Do it!" Helen spoke through gritted teeth without looking at the girl. Victoria obeyed as Terrie sent her a glare full of hate. "Get out of my way, Terrie. I'm leaving your little party. Go explain that face to my aunt."

"Did you fuck the little cunt yet, Helen? Was she any good? Maybe you like punk virgins. She probably isn't even legal age yet, is she?"

Helen slapped her again. Who gave a fuck if she filed some kind of charges? Not likely, since she wouldn't want to risk her career with the stink she knew Helen would make about it. Helen had nothing left to lose.

Nothing left to lose. Not good words to leave by. With a

sinking feeling in the pit of her stomach Helen got into the car before Terrie caught her breath again. She glimpsed Terrie in the rearview mirror as she drove off. Terrie was touching her mouth gingerly and staring after them.

"Helen? Where are we going?"

Helen glanced at Victoria, who hadn't stopped trembling. "California," Helen answered.

"Promise?"

"I promise." *I hope.* She kept driving north.

Chapter Nineteen

At first Helen barely noticed the truck rolling along behind her car on the highway heading to Memphis and the airport. The truck was perhaps a quarter of a mile distant, recognizable as some large vehicle of the four-wheel-drive variety, but not much more. Darkness was approaching — Helen marveled at how quickly summer faded into autumn, with its shorter hours and gathering gloom in the gentle curves of the low hills in north Mississippi.

"How long till we get there?" Victoria had asked that question at least six times in the last hour. Helen kept a firm grip on her patience and fervently hoped that Victoria's childish behavior was simply a reaction to the fear and tension of the past week on her part and not a permanent feature of her personality. A doubt began to creep across Helen's mind like an unsightly wrinkle encroaching on starched fabric. She'd been so intent on proving her points to an unwilling audience and finding out some version of "truth" about her uncle that the young woman now sitting beside her had perhaps never appeared to Helen as much more than some kind of symbol. Of what? Of injustice or lies or hypocrisy? Of the fruits of repression? Ignorance? Or was she in some sense a skewed mirror image of the self Helen was trying to save?

But as soon as these worries surfaced Helen pushed them back down into the silt of her mind. The important thing, she reminded herself, was simply to get away. Get out of Mississippi, leave her relatives alone to sort out their own lives, and get back to some semblance of normal life for herself. "It will probably take another hour or hour and a half, Victoria." Helen spoke slowly, forcing patience into her voice. "Just relax, okay? We'll get there when we get there."

As she spoke, her attention kept going back to the rearview mirror. The truck was gaining on them. Except for her car and this truck, which had shown up soon after they had left Tupelo, the road was fairly deserted. By this hour most of the citizenry would be sitting down to supper or switching on their televisions. Certainly this state road, a two-lane blacktop pitted and rutted with years of neglect, displayed few signs of life beyond some birds sitting on wires overhead. They wheeled and circled and screamed at the car as it passed, as though they were unaccustomed to traffic at this hour of the evening.

"Can't you go any faster?"

"Victoria, please. Just take it easy and give it a rest."

"Or you'll hit me like you did that woman?"

Helen kept her attention fixed on the road and her hands firmly gripped on the steering wheel. She couldn't really blame Victoria for that jibe, although it really pissed her off — indeed, almost to the point of slapping Victoria, too. So the comment wasn't so far off the mark. Helen's recent violent behavior in front of her Aunt Edna's home had in fact been the reason they were driving along this little-used road off the main highway, taking the long way to Memphis and adding considerably to their travel time. Between Helen's nervousness about the state troopers tracking her down and her fear that Terrie would go ahead and press charges against her for assault, it had seemed the better part of valor to take a roundabout series of detours from the highway, staying off of well-traveled roads and out of sight.

"Sorry, Helen," Victoria mumbled. "I'm just kind of freaked right now, you know?"

"Please. Just let me drive. And try to stay quiet for a few minutes." At the moment, the truck gaining on them presented more of a concern to Helen than Victoria's incessant questions. Helen had a good idea of who was in that truck. She cursed herself for slinking around on back roads. State troopers or no state troopers, Jimbo and Tommy would have had less opportunity to catch up with them on the main highway. "Victoria. Did you tell our friends from Biloxi we were going to the airport?"

"What are you talking about?" Victoria squirmed in the seat and unfastened her seat belt, sprawling her legs out as far as they would reach. "I never said anything to anyone."

"Listen to me. You told me at the halfway house that you'd made a deal with Jimbo and Tommy. Did you call them or contact them to let them know our plans?"

"Jesus, no! Helen, I swear it. Honest. Except for that phone call to Aunt Josephine at the gas station last night, I didn't tell anyone anything." Victoria's voice trailed off, and she pressed her hands to her mouth in horror. Helen glanced at the girl — even in the growing darkness she could see realization sinking in with accompanying horror. "Oh my god," Victoria gasped. "Aunt Josephine — maybe she said something. Maybe they came looking for us."

"Fuck." Helen muttered a curse against all the aunts of the world, both Victoria's and hers. Who knows how they'd represented themselves to Josephine? That didn't matter now, of course. Survival took precedence at the moment. "Get the map out of the glove compartment, Victoria."

"But I don't know how we —"

"And get that gun of Jimbo's out of my bag."

Victoria stared at Helen, frozen with fear. "The gun?" she whispered.

"Just fucking do it! Now!" Helen kept watching the rearview mirror while Victoria pulled out the gun and fumbled with the map. The gun lay like a big dead insect on the car seat between them. The truck was only five or six car-lengths behind them, but it was staying there. Yes, there were two figures in the cab, presumably male judging by their silhouettes against the reflected glare from the headlights. Helen seriously doubted they had been sent by R and F at this stage of the game — it was much more likely that they were hellbent on kicking the ass of the woman who'd gotten them into so much trouble to start with. And Terrie Muncie could have arranged to give them a little push in the right direction, outside of proper channels. She could have contacted the boys as soon as Helen had left the trailer park, and no doubt they'd been ready and waiting for her car to appear. Stupid, stupid, stupid, Helen chided herself. It was as if her brain had completely mushed into oatmeal during the past week. Was it personal involvement? A bloated ego? Maybe Helen had just used up her ninth charmed life and it was all over now.

Helen felt panic rise in her chest, burning like acid. Right now it didn't matter who'd sent them barreling down the road intent on revenge. What mattered was getting off this isolated stretch of the countryside and back to what passed for civilization. If they could just make it to the airport they'd be home free. Jimbo and Tommy, stupid though they were, wouldn't dare attempt anything in a bustling airport terminal. "Come on, Victoria, help me out here," she spat, not caring what she sounded like. Apologies could come later if they made it through this episode.

"Okay, okay." The girl's voice trembled, but at least she was looking at the map intently by the pinpoint of light from the glove compartment. "Okay. We just passed that place called Jefferson Point, right? There should be a road going off to the left a ways up — wait, that must be it!"

Helen saw only a narrow passage opening between banks of dense shrubbery that could have been anything from kudzu to poison oak. With a squeal from protesting tires Helen swerved the car off to the left, ignoring the whine of thorny brambles scratching the paint on the rental car. Right away the car hit a series of rocks that seemed to gouge the underside of the vehicle. Helen squinted into the darkness and switched on her high beams. They were entering an overgrown path of beaten red dust that snaked crookedly as far as the eye could see beneath overhanging branches and an utterly black sky. "How far to the main highway, Victoria?"

"I don't know. Looks like it's not very far, but I can't really tell." Victoria shifted around in her seat and stared out the back window. "I can't see anything, it's so dark." Her voice shook, and Helen could hear her heavy breathing. "Shit, they're back there!" she cried out.

Helen, who'd been staring hard at the road ahead and praying they wouldn't come across any fallen logs or immovable boulders, glanced in the rearview mirror. Amid the swirl of dust kicked up by her car she could see the twin balls of light behind them. Shit. Their truck was no doubt much better equipped than this little car to handle an unpaved road. Each jolt brought them nearer to damaging the car beyond use. "Victoria," she yelled out over the noise of grinding gears, "look at the map again. Is there any way off this road until we get to the highway?"

Victoria was openly sobbing now. "No, nothing. Just this big thing on the map next to the road. It's — I don't know what it is — something big. It's not a road, it's just like a big hole on the map, we don't have any way out of this."

She was almost hysterical. Helen ignored her, focused her

thoughts until there was only the dusty road, the trees, the truck gaining on them. Victoria's cries suddenly stilled when their car burst into a level space, free of trees and dust and rocks.

"What happened?" Victoria breathed.

"I don't know." Helen kept the car going at a furious pace, hoping to gain a little time. "Maybe it's your big hole on the map. Whatever it is it didn't come a second too soon." If their luck held, the road would stay like this until they reached the highway.

"Helen, oh my god! Look out!"

Helen didn't need Victoria's shout to see how the pavement swerved off to the right. At their left, just beyond the newly laid asphalt, she could see a gap in the earth. It was too dark to make out much of the terrain, but the dim glow of starlight, unobstructed now by trees, showed a long narrow chasm gorged out of the soil. Some kind of strip-mining procedure, perhaps?

Victoria confirmed her suspicions a moment later. "The map says this is going to be Palos de Monteia Estates, or something like that."

"Terrific," Helen mumbled. A plan was beginning to form in her mind. Behind them the truck rumbled off the dirt path and onto the pavement. Helen slowed the car and edged it as close as she dared to the yawning hole on her left. Her brain, as if dislocated from her body, kept making weird calculations. This paved stretch was probably meant for nothing more than the high-muck-a-mucks and grand pooh bahs overseeing the construction site. Dump trucks and heavy vehicles no doubt had their own entrance to the man-made valley below, far away from where they sped along now.

"Helen, what the fuck are you doing?" Victoria's shocked whisper hissed in her ear.

"Get off of me and shut up." Her hands were like ice. Every inch of her body fought in protest of steering the car leftward. She managed to keep her foot raised from the gas pedal long enough to get the truck very, very close. "Maybe we have something to thank land developers for, after all."

"Are you crazy?" Victoria's whisper grew into a terrified scream as she looked over her shoulder. The truck was close enough to bump into their car in a matter of seconds.

"Yes, I am!" Helen shoved her foot down hard on the pedal and jerked the steering wheel to the right, circling back around over the right-hand shoulder and pointing them back the way they'd come. In a strangely calm moment, like finding the eye of a hurricane, Helen felt light and free and empty.

And it worked. The driver of the truck — maybe Jimbo, since the figure of the driver seemed shorter and fatter than the man occupying the passenger's seat — gunned the truck's motor and tried to spin the vehicle around to pursue them. But the paved length of road was simply too narrow for the truck to safely maneuver at high speed. Helen kept going back the way they'd entered, her stare flickering between the dirt road ahead and the rearview mirror. As she watched, the truck swerved and veered on the dirt shoulder, first scraping up against the remains of trees and shrubs on the undeveloped side of the hill, then faltering on the tiny edging of sand separating pavement from artificial canyon.

It was a losing battle. The truck groaned and squalled as metal ground against metal. The driver lost control as the big fat tires slid in soft dirt. In a strangely beautiful precise arc the truck sailed up against the starry sky and plummeted into the canyon. The sound of the crash echoed through the trees in a lingering series of metallic thuds as the truck tumbled into the crevasse.

Helen stopped the car just before they reached the dirt road at the edge of the pavement. Her whole body shook like a leaf in a strong wind, and sweat greased her skin in a thick, oily film. Beside her Victoria stared out the window in horror, barely breathing. "Victoria," Helen managed to get out. "Are you okay?"

In response Victoria merely turned around to stare at her,

eyes wide and dark and blank in the dim light. Helen sighed and leaned her forehead against the steering wheel, closing her eyes and trying to get her heart to stop pounding. "Jesus, Jesus, Jesus," she whispered. Deep breaths, in and out, she schooled herself. It felt like eons before she could move or breathe with a semblance of calm. "Okay," she finally said. "We have to see if they might still be alive and let someone know."

"No, we don't."

"Victoria." Helen moved wearily in her seat, struggling to unfasten her safety belt. "I've done an awful lot of stupid things in the past few days, but I won't just leave them there. If they survived this there's no telling what kind of fallout we'll have to face."

"Let's just go! They tried to kill us, they tried to murder us out here!" Victoria's face, a pale mask in the moonlight, distorted in fear and fury. "We can just fly right out of this place, go to California, start everything over. You promised!"

"Listen, if they're still alive we can maybe find out if they really did kill your father and Dixie Mae," Helen protested. Her energy was almost completely drained. She didn't know if she had much fight in her and devoutly hoped Victoria would subside back into docility for the duration of the night. "Come on, just think for a second. It's going to be okay now. Those guys are either dead or so fucked up by the crash they won't be able to hurt us. All I'm going to do is see what state they're in and then go find a phone. We'll be okay —"

Helen stopped short at the sight of Jimbo's gun in Victoria's trembling hands. Fuck. In all the confusion she hadn't dreamed the girl would go for the weapon. "Victoria," she began calmly, "there's no call to do that. You don't know what you're doing."

"Really?" Shit, her hands were shaking so bad she'd probably fire the gun by mistake. Of course, Helen would be just as dead, mistake or not. "I think for the first time since

252

I met you I have a good idea of what I'm doing. Of what I need to do. Just drive."

"Please, please listen to me —"

"Just drive, bitch!"

Helen slowly steered the car around and drove across the paved stretch toward the main highway. As they passed the scarred earth where the truck had gone over, they saw flames shooting up from the canyon. Great. She seriously doubted Jimbo or Tommy had crawled clear of the fire. The truth about Victoria's father was turning into ash along with their bodies. After a quick glance at the wavering gun barrel held only inches from her side, Helen refrained from pointing that fact out to Victoria.

She drove in silence broken only by the sound of two women breathing heavily. Okay, big-city private eye, Helen told herself, get out of this one alive. That would be a nice piece of work. They reached a turnoff marked for the highway in what felt like years but what was probably only a couple of minutes. Made sense, a dislocated reasoning part of Helen's brain mumbled — the developers wouldn't want to deny the close proximity of the nearest mall to their potential inhabitants.

And maybe their quick arrival at the highway offered Helen her last chance of getting that gun away from Victoria. "I need to see the map," she said quietly, hoping her voice sounded a lot more placid and reassuring than she felt. "I'm not sure which way we should go." The car sat idling at a convenient crossroad. There were no markers to indicate which way Helen should turn if Memphis was her final destination.

"Didn't that sign say something? The one we just passed?" Victoria kept her gaze fixed on Helen, but her voice sounded nervous.

"It just said the highway was ahead. It didn't say which direction to go." Silence and stillness from her passenger.

"Look, Victoria, I can't get us to the airport unless I know which way to go. Someone out here will have seen that fire by now," Helen added in what she hoped would be a persuasive argument. "They'll be calling the police, and we're going to have company very soon."

As soon as Victoria relented and reached out to open the glove compartment, Helen grabbed at the gun. She tried to force the barrel up toward the roof of the car as they struggled for possession of the gun. The crack of the gunshot sounded strangely muffled, echoing dully inside the small rental car. Helen stared in shock as Victoria's eyes opened wide in confusion. Her mouth opened and closed as though she were about to speak but had changed her mind. "What happened?" she gasped out, still not understanding. "What happened?"

"Oh god, please not her, not her. Please let it be me," Helen moaned. She leaned away from the girl, the gun now safely in her hand. With a growing sense of horror Helen realized that she felt no pain from a bullet, no sensation of weakness or shock. Something dark and wet spread across Victoria's shirt, blooming like a flower that just kept getting bigger and bigger. Her fingers clutched at Helen's sleeve in a futile clawing gesture as shock and rapid blood loss took over. Her eyes gleamed brightly in the moon light, then faded into dull blank death as she died before Helen's stunned gaze.

Chapter Twenty

The orange jumpsuit issued by the county jail chafed on
Helen's skin. It had been a week now, and her body still
refused to get used to the stiff, coarse fabric. Somehow it
bugged her worse than the manacles the guards put on her
wrists every time she left her cell to meet with her infrequent
visitors. Perhaps because handcuffs were an accepted and
obligatory part of being in jail. Maybe the indignity of
constant itching seemed more like a personal humiliation.
Helen did her best during the long hours of confinement in
her cell not to scratch at the welts all over her body. It could
have been the soap they used, or just a physical reaction to
the ordeal she was facing. In any case, it was driving her crazy.
Funny — not the insolence of the guards, not the jeers and

taunts of her fellow inmates in the county jail, not the hours of solitude and boredom would do her in. It would be a simple skin rash.

Besides, if she ever said anything about it to anyone, she was sure to be harassed even more by the other prisoners detained here. No one had tried to injure her yet, perhaps just because they hadn't had a chance so far — but Helen was sure attempts at beatings were not going to be long in coming. Helen hadn't yet had time to piss off any guards. Possibly she'd avoid doing that, but it was highly unlikely. Depended on how long the trial took. If she was stuck here for more than a couple of months she'd be in deep shit.

At least, Helen mused as she felt her face freeze in the stonelike mask all the women here affected for the guards' scrutiny, she wasn't chained at the waist and ankles like some of the others. It wasn't hard to see that the darker your skin, the more physical restraint you could expect. For the most part the guards had paid little attention to her, anyhow. Her stay here would no doubt be relatively brief. As Helen moved with lowered head and shambling gait behind the guard down the long, gray corridor that smelled of piss and vomit overlaid by disinfectant, she went over in her mind for the millionth time the sequence of events she could expect. Each step taken by the Mississippi legal system, as explained by the exasperated and exhausted court-appointed lawyer, was as fixed in Helen's mind as the gray squares of linoleum laid out in a straight path toward the visitors' rooms. Jury selection for her trial would begin next week, and she could expect swift justice in perhaps a month after that.

The lawyer, a balding young man who looked like he'd graduated from law school just hours previous to meeting with Helen, had at first gotten her case confused with a couple of others assigned to him. When he'd finally pulled the right file from his bright, shiny new attaché case, it hadn't taken long to lay it all out for Helen. Second degree was the best they could hope for — a stretch of several years less than the prescribed amount of time if she kept her ass out of trouble while she was inside.

"I don't see any way around your doing some time," he'd said as he packed up to go. "Not with being gay and from California and having made a nuisance of yourself in two different counties."

Helen had barely uttered two words to him, accepting that this little asswipe was the best she could hope for from the gracious mercy of the Mississippi courts. She didn't even bother to tell him that he was her last option since she'd steadfastly refused any help from Aunt Edna.

"But, darling, your uncle would have wanted it this way. He would never forgive me if we didn't get the best lawyer for you." Aunt Edna seemed to have developed a tremor in her hands that wouldn't go away. Even in her Sunday best, dressed up with carefully applied rouge and lipstick for a visit to her wayward niece, her astonishment and anguish was evident in the way her fingers kept twisting the shredded tissue balled up in her hands.

"No. That money is for you and Bobby. I absolutely refuse to let you spend a cent of it on me."

That was the only time Aunt Edna had visited. Helen had a small package of toiletries and a picture drawn by her cousin Bobby to keep in her cell — her only proof that she'd once had a life of some kind in the world outside. Sometimes she would look at the crayon drawing Bobby had made, trying to decipher what winged animal in purple and green he had imagined. It looked like a dog, then maybe like a cow. Or a bear. Whatever it was, it flew free in an orange sky.

The slamming of doors and buzzing open of gates brought her thoughts away from the soaring mythical animal and placed her back in the gray blank world she now called home. Who the hell could be visiting her? Her lawyer had told her he probably wouldn't see her until the court date, and she'd gotten Aunt Edna to agree to stay away. She seriously doubted it could be Beth. Helen had only a dim memory of her former lover, garbed in her uniform, standing against a backdrop of whirling red and blue lights and looking with horror and disgust at the woman she'd thought she'd known. In the fuzz of her mind, through the thick fog that seemed to have permanently settled over Helen, she sort of remembered seeing Beth once or twice at the jail. But she couldn't seem to recall anything said or done by either one of them. Maybe it hadn't even happened.

But when Helen saw Terrie Muncie sitting on the other side of the thick glass she felt something for the first time in weeks. It took her a few seconds to realize that she felt rage.

Terrie picked up the phone that would allow her to talk to Helen. She stared unsmiling at the woman garbed in orange and sporting handcuffs, waiting for Helen to pick up the receiver on her side. After a few moments of registering the amazing fact that Terrie was at the jail, Helen clumsily picked up her phone and put it to her ear, fumbling because of the manacles.

Even over the scratchy phone line Terrie's voice was soft and seductive. "You don't look happy to see me."

Helen cleared her throat — she was hoarse from not talking for days on end — and answered, "This isn't exactly the right setting for you."

"You either." Terrie licked her lips — the bruise Helen had left on her mouth had long since healed — and sighed heavily. "I never thought I'd see you like this."

Helen shrugged. "Life is just full of little surprises. Like why the fuck you're here right now. Go ahead and gloat, if that's what you came for — knock your socks off."

"That's not it, not at all." Was that actually sweat beading on Terrie's upper lip? The lip Helen had licked and sucked for one incredible night of fucking only a few weeks ago? Maybe it was just stress at being surrounded by low-life peasantry for the first time in her privileged existence. "I'm here to say good-bye. I'll be back for the trial if I'm summoned, but I'm leaving Tupelo. Roberts and Farrell is sending me to their offices in Florida."

"Is this a promotion based on your public relations skills?" Helen asked with false brightness. "I'd be happy to add my testimonials to those of your lords and masters. In one phrase, Terrie — fuck you and the horse you rode in on."

"Look, I came here to see if you'd accept my help." Terrie struggled with the words, spitting them out as if they tasted bad. "I never meant — no one should have died over this. You didn't have to kill them."

"Your help. That's a good one. Listen, if it's all the same to you I think I'll pass."

Terrie leaned her head on her hand, rubbing her forehead as though it would wipe out ugly thoughts in the simple gesture. "I want — I need to do something to help make things right, Helen." She looked up again. Helen was surprised to see something like feeling in the other woman's eyes. Or was it yet another act? Impossible now to tell. And to Helen's amazement and relief she really and truly didn't care anymore.

"Really? Well, that's nice." Helen gazed expectantly at Terrie, who began to squirm in her chair. "Is that all? If you're finished I have to get back. The ladies' tennis club is about to meet in the courtyard, and I simply must be there for the big match."

"Helen — please." Terrie laid her hand flat on the glass and kept it there until a guard standing just the other side of the glass door rapped on the door's small square window. "Won't you just listen to me? Won't you just let me help?"

"Don't you think you've done enough already?"

"I can get a lawyer for you. He's good, he's worked for R and F before. I'll manage the cost myself —"

"Yeah, right. You and what army? You listen to me, you fucking bitch," Helen murmured, leaning close to the glass. "I know damn well you just want to make sure that R and F's big corporate ass is covered, that nothing comes out at the trial to damage the profits their stockholders have come to rely on. Don't even think about trying to sell me on your bullshit any more."

The expression of sorrow and pity drained away from Terrie's face as Helen spoke, leaving only the lovely features Helen now loathed set in wry amusement. "Oh well," Terrie sighed. "It was worth a try, I suppose."

"Go back and tell your owners I'm not betting on their pony, now or ever." For the first time since Victoria had died at her hands, Helen felt a surge of life inside her. It was only a faint pulse, a small glimmer of something beating with fragile wings somewhere beneath the orange jumpsuit and the rash and the sullen husk she was becoming with every passing hour. She sat still and silent for a moment, savoring the sensation while it lasted. It would come again, she was sure of it. For now she had to simply be quiet and listen for the inner signal, then harbor it in secret.

"By the way," she went on, "is Beth going with you to Florida?"

Terrie froze for a moment, then the smile came back across her lips. "You know damn well she's staying behind. I guess I have you to thank for that, don't I?"

"You screwed things up with Beth all on your own, sweetheart. You get all the credit for that. Both me and Beth are sticking around here for a while, I guess."

"So you'd prefer all this, then?" Terrie asked, sweeping her arm around her at the barren room. "This is your choice — to stay here with a bunch of killers and drug dealers and whores instead of a chance to go back to everything you left behind?" She shook her head, and her smile widened. "I know you're not too bright, Helen, but you don't have to be a rocket scientist to see which choice is the right one. What did you prove, anyhow?"

Helen shrugged, and the jumpsuit rustled around her

shoulders. "Maybe I only proved that sometimes the good guys finish last."

"Good guys. I take it you're including yourself in that crowd, Helen? Think again."

Drug dealers, killers, whores — scum of the earth. That's where I am now, Helen thought. Lowest of the low, irredeemable criminals, not worth the effort to house and feed them. That's where the state of Mississippi thinks I belong. "Hmm. Well, you know, Terrie — I've been out there with the nice normal types like yourself. The so-called law-abiding citizenry with the nice houses and money in the bank and stable careers on the rise." Helen stood up, shoving the wooden chair back with a clatter. "I think I'd rather take my chances in here."

She slammed the phone down and went to the door to knock for the guard to escort her back to her cell. Helen didn't look back to see the last of Terrie, so she never knew if the other woman tried to respond.

Helen and the guard walked back down the corridor. There was no need to hurry — nowhere either of them had to be. The walls, thick concrete, muffled the slide and scrape of her slippers on the cheap linoleum as well as the click of the guard's heels. Along the top of the wall a row of narrow windows, paned with frosted glass, allowed weak rays of sunlight to spread a thin yellow, like fresh butter, in the dust-moted air. It was going to be a very hot day.

Helen sat down on her cot as the guard clanged the metal gate shut behind her. On either side she heard curses and mutterings from women whose names she didn't know — not yet — and maybe never would. A single big bulb glared like a huge white eyeball from the whitewashed ceiling. Someone was watching television — a game show with prizes of trips to Hawaii or Puerta Vallarta, places no one here would ever see.

From underneath her pillow she took out the folded newsprint that bore a grainy photograph of Victoria Mason's face. It wasn't a really good picture. Not a good likeness at all. But the high-school yearbook photograph had captured a small hint of those wistful dark eyes, the wry smile, the tilt of her head as she viewed the world in confusion and pain. Helen wished she could risk putting the creased and yellowed portrait in a frame and keep it with her. She glanced up again to the cracked mirror over the brown-stained sink. Strange they'd allow a mirror in here — someone had slipped up there. Maybe she could put the clipping there one day. Until then — she folded it and tucked it safely away under her pillow.

Bits and scraps, Helen thought, lying down flat on the cot. That's what she had left now. Nothing completed. Loose ends flapped everywhere. R and F had gotten away with murder, and even rewarded Terrie for her assistance. She'd probably never see Aunt Edna or Bobby or Beth again. No bad guys in black hats shot down by the sheriff or the rangers or whatever. The knight on the white horse had definitely fallen on his ass with this whole tragedy. Just a few people dead, and a new kid on the cell block. Nope, the only thing settled now was where Helen would be spending the next twenty to thirty years.

She shut her eyes against the tears that fought to spill down her cheeks. Strange — somewhere deep inside, beneath the jumpsuit and the handcuffs and the conscious mind stunned into numbness, some sliver of herself was relieved that the tears could still come.

On the wall beside the cracked mirror Helen studied, for the thousandth time, the prayer meeting schedule. Mrs. Muncie and her comrades in Christ would be here again at two-thirty this afternoon. Helen never missed. It got her out of the cell, at least, for a couple of hours. Besides, a couple of these women could really belt out the gospel tunes. Worth the piercing gaze of Mrs. Muncie to hear the singing. And Helen always tried to say or do something memorable for Mrs. Muncie to report back to the suits and the authorities. Maybe today she'd convert or speak in tongues. No — maybe not —

it might prevent her from being able to come back if she got too rowdy with it.

She turned her gaze to Bobby's drawing. Would she ever figure out what the hell that winged creature was supposed to be? Maybe. She had a lot of time to think about it.

About the Author

Pat Welch was born in Japan and grew up in small towns in the South. She has lived in the San Francisco Bay area since 1986. This is her first novel with Bella Books.

Visit
Bella Books
at

www.bellabooks.com